A Village Deception

REBECCA SHAW

An Orion paperback

First published in Great Britain in 2011
by Orion
This paperback edition published in 2011
by Orion Books Ltd,
Orion House, 5 Upper Saint Martin's Lane
London WC2H 9EA

An Hachette UK company

1 3 5 7 9 10 8 6 4 2

A CIP catalogue record for this book
is available from the British Library.

ISBN 978-1-4091-2073-5

Typeset by Deltatype Ltd, Birkenhead, Merseyside

Printed in Great Britain by Clays Ltd, St Ives plc

The Orion Publishing Group's policy is to use papers that
are natural, renewable and recyclable products and
made from wood grown in sustainable forests. The logging
and manufacturing processes are expected to conform to
the environmental regulations of the country of origin.

www.orionbooks.co.uk

INHABITANTS OF TURNHAM MALPAS

Willie Biggs	Retired verger
Sylvia Biggs	His wife
James (Jimbo) Charter-Plackett	Owner of the village store
Harriet Charter-Plackett	His wife
Fergus, Finlay, Flick & Fran	Their children
Katherine Charter-Plackett	Jimbo's mother
Paddy Cleary	Gardener
Alan Crimble	Barman at the Royal Oak
Linda Crimble	His wife
Lewis Crimble	Their son
Maggie Dobbs	School caretaker
H. Craddock Fitch	Owner of Turnham House
Kate Fitch	Village school headteacher
Tamsin Goodenough	Organist
Zack Hooper	Verger
Marie Hooper	His wife
Gilbert Johns	Church choirmaster
Louise Johns	His wife
Greta Jones	A village gossip
Vince Jones	Her husband
Barry Jones	Her son and estate carpenter
Pat Jones	Barry's wife
Dean & Michelle	Barry and Pat's children
Revd Peter Harris MA (Oxon)	Rector of the parish
Dr Caroline Harris	His wife
Alex & Beth	Their children
Jeremy Mayer	Manager at Turnham House
Venetia Mayer	His wife

Tom Nicholls	Assistant in the Store
Evie Nicholls	His wife
Dicky & Georgie Tutt	Licensees at the Royal Oak
Bel Tutt	Assistant in the village store
Don Wright	Maintenance engineer (now retired)
Vera Wright	His wife and cleaner at the nursing home in Penny Fawcett
Rhett Wright	Their grandson

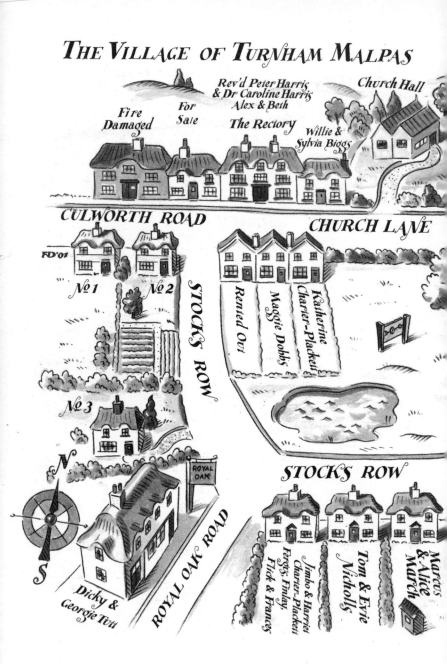

Chapter 1

By nine o'clock, Zack Hooper, well pleased with his attempts at getting the Church of St Thomas à Becket thoroughly organised for the wedding later that morning, decided to have a brew up in his new shed in the churchyard. It had a window along one side so he had a good view of the flowerbeds he'd planted and the ancient trees. Halfway through his mug of tea he became aware of a man studying the inscriptions on the gravestones. Not someone he knew, though. He must have come early for the wedding, he thought. His tea finished, he tossed the tea leaves out on the grass with a practised aim and suddenly the man was beside him.

'Morning, sir, here for the wedding?'

'Er, yes. Yes, I am. Yes, got here a mite early. Is it all right if I walk around for a bit?'

'Of course, the main door's open when you're ready to go in.'

'Lovely morning for a wedding, if it's ever a good morning for one.'

'Ah! Well, the two of them have found love for the first time very late in life, as you will know, so it's a very happy occasion.'

'Of course. Yes, you're right.' The man nodded his head in agreement.

'Relatives of yours, are they?'

'Distant. Come for my mother's sake, really, she can't manage to get here herself. She's confined to a wheelchair, you see.'

Zack's eyes followed the man as he wandered about.

Good-looking chap. Well dressed too, though the suit might just have seen better days. Tall, held himself well, might be an army man, fifties? No, perhaps late forties. Nice thought that, coming for his mother's sake. Showed respect, like.

There were only six guests at the service, not including the man who'd spoken to him, who sat at the back, kind of half there and half not.

Zack tidied up after the service, checked the flowers had plenty of water, turned out the lights, and decided he'd done for the day. But the tall chap was still around.

'Anywhere I could get lunch later on?'

'The Royal Oak has a dining room. Very nice food.'

'Do they have bedrooms?'

Zack shook his head. 'No. Are you wanting somewhere for tonight?'

'Well, yes, I could be.'

'The only place in this village is my wife's B&B. Down Shepherd's Hill, go left at the shop. Or else it means going into Culworth, there're hotels there.'

'I like the idea of staying in this village. Has she a room for tonight?'

'By chance, yes, she has.'

'I'd like to take it. My name's Harry Dickinson.' He held out his hand and Zack found it a no-nonsense handshake, strong, firm and reassuring.

'I'm Zack Hooper. My wife's Marie Hooper, and the house is on the left-hand side going down the hill, Shepherd's Hill that is, and it's called Laburnum Cottage. It's bigger than it looks.'

'Thanks, I'll go down there shortly. I'll have a look round the village first though.'

'Tell her Zack recommended you.'

'I will. Certainly. Thanks.'

'I'm off into Culworth now. Perhaps I'll see you later.'

'Indeed.'

Zack gave Marie a brief blast on his mobile to warn her the chap might be coming, then went into Culworth for lunch and a pint at the Cricketers Inn and a visit to the betting shop. He missed his weekly racing tip from Barclay Ford, such a pity he'd had to do a moonlight flit. Altogether, he'd made about £500 from his tips and his luck hadn't really been in since.

While Zack was lunching in Culworth, the man from the wedding, having bought some chocolate in the village shop, had a coffee in the bar of the Royal Oak, then sat on the seat on the green and watched the geese, was now walking down Shepherd's Hill.

Harry Dickinson liked the look of Laburnum Cottage. A house rather than a cottage, and very smart in a country way. The front had no garden, nor pavement to separate it from the road, and its age showed in the old sash windows and the slightly bulging walls, which were painted yellow as befitted a cottage with the name of laburnum. The door was a gleaming, spotless black with an unusual knocker in the shape of a tree, polished to within an inch of its life. Looking at the upstairs windows he noted the immaculate lace curtains neatly draped and the flowers, real or fake, in each window. Yes, Harry thought, just the place for me.

He gave three loud, positive bangs with the brass knocker and waited. He must be living in country time because there was a long delay before the door was opened. When it did, he was confronted by a small, round woman looking remarkably like a rosy red apple just plucked from the tree; not a blemish on it and ripe and ready for eating.

'Good afternoon. My name's Harry Dickinson. You must be the verger's wife? He said you might have a room available?'

Marie saw a tall, well-dressed man with a charming smile and something about him made her heart skip a beat. 'That's right.

I'm Marie. I do have a room with a lovely view of the garden and Sykes Wood at the back. Would you like to see it?'

Harry nodded. 'Yes, please. It's just for a couple of nights.' He followed her into the house, remembering to wipe his feet on the doormat to make a good impression. The stairs led straight up from the tiny hall and he followed her up the shallow stairs, liking the pictures which scaled the wall as they went upwards. Not a speck of dust was lurking anywhere and the upstairs showed great promise.

She turned to the first door on the left and opened it, inviting him to go in ahead of her. The bedroom glowed with light, the duvet cover and the curtains matched, the carpet was rose coloured, and there was another door which Harry hoped would be an en suite, for he hated sharing bathrooms with strangers. He'd had enough of that.

Harry asked, 'En suite, is it?' Pointing to the door.

'Oh! Yes, my rooms are all en suite. Everyone expects it now, don't they? Gone are the days of nipping down the landing in your shimmy.' She grinned at him and her rosy cheeks became more rounded. He liked her very much indeed.

'I might stay a week, would you have room?'

'At the moment, yes I have. If it's a week, then it's seven nights for the price of six.'

'Which is?'

'Twenty-five pounds a night with full English, access to your room twenty-four-seven and use of the sitting room.'

'I wouldn't want to be in your way.'

'You wouldn't be. Zack and I have ample space in the attic rooms, so you have the guest area to yourself.'

'I see.'

Caution, born of experience, prompted Marie to say, 'Your luggage?'

'In my car. I parked in the village. If I may, I'll go and get it now.'

Marie beamed at him. She pointed to the hospitality tray. 'I keep it well stocked.'

'Thank you, I can see I shall want for nothing. We'll shake hands on the deal.'

And they did and somehow he held her hand a little longer than he should have done, but she didn't mind, he had such a lovely smile.

'You can park round the back. It's better than in the road, sometimes they come charging down the hill as if they were in a Grand Prix race.'

'And parking too. Wonderful. Won't be long.'

Marie then remembered that she'd omitted to take his credit card number as a surety. Well, she'd ask him when he came back.

Harry Dickinson kept himself to himself at first, he had a key so he came and went at will. Once Zack met him in the bar and they had a drink and walked home together but really that was all. He always ate a hearty breakfast, having something of everything and a pile of toast, but then he had paid for it so that didn't matter.

He said he was thinking about staying on and, naturally, Marie agreed because he was no trouble at all. In fact, they'd settled down to a very comfortable going on. She'd already invited him to have Sunday lunch with the two of them and they'd had a nice chat about politics and present-day country life and how it had changed, then he'd gone out for the rest of the day so that was that. He used his car a great deal for going here and there, he'd bought a map from Jimbo's store, and popped into the Royal Oak. One day, when Zack couldn't get the mower to work, Harry had gone to the church and given him a hand and solved the problem almost immediately, so that night he and Marie had gone to the bar and bought him a couple of whiskies as a gesture of thanks. He was so appreciative it was almost embarrassing. 'I don't drink very much, you see. I like to be on the abstemious side, it's all too easy to slip into being dependent on it and that's not my style.'

'Nor mine,' said Zack, 'too many lives ruined by drinking too much.'

'Exactly,' said Harry, staring into his whisky glass. He looked up as though he was about to add some intimate revelation, but closed his mouth and looked bleakly out of the window.

Marie touched his hand gently. 'You look sad.'

He gave her an apologetic half smile and said, 'You don't want to hear my troubles.'

'A trouble shared is a trouble halved.'

But he refused to reply and somehow the pleasure went out of the evening and, before long, Harry asked to be excused and disappeared out of the door with only the briefest of thank yous.

'The poor chap, he's very upset.'

Zack looked at Marie, wondering what was going through her mind, but before he could ask, Paddy Cleary came across.

'Evening, Zack. Marie, how're things? That one of your B&B guests?'

'Yes he is, actually. He's booked to stay a week but he's fancying staying a fortnight.'

'He's a nice chap,' said Paddy.

'Sit down, Paddy, we're about to have another drink. You've met him then?'

'Yes. He came up to the big house thinking it was open for viewing like a stately home is, and I met him in the garden. He gave me a hand loading some new paving stones on to my truck. He wouldn't take no for an answer. Insisted, he did.'

Marie smiled. 'That's typical of him, he gave Zack a hand getting the church mower going when he couldn't fathom what was wrong with it. Such a nice man, so well mannered and no trouble at all. I wish all our guests were as good as him. Two new ones came yesterday and they are a pest.'

'Picky, are they?'

Marie nodded her head emphatically. 'You can say that again. They turn their noses up at my cooked breakfast and want yoghurt and fresh fruit and brown toast and something funny called organic something or other, can't even pronounce it, which I haven't got. If they think they'll get money knocked off for not having cooked, they've got another think coming.'

'Well, if that's the agreed price they can't ask for a discount, can they?'

'Can't they? We'll wait and see.' Marie studied Paddy's face and decided to take the plunge. 'You know, Paddy, I've been thinking, why is it a charming chap like you, in a good, steady job and with this new horticultural qualification Mr Fitch has paid for you to get, why aren't you married?'

Paddy took a long drink of his home-brew before he answered. Those Irish blue eyes of his with their dark lashes twinkled as he said, 'To be honest, Marie, if you were free, I'd ...'

Zack laughed like a drain. 'Too late, Paddy. I found her first, and it's staying that way.'

'You're greedy, Zack, keeping her all to yourself.'

Marie blushed. 'I'm too old for you anyway.'

'I like older women, they know how to look after a chap.' Paddy raised his eyebrows at her and then winked.

'Well, really! You've all the blarney of the Irish and then some, Paddy Cleary.'

Tamsin Goodenough came by, glass in hand. Glad of something to divert Paddy's attention from her, Marie said, 'Oh! There's Tamsin. Come and join us, Tamsin, it's been ages since we saw you. What have you been getting up to lately?'

Tamsin wandered over, Martini and lemonade in hand. 'Hi, Marie. Good evening, Zack.' She nodded to Paddy, who moved his chair a little to make room for her. 'Busy, busy as usual, you know how it is.'

Marie was eager to know, for she was envious of Tamsin's musical success. 'Well, tell us then.'

'Gave an organ recital in the abbey last week, and I've another one in London on Friday evening. Keeps me going.'

Zack, who knew Tamsin well due to her being St Thomas's organist, said, 'We're proud of you, you know. People might not say much, but they are. You're always such a joy to listen to. Have you heard her play, Paddy?'

'No, never. I don't go to church.'

'You can always go to a recital, even if you aren't a church-goer. I'm not, but I go to her recitals when I can.' Marie smiled at Tamsin, thinking as she did so that maybe a bit of matchmaking with these two might be a good idea. Paddy, being lightly built, appeared smaller than he actually was when he stood up, and Tamsin, well, she was just the right size for a woman; not too big and not too small. 'The rector is one of your biggest fans, isn't he, Tamsin?'

'He is, but he plays the organ well too, you know, with no training whatsoever. You've heard him, haven't you, Zack?'

'I have, it can be tear-jerking when he plays sometimes. On the other hand, it can be very jolly. Yes, jolly, that's right and it can lift your spirits. You'll have to go to one of Tamsin's recitals, Paddy, see what you think. Her playing isn't all solemn, it can be funny too and make you laugh.'

'Another drink, anyone?' Paddy wasn't going to let himself get involved with anything at all to do with the church. The further he stayed away from it, the better, in his opinion.

Things got quite lively later on. Dicky Tutt came out from behind the bar to give one of his comic performances, complete with new jokes, and Vince Jones was turned out by Georgie Tutt for becoming truculent, having drunk too much as he cele-brated a win on the lottery. Someone also brought in a dog that threatened to clamp its jaws round Paddy's ankle when he trod on its tail as he passed it on his way to the bar again. Altogether, Marie wished Harry had stayed and witnessed a typical night in the Royal Oak saloon bar.

They'd decided to walk to the pub as the evening was fair but, when it came time to go home, Marie wished they'd brought the car. It seemed a long way home, even though it was downhill all the way. Then, as luck would have it, Harry came past in his car and stopped to give them a lift.

'You should have stayed, Harry. We had a right laugh after you'd gone.'

'Had other things to do.'

'Oh! Right.'

When they got back to Laburnum Cottage, Marie suggested Harry might like a hot drink with them before he went to bed. 'I'll gladly make you one. I can offer you tea, coffee, Ovaltine or Horlicks. I think we've got some ...'

'That would be lovely. Add it to my bill, I insist.'

'Oh for goodness sake! One cup of whatever isn't going to break the bank.'

'Please, I insist.'

'Very well then. What shall it be?'

'I fancy a Horlicks. Please.'

'Come in the kitchen then, while I make it. Zack, what about you?'

'No, thanks. I'm off to bed. Goodnight, Harry.'

While Marie was making Harry's Horlicks, they heard the couple in the front bedroom come in. Marie listened for them going up the stairs and she was glad they did so without calling in the kitchen like they normally did with some complaint about the weather or some outlandish request for their breakfast that she wouldn't be able to cater for.

'Here we are. Horlicks, as requested.'

She sat down with her cup of tea and dared to ask him, 'You

seemed sad in the pub. I hope it wasn't anything me or Zack said.'

Harry's dark-brown eyes focused on her. 'This Horlicks tastes just like my granny used to make.'

'She was a good granny then?'

Harry nodded. 'Drink ruined our family, you see. That's why I'm careful in the pub.'

'Ah! Right. Alcohol has a lot to answer for.'

'Exactly. Both my mum and my dad drank to excess and it made for a rotten childhood.'

Marie felt so sorry for him. She'd had a brilliant childhood, loved and cared for, even though there wasn't that much money about when she was growing up. 'That's hard.'

Harry nodded again. 'They used all the money for drink and then had nothing left to provide food for us all. It was hard.'

'It certainly is.'

'I guess, from the kind of person you are, your childhood was as every child has a right to?'

'Well, we hadn't much money, but we were loved and cared for.'

'That makes such a difference. It spoils your life otherwise, the whole of your life. I joined the army to get away from it all. It's so lovely here, being looked after by you.'

'Pleasure. I suppose at least you got fed well.'

'Yes, but the Falklands and then every unmentionable place you could think of after that, didn't exactly help.'

'You're a Falklands veteran?' Marie reached across and patted Harry's hand. 'Then you're a hero in my eyes. And Zack's.'

He gave her half a smile, then a shadow crossed his face and the sadness was back. 'I was just eighteen. I think I'll drink the rest of this in bed. Do you mind?'

'Of course not, Harry. Feel free. Goodnight.'

As Marie listened to him climbing the stairs, all her mothering instincts sprang to the fore. The poor, dear chap. The

Falklands at eighteen! Just eighteen. Far, far too young for such an experience, and such a sensitive man would find it very hard. If he was eighteen in 1982, what did that make him now? Forty … Forty-seven, if her maths was right. He hadn't mentioned a wife, though. Come to think of it, he hadn't really mentioned anything at all in detail. Perhaps that was part of being a soldier, you learned to shut out the things that you hated. Poor Harry. When he paid her tomorrow she'd find out if he wanted to stay a while longer, except not much longer, because she was already fully booked for some weeks in the summer. Anyway, his money was as good as the next one's, so perhaps she could squeeze him in somehow.

But the day for Harry to pay his bill arrived and he made no offer to pay at breakfast. She'd mention it when she met up with him during the day, Marie decided. Perhaps he was planning to go to the bank today anyway, or pay by credit card. That would be the easiest for her, by credit card.

When she casually reminded him that same evening, on his return at about eight o'clock, he was genuinely sorry. 'My God! What am I thinking about? I've so enjoyed myself here I didn't realise I'd been here a whole week. Tomorrow, first thing, I shall go straight to the bank. I shall draw it out as the clock strikes nine-thirty. In fact, I could go now, couldn't I, and get it from the cash machine instead? I will. I'll go right now. Right away. Please, Marie, please forgive me. It's so careless of me and I wouldn't want to cause offence, not for anything. I'll be back in about an hour.'

He struggled to put his jacket on, but one sleeve somehow managed to be inside out and his hand caught in it and …

'Look, Harry, please don't rush out now. It'll do in the morning. Honestly.'

He stopped struggling with his jacket and looked Marie full in the face. Honesty was in every millimetre of his smile as he said, 'Are you sure, because ...' and continued the battle with his jacket sleeve.

'Just do as I say, pay me in the morning.'

'Well, I have had a busy day ...'

'There you are then. Tomorrow will do. I get the days mixed up sometimes too, it's easy done when you're busy.'

Harry left the moment he finished his breakfast without even cleaning his teeth, which she knew he always did before he went anywhere at all, and was back with the cash by ten-thirty. He insisted on paying her for seven nights seeing as he was paying late. She didn't want him to, but he persuaded her to accept it in the end so his conscience would be clear.

Chapter 2

Despite the downturn in the economy, Jimbo's Turnham Malpas village store was thriving. He'd carefully taken on board a few basic lines that customers could buy more cheaply and yet feel they were buying good food and getting real value for money. Also, and he never let on to Harriet, nor anyone else for that matter, sometimes when his customer was elderly, he added up wrongly on purpose and very few people noticed he was quietly cutting their costs.

The day after Marie had been paid for his week's stay, Harry walked into the store and Jimbo met him for the first time.

'Good morning!'

Jimbo looked up to see who was speaking. 'Good morning. You must be new round here?'

'Well, I'm staying at Laburnum Cottage with Marie and Zack—'

'I've heard about you. Falklands War veteran?'

Harry nodded. 'Name's Harry Dickinson.'

'Yes, that's right. I'm Jimbo, the owner of this establishment.'

'Ah! Right. Nice to meet you. I have been in before, but not when you've been around.' Harry reached out to shake hands.

Like Zack, Jimbo found Harry's handshake very agreeable. 'What can I do for you this bright morning?'

'Because Marie has been so welcoming to me, I'd like to make a meal for them this evening. Just a gesture, you know … of gratitude.'

'They are very genuine people and I'm sure they'll appreciate that.'

'I wondered if you knew something that they would enjoy? I assume they shop here?'

'They do indeed. Something easy?'

'Well, yes. I'm not really very accustomed to cooking. I'd rather pay someone else to do it.' He grinned at Jimbo, who had to grin back. He was that sort of man was this Harry. Very relaxed and friendly, a really nice man.

'They both like fish and, this week, I have a new line in salmon. It comes already cooked, in herbs and wine, so it's just a question of tipping it out onto the plates. I'd also suggest a very nice French mayonnaise to go with it and a pack of new potatoes, scraped and cleaned, all ready for the pan. And perhaps some fresh artichokes? No, maybe not, artichokes could cause you problems if you're not good at cooking. How about frozen broccoli? The cooking instructions are on the packet.'

'Sounds just what the doctor ordered, I'll take your advice.'

In less time than it takes to tell, Jimbo had all the items in one of his smart carrier bags and registered on the cash till but, just before he touched the button for the total, he paused. 'How about wine? Thought about that?'

'Ah! Right! Yes. Wine.'

From the fleeting look of hesitation on his face, Jimbo did wonder if he'd embarrassed the chap moneywise by suggesting wine. 'You don't have to ...'

'Yes, of course. Why not?'

A choice was made after an informative discussion about wine.

'You take credit cards?'

'Wouldn't still be in business if I didn't.'

'How right you are. They are so useful, aren't they?' Harry did the chip and pin and then made to leave, but not before another customer spoke to him.

'Couldn't let you go without saying, "Hello". I'm Venetia

Mayer from the big house. I'm in charge of leisure activities for Mr Fitch's staff. You must be the new man staying with Marie Hooper? Nice to meet you. Your reputation goes before you.'

Harry looked at the vivid creature holding out her hand to him. She was dressed, from head to toe, in a pink sports outfit, including trainers, and a mass of sizzlingly curly black hair fluffed out around her face. She was giving out all kinds of messages. Not village material at all, Harry thought. 'How do you do? I'm not sure I like the idea of my reputation going before me!' he laughed and shook her hand.

'Don't worry, it's only good things about what a nice man you are. You should be flattered, they don't take to strangers quickly round here!' Venetia laughed, showing her startlingly white, perfect teeth which Harry guessed had had hours of work devoted to them by some dentist specialising in cosmetic work.

'That's all right then. I wouldn't want the story of my mis-spent youth to be broadcast all round here!' He flirted with her with his eyes, just enough to excite her. After all, you had to spread a little sunshine on your way through life.

She confidentially tapped his forearm saying, 'What nonsense! I'm quite sure you had an unblemished youth!'

'Well, we won't enquire too closely into that.' He grinned at her and made to leave, but she stopped him by softly suggesting, 'If you have time to spare, you could come during the day and swim in the pool at Turnham House. You could have it to yourself, the students attend lectures most of the day.'

'I might just do that.'

'Are you here for the summer?'

So she was fishing for more information about him, was she? Well, he'd keep her guessing. 'Haven't made up my mind yet, though I must say I'm very comfortable at Laburnum Cottage.'

'Well, any time during the day in the week, except lunch-time. Any time weekends, too, the students have all left then, you see. Ask for me when you come. OK?' She twinkled her fingers at him and he noted the long, well-shaped nails with their matching pink lacquer. She took good care of her body too, he guessed. 'Bye, be seeing you.'

'Thanks. Good morning, Jimbo. I'll let you know how my cooking goes!'

Venetia watched him leave. Jimbo had noted her reaction to Harry and smiled to himself. Well, he thought. She *has* behaved herself for years, ever since her husband Jeremy had his heart attack. Maybe she thinks it's time to go off the rails a little.

'What a nice man. So pleasant.'

'Yes, he is. What can I get you, Venetia?'

'A bottle of vodka please. Craddock is on an economy drive and our free drinks have been banned. He can be so domineering, can Craddock. I like powerful men but ... Now, take you for instance, Jimbo. You have authority, without being a pig. How do you do it?'

'Just my charm. Always got charm, I have. I find it works. Vodka then.'

He slid back the heavy glass door that fronted the drinks shelves and took out a bottle of vodka. 'Anything else?'

'No thanks.' She handed over her credit card.

'I notice *I* don't get an invite to swim in your pool.'

Venetia looked very seriously at him before she replied, 'I ... Well ... You're a happily married man, and very moral to boot. I'd be wasting my time with you. In any case, I don't want your Harriet after my blood, she's a very formidable woman.' She grinned very sweetly at him and Jimbo was forced to acknowledge the truth in what she said. She did the chip and pin and then left. Jimbo watched the swing of her hips as she went out of the door and sensed trouble in the air.

As he stood staring into space, thinking about the trouble Venetia Mayer had caused in the past, Harriet appeared. 'Got nothing to do? Come and give me a hand up at the Old Barn for an hour.'

'Can't, it's Tom's day off.'

'Oh! Of course. What's troubling you?'

'Nothing. Nothing at all.'

'Do I smell Venetia's perfume?'

'Yes.'

'She been flirting again?'

'Not with me.'

'Who then?'

'Harry Dickinson, the man staying at Marie Hooper's.'

'I haven't met him yet. Is he worth her flirting with him?'

'Very well could be. Time on his hands and I suspect there's more to Mr Dickinson than meets the eye.'

'Such as?'

'On the surface he's a very pleasant man; friendly, well spoken and good-looking but ... I don't know, there's a kind of depth to him ...'

'If he's ex-army, perhaps there is. You know, terrible things he doesn't want to remember.'

Jimbo shrugged. 'You're probably right. Will this formidable woman give her old man a kiss before she goes?' He pursed his lips, ready.

'Me? Formidable? Was that Venetia saying that?'

Jimbo nodded, lips still pursed.

So she kissed him. 'Less of the old man! If you're old, then so am I, and I'm not. Bye bye!'

'Bye!' Jimbo thought he was right about Harry. He probably wasn't hiding *unpleasant* thoughts, it was more likely that he was simply a very private person. That could very well be it. A very private person.

All morning, business had been slow and then suddenly, the doorbell, the love of his heart, didn't stop ringing and he was too busy on the till to be thinking about Harry and about him going to be ensnared by Venetia, if he let her.

At Laburnum Cottage, Harry was carefully explaining to

Marie that he was cooking supper that night. 'I don't wish to cause offence, but I thought I should like to do it. So, please, do you mind?' He smiled the gentle smile of a very genuine man, and Marie was won over.

'Of course I don't expect it of my guests but, yes, that's fine. Zack and I will be delighted to have supper with you. The kitchen is yours.'

Harry hoisted the carrier bag onto the hall table. 'To be frank, Jimbo has recommended some very simple things for me to prepare. A couple of things will need to go in the fridge until tonight. Is there room?'

'Of course there is.'

'It's just occurred to me, I've completely forgotten about a dessert! I'll go back and ...'

'You'll do no such thing. I've a box of Cadbury's roulade in the freezer, that can be our contribution.'

Harry thanked her profusely. 'I didn't intend ...'

'Think no more about it. Give me what needs to go in the fridge and I'll put it away. Right?' Marie's lovely country face was lit with a beaming smile and Harry couldn't stop himself from responding to it. He quickly kissed each of her rosy cheeks saying, 'You're too kind.'

Marie blushed bright red.

'Sorry, shouldn't have done that, but you are so very kind to me.'

He handed her the carrier bag and when she noticed there was a bottle of wine in there she said, 'You naughty boy, wine too! Zack will be set up.'

'Jimbo advised me which one to buy. I'm not very well informed about wine, you see.'

'I'm certain it will be lovely then, he's very knowledgeable.'

Harry stood watching her as she disappeared into the kitchen, thinking how lucky he was to have found such a nice place to stay. He almost wished he could stay for ever, but staying in one place for a long time wasn't his scene. He preferred to move on, it was much easier that way. He wandered into the sitting room and sat down to read Zack's morning paper.

He heard Zack shouting to Marie that he was going to do the mowing at the church and that he'd be a couple of hours. Harry, already bored with the day, jumped to his feet. 'Zack! Zack! I'm at a loose end this morning, the friend I was going to meet can't make it. Could I come and give you a hand?'

Glad of the company, to say nothing of the help, Zack welcomed his offer. 'You can use the small cutter and do the awkward bits, if you like. But those shoes of yours will get spoiled.'

'I've got some old trainers.'

Zack nodded his approval and within minutes they were striding up Shepherd's Hill together like old friends.

It took a while for Zack to get the big mower out of the shed and set it up, then he got the small, old-fashioned mower out for Harry to use. 'You don't need me to tell you which bits this little one is for. At one time old Willie Biggs used this for everywhere, but a kind benefactor bought me this big one and it's made all the difference.'

'Not much technical expertise needed with this little one then, just elbow grease!'

'Exactly. When you're fed up, just stop and I'll finish it off.'

'Absolutely not, it will do me good to get my teeth into something and see it through to the end.' Harry switched on the old mower and set off between the graves. Zack studied his purposefulness and thought he really was a grand chap. Such determination and such vigour. He could do with him every week right through the summer.

The two of them worked for the next hour and a half without exchanging a word until Zack felt in need of his morning tea. He switched off the big mower and shouted, 'Just going to put the kettle on.'

Harry acknowledged what he said, then went to the end of the narrow path he was mowing and switched off.

Zack had quite a comfortable set-up in the shed. There was an old kitchen cupboard that provided him with a workspace for his kettle, bottle of milk, mugs and spoons and a trio of old kitchen canisters held the coffee, tea bags and sugar. There was an electric socket just above the worktop. 'Sit yourself down. It won't take long with this kettle, it used to be Marie's but when she decided to do B&B, she bought a new one and I got this.'

'You're lucky with Marie, she's a lovely lady.'

'You're right there. I'm the luckiest man alive, and there's not many that can say that after thirty years of marriage.'

'Thirty years, that's a long time.' Harry sat ruminating on this matter while they waited for the kettle to boil. 'My parents weren't even married. It might have been better if they had been, they might have felt more commitment, you know.'

'There's lots nowadays aren't married, isn't there? They seem happy enough, but it's not quite the same, I always think.'

'Children?'

'One daughter in America, and she's the spitting image of Marie. Always wished we had more but it didn't happen. You got brothers or sisters?'

'Two brothers and we fought like hell. Dad encouraged us.' Harry sighed. 'He favoured first one, then another. He put us at each other's throats, to make men of us, he said. The idiot. He drank himself to death, literally. I don't remember him ever being in work.'

Zack detected a slight tremor in Harry's voice and wished he'd never brought the subject up. Poor Harry, what a life. It took a lot of character to overcome a childhood like that and become such a decent man. 'Here's your tea. I never thought to ask, is tea OK or would you prefer coffee? Is that enough milk?'

'Tea's fine.' They sat, drinking in silence, until Harry

eventually said, 'That's why I joined the army. To get out of the way, have a roof over my head and some half-decent food.'

'First time I saw you, I thought you might be army. It was the way you walked; upright, shoulders back. You always look as if you're going somewhere too, not just idling about.'

The light flooding in from the wide open doors of the shed was unexpectedly blocked by a tall figure. 'Good morning, Zack.'

Zack leaped to his feet. 'Good morning, sir. Another beautiful day. What can I do for you?'

Harry got a nod from the intruder and Zack introduced him, 'This is Harry Dickinson. He's staying with us for a while and he's been helping with the mowing. Harry, this is our rector, Peter Harris.'

Harry stood up and shook the hand he'd been offered. 'Good morning, Rector. A lovely day.' Harry found himself looking up into a pair of startlingly blue eyes that seemed to bore into his very soul. It took some strength not to feel intimidated by him. This man had the kind of aura that Harry found disturbing, so he sat down again, eager to avoid his thoughtful eyes.

'Just a message, Zack. I had a phone call this morning from the undertaker in Culworth to say that the last of the Gotobed sisters has died in the nursing home. Not unexpected, I must say. I saw her a week ago and her Gotobed sparkle had seriously diminished. We've arranged the funeral for next Monday at two o'clock, refreshments afterwards in the church hall. The last of a long line of Gotobeds, I'm afraid. None of the three girls, nor their brother, ever married, you see. A hundred and one she is ... Was. I'll put the details in the book for you. Right? You know which grave, don't you? The Gotobed one under the apple tree, not the one out by the yew tree.'

Zack nodded. 'Right you are, sir.'

'Nice to have met you, Harry. See you again sometime.'

'I'm sure you will.'

'Kind of you to help Zack with the mowing.'

'A pleasure ... Sir.'

Harry didn't speak for a while after Peter had left then, having finished his tea right to the bottom of the mug, he said, 'Nice man?'

'The day he leaves here, and please God it won't be for years yet, will be a bad day for this village. He's seen us through a lot these last years. He's always there if you need support and whatever you tell him, it's absolutely confidential. He never breathes a word, even though some of the busybodies round here try to get him to say what he knows. A wonderful rector, couldn't be bettered.'

'Good-looking man. Is he married?'

'He is. Married to a doctor. She's a lovely lady who sees the best in everyone and brings out the best in everyone, believe me. You seem very interested.'

'The clergy interest me in general. I just can't understand why they do it. A fine, upstanding chap like him. He's obviously intelligent and has a lot going for him, and he becomes a rector. I mean, you know. Clerical collar, and all that. It's a funny occupation for a real man.'

'Well, he's a real man and he's good at his job.'

'Didn't say he wasn't.'

'And, what's more, he means every word he says. He prays for half an hour every morning in church from six thirty to seven, then he does a three-mile run, home for his breakfast and then on with his work.'

'He has a pretty penetrating stare.'

Zack grinned. 'You've noticed. Nobody can hide things from him. He knows you inside out, so you'd better watch out!' Zack nudged Harry and laughed out loud, 'Come on then, let's get cracking.'

'Let's go to the pub after and you can introduce me to some of the others. Right?'

'Great.' Zack glanced at his watch. 'Half an hour should see us finished. Come on then.'

Harry went back to finish his mowing and started raking up the grass, thinking hard. The less he saw of that rector, the better it would be for him. He hated it when he met people who wanted to find out too much about him. He liked to keep his life private, after all, his life was his life and no one else's, and that's how it should be. He'd never been close to anyone in his life. In fact ...

'I'm done, are you? I'll rake this bit here up for you and that'll be it, won't it?'

'OK, Zack. Thanks.'

They each had a ploughmans. The cheese was wonderful, the salad fresh and the pickle homemade. A glass of Dicky's home-brew topped it all off wonderfully well. Harry enjoyed meeting Dicky properly. He was a 'hail fellow well met' kind of person, there didn't seem to be any unknown depths to him, nor his wife Georgie, who was bright, blonde and jolly. Just the kind of wife he would ...

'Hi there!' It was Jimbo from the store, delivering a side of cooked ham for the dining room. 'Mind if I join you? I just fancy a glass of ale. I'll see Georgie first.'

Jimbo exchanged the side of ham for a fistful of notes from the till and ordered his ale. 'On the house, Jimbo, you dear boy. We've run out of ham and I never thought you'd deliver today. You're special, you are.'

Jimbo came across to sit with Zack and Harry and a general conversation ensued, in which they told Harry all about the advantages of living in Turnham Malpas. Some things they thought were good, Harry knew for sure he wouldn't like, but others he could see the advantage of, and wondered why he'd never chosen to live in a village before.

Jimbo downed the last of his ale and, after wiping his

moustache in case of froth lingering on it, said, 'I don't suppose you're a bell-ringer, are you?'

'A bell-ringer?' Harry almost choked on the last of his pickle. '*Me,* a bell-ringer?'

'I only meant it if you intend staying in the village. Do you?'

'Well, not really. I'm just here for a week or so to get my bearings and such, but no intention of staying for a lifetime. No, no. I'm terribly sorry.'

'Have you any experience in that field?'

Harry laughed. 'Absolutely none, sorry. I can't help you with that.'

'Ah! We're desperately short of volunteers, you see. I saw you helping Zack and thought that perhaps you were thinking of staying.'

'No, I'm not. I was just at a bit of a loose end this morning, so I thought I'd give him a hand, that's all. Thanks for thinking I might be a suitable candidate, though.'

'What is your forte?'

'Accounts, mainly.'

Jimbo came alive. 'Accounts! I could give you two weeks' work, immediately. My accounts person is just out of hospital after an operation, and I'd be grateful for you to take over the basic running of the accounts for me. He'll be back at work two weeks from now, he says, though I doubt it.'

'I haven't any references with me.'

'Not to worry, you won't be handling money. I always do that side. It's entering the data that's the bit that bores me and takes up too much of my time. Overheads, wages, writing cheques for me to sign to pay my suppliers etc. Would you? You could start tomorrow. I'd be ever so grateful. You'd be working up in the office at the Old Barn. Lovely working conditions.'

'Well, I am computer literate. But ... You're taking a risk ... No, maybe I'd better not.' Harry shook his head, a grave expression on his face.

'Really? My daughter Fran helps out sometimes with the data-entering, but she's busy at school at the moment. GCSEs and all that. Come on, how about it? I pay good workers, good money. I'm not a penny pincher, honest.'

Harry hesitated. He could do with the money ... He'd get a reference out of it too, he supposed. 'Shall I? OK then, I will. As long as I'm not outstaying my welcome at Marie's.'

Zack emphatically declared he would not be, privately thinking of the £150 a week Harry would pay for the privilege.

'Tomorrow morning. Eight-thirty start, four-thirty finish. I'll be up there and I'll explain everything. I'll be so glad to have someone reliable.'

'You don't know if I'm reliable. Not yet, anyway.'

'If you're not, then I shall give you the elbow. I'm not in the business of paying people to play when I'm paying them to work. I'm a tough but fair employer.'

'I like the sound of that. You're up front and that pleases me. I like to know where I stand. I like that kind of honesty. Right, you're on. Eight-thirty tomorrow morning, for two weeks.'

Harry watched Jimbo leaving, lost in thought. Suddenly he said, 'That all right with Marie, Zack? I don't want to upset her plans in any way.'

'There're two guests coming this Friday for the weekend, that's all at the moment. Things don't hot up until the summer, you see. June, July, August time. We'll both be glad of your company until then.'

Harry left the Royal Oak delighted by the prospect of working for Jimbo. He'd been at a loss for things to do these last few days, there was a limit to the sightseeing one could do without travelling miles, and petrol wasn't cheap. Two weeks' work. First thing tomorrow, he'd ask what the pay was.

That same afternoon he walked up to Turnham House for a swim.

Chapter 3

So the next morning, as promised, Harry arrived at the Old Barn at eight twenty-five to find Jimbo ahead of him, opening up the staff door.

'Good morning. You've walked up.'

'Yes. I didn't know the parking arrangements and thought that, as I would be sitting down most of the day, the walk would do me good. First of all, I would like to thank you for the opportunity to help you out. I'm used to being busy so I'm not very good at hanging around. I just hope you'll be satisfied with my work.'

'We're doing each other a good turn. Here we are, this is your office.'

Jimbo flung the door wide open and Harry thought: Could there be an office anywhere in the world better placed? The room was ablaze with the early morning sun streaming in through a vast window that overlooked the parkland and, in the distance, a lake fringed by trees newly burst into life. Someone was riding a rather splendid horse down to the lake and, unwittingly, brought the whole breathtaking scene to life. The beauty of it all illuminated Harry's very soul.

'My word! Isn't that wonderful? And, by the looks of it, water-fowl too. Not black swans, surely? Yes, they are! Marvellous!'

Jimbo, accustomed to the beauty through familiarity, nodded his agreement. 'This is your desk.' It was one of two bright, up-to-the-minute desks with the latest computers. Beside the one he would be using was a pile of paperwork and Harry longed to get his teeth into it and do something worthwhile at last.

Jimbo sat with him for a valuable half an hour, pointing out the mistakes people tended to make and the ease with which the computer gave out figures with the simple pressing of keys in the right order. 'Well, how do you feel about it? Is it within your capabilities?'

'I shall be slow to begin with, but it appears to be a very smooth system, well put together. I'm keen on everything being correct, you see. I hate mess with figures, figures have a right to be accurate, that's what they're for.'

'That sounds like the kind of person I need. Too many people claim to be computer literate and scarcely know how to switch the damn things on, never mind put in data correctly. I shan't be hovering all morning, but I will come back in an hour just to check you've got the hang of it. Facilities through that door over there. There's a small kitchen so if you fancy a drink help yourself. Lunch is one till two. You're free to have food in the kitchen on the ground floor, I don't like the smell of food in the office, you see. A pound for lunch. The girls are very helpful. OK?'

Jimbo swung away out of the car park, well satisfied with his newest member of staff. If he made a success of it, he might just offer him a permanent job to take some of the pressure off himself. Perhaps then he might have more free time.

Upstairs, alone in the office, Harry stood looking out of the window, indulging himself with the view. He imagined what it would be like to own it all himself, to ride that magnificent horse across his own park, across his own field. What would it be like to live in the wonderful house he could just glimpse through the trees? When he'd been up there the other day for his swim, he'd had no idea of the extent of the estate. Money. That was it. Money. Just paying the wages of the people working there would need a stack of it. Up the narrow lane came a battered red van with planks of wood sticking out of the back door. The driver pulled up outside the Old Barn and leaped out, leaving the engine running. Harry could hear him racing up the stairs to his office.

'She's not here then?'

'Only me, I'm afraid.'

'Harriet, I mean. They said she'd be here.'

'Sorry.'

'I'm Barry, the estate carpenter. If she comes, will you tell her I've got the planks and I'll start on that job for her tomorrow. She'll know what I mean.'

'Right.'

'You are?'

'Harry Dickinson. I'm inputting data for Jimbo, temporarily.'

'Better get cracking then. He doesn't pay for people to be idle. When he comes back, he'll expect three days' work done in half a morning, believe me.' Barry laughed as though he'd been caught out more than once.

'He's a right to expect it when he's paying.'

Barry nodded. 'I'll be off then. Tell her I've left the planks round the back.'

'OK. Be seeing you.'

'I expect so.' Barry wagged a finger at Harry and then pointed it at the computer. He left, his laughter curling back up the stairs as he went back to his van.

Harry sat down to begin work, somehow more cheered than for a long time.

He had his swim gear in his backpack so, if he finished at four-thirty like Jimbo had said, he'd go for a swim. After all, Venetia was well worth pursuing. Though he couldn't decide if it was him doing the pursuing or Venetia ... Whatever, she held a lot of promise and it had been a long time.

★

Later that morning, Harriet arrived, introducing herself immediately as Jimbo's other half. She held out her hand. 'You must be Harry. How do you do? I'm Harriet, Jimbo's wife.'

Harry got to his feet and found himself looking into a pair of kindly brown eyes. He warmed to her immediately. She was wearing a kitchen uniform, it was snow white and flattering and her brown hair peeped out round the edges of her black-and-white checked hat.

'That's right. Harry Dickinson.'

'Jimbo was coming to see you at ten, but he's been inundated with reps this morning and hasn't been able to escape. Is everything OK, he says.'

'Absolutely. The system is unbelievably simple and does the trick marvellously. Whoever wrote the program must be a genius.'

Harriet smiled. 'I'll tell him, he'll be flattered.'

'Jimbo did it then?'

'He did. Hours of sweat and toil ironing out the gremlins, but got there in the end. Must go. Busy, busy. He told you about lunch?'

'He did.'

After Harriet left, Harry sat down to contemplate his good luck. Never in the whole of his life had he fallen on his feet to such an extent as now, and how he relished it. Such trusting people, that was what surprised him. They'd never met him before and they hadn't even asked for references before entrusting all this to him. He looked round the office at the thoroughly pleasant surroundings, the thick carpet, the marvellously contoured chairs provided; he wasn't going to get backache sitting in one of these all day. Oh no! Top of the range, they were. And that wonderful view from the window, now that he really did enjoy. Back to work.

★

Jimbo came to see him towards the end of the afternoon, apologising for having neglected him.

'Please don't worry. I haven't felt neglected, and I've processed three quarters of the pile.'

'You have! That's terrific! I thought you said you would be slow to begin with?'

'I did say that, but I only meant the first hour and since then I've been rattling away. I rang Mrs Jones in Mail Order with a query which she was able to sort out for me. Other than that ...'

'She's usually right. Not always, of course, but more often than not. Works like a slave, does Greta, and well worth her money. Ten pounds an hour, is that all right?' Jimbo's eyebrows arched a little as he waited for his answer.

'That's absolutely fine. Yes, absolutely fine.'

'Feels fair?'

'Of course.'

'Lunch OK?'

'Yes, thank you. I paid my pound.'

'Did you get a receipt?'

'No.'

'Damn. I shall go down there and play hell.'

'Not on my account.'

'No, on mine. Four-thirty, it's time you weren't here. I don't pay overtime unless it's agreed beforehand.'

'I won't ask for extra payment, but I want to finish this batch before I go for my own satisfaction.'

Jimbo studied Harry's expression. 'Very well then, that's your choice. Bye.' He liked the chap, he really did. He'd taken a risk with him, but it seemed to be justified. He liked that phrase of his, 'for my own satisfaction'.

Before he left, he went into the kitchen to play hell like he'd promised Harry he would. He found a few things he wasn't exactly pleased with in the kitchen hygiene routine so he was longer than he intended and, when he was leaving, he saw Harry going into the big house through the student entrance. Now what was he up to? Ah! Yes, just what he'd suspected might happen. Oh, Venetia! Oh, Harry!

But Venetia and Harry were behaving very circumspectly. They were seated on sunloungers after a rigorous fifteen-minute session racing each other up and down the pool. Venetia was fitter by far, and it had been Harry who'd suggested a rest.

'Terribly sorry, I've just not had the opportunity to keep fit lately.'

'Why, what have you been doing?'

'That and this, this and that. Very busy doing lots of hours, earning a living wage.'

'Well,' Venetia patted Harry's forearm, 'You've a job now. Paying well, I assume, with reasonable hours, so now's the time to get fit again.'

'I'm certainly well paid for what I'm doing.'

'That's typical Jimbo. He pays above the odds for the area, so he gets people clamouring to work for him. He never appears to have problems filling vacancies. And what's more, everyone loves working for him, even if they do complain what a taskmaster he is.'

Venetia's eyes strayed to Harry's chest, then his thighs. Then she found that she was being scrutinised too. She was aware that there was nothing but approval in her eyes and hurriedly veiled them in case he ...

'Like what you see?' Harry asked her.

Venetia's excuse quickly sprang to mind. 'I was just thinking what pale skin you have, as if you've not been outside for yonks.'

'I never stay out in the sun because I get sweat rashes if I do, so I always look pale. Obviously you aren't affected by the sun, you've a lovely tan.'

It occurred to Venetia that Harry was as skilled at finding reasons as she was, but she dashed that idea aside because she liked him and he was the first man she'd properly flirted with since she'd turned over a new leaf after Jeremy's heart attack. She thought about her Jeremy and how much he loved her, and all the times she'd been wayward in their marriage. Well, she deserved a bit of waywardness now considering how long she'd been faithful to him. Venetia laughed deep down inside herself, and decided: blast it, I'm going for this one, he won't be staying long. Two weeks of fun, that's what. Just two weeks.

Harry had identical thoughts and ran the tip of his tongue around his dry lips. He looked deeply into Venetia's eyes, a half smile on his face. She was brazen with her flirting, totally brazen. She could make the slightest movement of her body into a promise and he sensed she wouldn't be hurt by the brevity of a whirlwind relationship.

'Another swim?'

Harry nodded, 'Leisurely though, not racing. I've got to get myself fitter before I race again. Obviously you're never out of the pool.'

'That's my job; teaching swimming, diving and organising leisure time fun for the students. Work hard, play hard is Mr Fitch's motto.' She grinned at him, but dropped her glance when he raised his eyebrows. Damn the man, he could read her every thought and it wasn't on, but at the same time she loved the danger of it.

'Mr Fitch, who's he?'

'The boss. Fitch Enterprises Europe. He's wealthy beyond belief. All this,' she waved an arm around the pool complex, 'is for staff training. My husband runs the estate and I do the leisure and sports bit.'

'Where do you live then?'

'We have a maisonette on the premises. Our own front door, but it's part of the big house.'

'Very useful, I should think, your own front door.' He flicked an amused glance at her.

'You're flirting with me!' Venetia leaped up, braced herself on the edge of the pool and dived gracefully into the water, making scarcely a splash but a big impression on Harry as he watched her body curve down towards the water. His eyes scanned the pool until, almost halfway down the length of the pool, her head bobbed up and she rolled over onto her back. My God, she was fit. He guessed she was older than she would like to be, but what the heck! So was he; they made a pair. Harry dropped into the pool and, doing his clumsy front crawl, caught up with her. They both burst into laughter as he caught hold of her round her waist.

Neither of them noticed Jeremy who, having finished his day's work, had come to look for her. He turned away, silently closing the door behind him, not able to face what he recognised would inevitably happen between the two of them. His heart lay heavy in his chest. This time he couldn't possibly ignore it, not like he'd done all the other times. Love was the very devil.

Chapter 4

Harry might have imagined that no one knew about his assignation with Venetia, but then he'd never lived in a village before. Jimbo knew, and thus Harriet had been informed. Maggie Dobbs, who kept the school clean and sparkling, also knew because she had, quite by chance, met Harry walking back to Laburnum Cottage as she left the school and walked down Shepherd's Hill with him on her way to Dottie Foskitt's.

Maggie greeted him by introducing herself and good manners dictated that he should tell her his name. 'Oh! You're the gentleman who's started working for Jimbo Charter-Plackett?'

'That's right. First day today.'

'It's good working for him. I look after the school during the day but I help Jimbo on the catering side with the events at the Old Barn in the evenings and weekends. It's a lovely job, it keeps me busy and the money's very welcome.'

She could smell the chlorine on him and noted his damp hair and backpack. 'Been swimming?'

'Yes. I got invited. It's a lovely pool.'

'You'd have seen Venetia then?'

'That's right. I did.'

Maggie had to laugh. When she did a quick glance sideways, it told her Harry looked a mite embarrassed. She'd guessed, and yes she'd guessed right. There was something going on there. She must be wrong though. He seemed to be a gentleman and Venetia had been behaving herself for years.

Harry, always on the qui vive where his private life was

concerned, diverted her attention by asking her how far down the hill she was going.

'Right to the bottom, to that very old cottage. Well, three years ago it was improved a bit. Dottie rents it. She wishes she owned it, after all, it'll be worth a fortune now with the new kitchen and bathroom and the garden made lovely.' She sounded envious.

'Like gardening, do you?' Harry asked.

Maggie stumbled and Harry caught hold of her elbow as her ankle twisted in a hole in the tarmac. 'Whoops! Thanks. This road is always the very last on the council's repair list. That hole's been there for months. You'd think I'd learn, wouldn't you?' Maggie rather liked the firm grip of Harry's hand on her arm, it was the kind of grip that made you feel the owner of it was reliable.

'OK?'

'Yes, thanks.'

Harry released his grip saying, 'Well, this is me. Laburnum Cottage.'

'You're lucky. They're a very nice couple.'

'You're right, they are. Be seeing you around, no doubt.'

'I'm in the Royal Oak in the evenings sometimes. Might see you there?'

'Very likely. Bye, Maggie. Nice to have met you.'

'And you. Bye.' Maggie strode on down the hill to Dottie's. So that was the Harry Dickinson they were all talking about. Well, she liked him. There was something very pleasant about him, there really was. Gentlemanlike, he was. Consequently, she made a point of being in the Royal Oak that very night. Not to see him, of course, but to relay the information she'd gleaned.

She found herself to be the very first of the group who regularly sat together on the old table with the oak settle down one side of it. She carefully avoided sitting in the chair that had always been Jimmy's; no one did, you see. His chair was always felt to be his and no one else's. Georgie came across to have a word. 'Hello, Maggie. All alone tonight?'

'The others will be in before long, I expect.'

'It'd feel funny if they weren't.'

'Has the new chap, Harry Dickinson, been in?'

Georgie nodded. 'He's been in a few times. He's got a job now, I understand.'

'Accounts for Jimbo, till his accounts person gets over his op. He's a nice man.'

'I thought so too. Very polite, almost shy.'

'Not that shy!' Maggie laughed.

With raised eyebrows and a grin on her face Georgie said, 'What do you mean, Maggie Dobbs?'

Maggie tapped the side of her nose, 'Been swimming up at the big house.'

'Not ...' Georgie glanced round to make sure she wasn't overheard, 'Venetia?'

'Now, did I say that?'

'No, you didn't, but you might as well 'ave. Oh! Here they come.' She patted the chair that had been Jimmy Glover's. 'I miss him. I expect you do, too.'

Pat Jones had arrived, along with Sylvia and Willie Biggs and, trailing a long way behind, Don Wright, but no Vera.

'No Vera tonight, Don?'

'No. My turn for the first round. No, there's been a crisis at the nursing home, all hands on deck job.'

'Somebody taken poorly?'

'You're right there, Maggie. Lovely old chap. My Vera's right upset, she really took a shine to him she did. Always the gentle-man. Lancelot Lewis-Figges is his name. Lewis-Figges with a hyphen. From a posh family, he is and ...'

'Don! Are you getting the drinks in then, or not? I'm parched.' Willie was impatient, he could see this conversation might go on for an hour or more. Once Don got going, he didn't know when to stop. He hadn't been quite the same since his accident, it had addled his brain, for sure.

'All right, all right.'

As Don headed for the bar counter, in came Harry. He stood looking around as though hoping he'd see someone he knew. Georgie waved to him and called, 'Good evening!' and Maggie called out, 'Come and sit with us, we're just getting the drinks in.'

Harry gave her a thumbs up and went to the bar to order his own drink.

Maggie leaned forward and whispered, 'He's been swimming with Venetia!'

'No!' said Pat Jones, 'Oh, my word! I thought she'd stopped all that? Perhaps there's nothing in it, maybe it happened by chance?'

Maggie raised her eyebrows in disbelief.

Harry came to their table, and seeing Jimmy's chair empty, sat down in it. 'Good evening!' He raised his glass in greeting and drank a good half of his pint all in one go, wiped his mouth, and looked at Maggie. 'I don't know anyone. Maggie, will you introduce me? I'm Harry Dickinson, by the way.' He smiled at everyone in turn.

His smile was met by frozen faces. Someone had to tell him and, finally, it was Sylvia who plucked up the courage to explain, 'I'm Sylvia, Harry. Married to Willie here,' she said, tapping Willie's arm. 'I hope you don't mind, but we're careful not to sit in that chair at the moment. A dear friend of ours died rather unexpectedly sitting in it only three weeks ago so we're a bit touchy about using his chair. We're not being unfriendly, just a bit touchy.'

Harry shot to his feet, white-faced and apologetic. 'I'm so sorry, I'd no idea.'

'Of course you hadn't. Here look, sit next to Don. Anywhere

but there!' said Sylvia sympathetically, moved by Harry's obvious distress.

'I am indeed very sorry. A dear friend, you say?' Harry pushed his glass of home-brew further along and slipped into the chair next to Don.

Don said, 'That's my Vera's chair.'

Harry shot to his feet again. 'I'd better sit at another table, I'm so sorry. Has she died too?'

'My Vera? No, of course not! She's just having to work late at the nursing home as someone's not turned in, so she won't be coming. But it is.'

Willie, unable to cope any longer with the confusion they were causing between them said, 'Look, Harry, stay where you are. Vera usually sits there, but she's not coming so it's fine. He's being difficult on purpose. You're very welcome. We're all friends round this table, believe me. Go on, sit down.'

Don, in a huff, complained, 'I didn't mean nothing at all, just mentioned it, that's what.' Those who knew him could sense he was brewing for a serious row, sometimes it happened all over nothing with Don.

'You should engage your brain before you speak, Don.' Willie reminded him.

'That's not very kind saying that. Poor Don.' said Pat Jones.

'Are you claiming I'm not right in the head no more? Because I am all right, our Vera says. Ask her,' Don said with a belligerent tone to his voice.

'No, I wasn't, but you should,' replied Willie.

'I know I'm not all that good after my accident, but I'm not rude.'

'I never said you were.'

'You did.' Don fidgeted with his glass, straightened the beer mat, ran his fingers through his snow-white hair and, before anyone managed to say something to calm his ruffled feathers, he leaped to his feet, well, as fast as he was able nowadays, reached across the table and landed a punch on Willie's nose. Blood immediately streamed from it. Sylvia screamed, Maggie began laughing, Pat Jones searched in her bag for a tissue or two for Willie, and uproar ensued. Georgie came across with a tea towel to catch the flow of blood, except initially it had spurted into Willie's half-full glass of home-brew. Sylvia then began to cry, she was so upset. Altogether, mayhem had erupted.

'You can apologise for that, Don, that was unnecessary in the extreme.' This came from Georgie, who'd had a heavy day brought on by the good weather, which meant that the bar had been extremely busy right from first thing.

'Not my fault. It was Willie, that's what.'

'Now, see here ...'

But Harry interrupted Sylvia by saying, calmly, 'It was no one's fault. I was to blame, through ignorance of whose chair I'd sat in, so let me sort things out. Willie, I'm buying you a fresh glass, home-brew, was it? Don, of course you didn't mean any-thing by what you said, and I haven't taken offence. Next round on me. Can Willie have another glass, Georgie, right now?'

'Of course. Thanks for taking it so kindly. Lovely manners you have indeed. I'll bring it straight across. All right now, Willie?'

Willie's nose was still running a little but the flow caused by the initial impact had definitely lessened. 'Much better.'

Harry spoke again, even more calmly than before, 'Tell me something about this dear friend of yours who so unexpect-edly went to heaven sitting in that empty chair. You must have valued him to feel like you do.'

Harry's softly spoken request drove them to reminisce about Jimmy Glover and his escapades, which kept them occupied right through the drinks Harry bought for them, and through the next round bought by Willie. Good humour was finally restored when they remembered the story about Jimmy's dog, Sykes. It took some telling, but Harry appeared to be enjoying it so they carried on. 'But you see this dog that turned up *after* the *first* Sykes had died, looked identical to Sykes number one and, what's more, it adopted Jimmy. It even knew where Jimmy had always put the water bowl and where it was supposed to sleep. It gave us all the shivers cos it seemed as though it was the old Sykes come back from the dead. It even liked going to church, just like the old Sykes did.'

'I can see why you felt it was creepy. Bit unnerving, wasn't it?' Harry declared.

'It certainly was,' said Sylvia.

'Where's Sykes two now then? Since, you know ...'

'Well, Grandmama Charter-Plackett from next door's taken him in but, to be frank, dogs aren't her thing and she'd be glad for it to have a home somewhere else. She only took the animal in because of her fond memories of Jimmy. He was her longtime neighbour ...'

'I see. Poor Sykes.'

'Yes, poor Sykes.'

Harry had been taken into their circle of friends in the space of an evening and they all went home delighted about him being so friendly and interested in the village.

'What a grand chap he is,' said Willie to Sylvia.

'He's such a nice man,' said Maggie to herself, having no one to listen to her.

Don told Vera when he got home what a lovely evening they'd had talking to Harry.

Harry went home almost feeling as if he belonged, which was an emotion he was totally unaccustomed to and he felt pleased ... but, at the same time, he knew it couldn't last. The job with Jimbo would only last two weeks and then he'd be off on his travels. Where though?

But fate took a hand and Harry got a shock the next morning when he found Jimbo waiting for him in the office, his face drawn and anxious, his eyes glazed by distress and his attitude thoroughly downbeat.

'Why, Jimbo, whatever's the matter?'

'Well … There's no easy way to say this, but my accounts person, Ken Allardyce, died last night.' Jimbo took a deep breath to get his voice under control.

'Oh! I'm so sorry.'

'Heart, you see. They rushed him back to hospital, but they couldn't revive him. It's a terrible shame, he was such a grand chap and a pleasure to work with. He was only thirty-nine. Dodgy, unpredictable things, hearts. He was the apple of his mother's eye. Lovely chap, straight as a die, and a real friend to me. Thirty minutes with Ken, and you'd be laughing for twenty-nine of 'em. Great chap.' He went to gaze out of the window.

'That is so sad.'

'I'll be off. I can't face the day, really. You OK with the accounts?'

Harry nodded. 'Leave the accounts to me. It's one less thing for you to worry about right now.'

Jimbo nodded. 'Thanks for that. Very kind. Perhaps see you later.' He gathered his bits and pieces together, took a long look round the office as though recalling seeing Ken working there, shook his head, and out he went.

Harry worked all day without giving a thought as to what this sudden death might mean to him. He couldn't grieve, after all he hadn't known the man, but he felt impressed that Jimbo, as an employer, was so upset. It said something rather special about him. It wasn't until he was clearing up at half past four that it occurred to him that this might be a fortuitous occurence for himself. Might Jimbo ask him to stay on? If he did, he couldn't stay at Marie and Zack's. One hundred and fifty pounds for a week or two, yes, but not indefinitely. He checked the clock. Four thirty-one. Better be off. Venetia would be waiting. God, she was an exciting woman. He found her utterly irresistible. She doubled, no trebled, every emotion he had ever experienced with a woman. His mother would have described her as a real cracker of a woman and, what's more, she was just what he needed right now, this very minute, this very day.

Harry went straight up there but today, instead of going so publicly into the leisure centre part of the building, he went round the back to knock on the front door of Venetia and Jeremy's maisonette. She'd said he could and he knew exactly where that would lead him; straight into her bed.

Venetia opened the door so quickly that she must have been standing behind it waiting for him. She drew him into her arms and they were kissing before the door closed. They stripped off as they finished their first kiss and were upstairs in the bedroom in far less time than it takes to tell.

Breathless, the two of them eventually rolled apart and Harry's first words were, 'What about Jeremy?'

'He's out for the day with Mr Fitch, looking at a new place he's thinking of buying. In any case, don't worry about him, he lets me do as I like in all matters. We have that kind of a marriage.'

Harry, for a reason quite unknown to him, suddenly went on red alert. 'I can't believe that. If you were married to me, you wouldn't have carte blanche, not likely.'

Venetia turned towards him saying, 'What would *you* do if you caught *your* wife in bed with a man?'

'Cut his throat.'

'Well, Harry dear,' she stroked his throat with a lingering finger, 'no need to worry about your throat because Jeremy wouldn't do a thing. He never has done, and he never will, believe me. Wouldn't say boo to a goose, would our Jeremy.'

The wickedness of her attitude thrilled Harry. It made her even more tempting than she already was. 'He's caught you before?'

'Not *caught* me, no, but he has known what was going on and he didn't say a word.'

'A very tolerant man, then.'

'He loves me, you see. Strange, isn't it? Perhaps if he *didn't* love me, he'd have cut my throat long ago.'

'Not this perfect, perfect throat?' Harry said, even though he could see the wrinkles starting to appear.

'Even this perfect throat. You are such a handsome man, Harry. So perfectly mannered and so confidence-boosting. Shall we?'

He couldn't resist her, but he wouldn't come to the house again. Taking a quick passionate moment in the changing rooms round the pool was fine, but this was altogether too risky. He also felt bad doing it in the excessively tolerant Jeremy's own bedroom. One had to have some standards.

'See you tomorrow?' she asked as he was leaving.

'Possibly. It just depends. You've heard Ken Allardyce has died? It might mean extra work for me. I don't know, Jimbo's very upset.' A thought occurred to him. 'He's not ...?'

Venetia roared with laughter. 'That man is so moral it's unbelievable. I had high hopes, with all that money, but no, he's strictly off limits.'

Harry humbly remarked, 'I'm glad I'm not.' Then he kissed her luscious red mouth and left with a spring in his step and a smile on his face. Best keep her guessing a bit, he thought to himself. If he fell completely under her spell she'd be capable of making his life hell, he knew that without a shadow of a doubt. A nice kind of hell, though.

He became aware of someone following him as he passed through the village down Jack's Lane and turned to make sure it wasn't Jeremy Mayer, bent on throat-cutting.

It was, however, a Jack Russell terrier. He stopped when

Harry stopped and when he began walking again, so did this strange little dog. The story about Sykes, owned by the now-deceased but greatly lamented Jimmy, came into his mind so he turned round and bending down said, 'Hello! Sykes, is it? Are you Sykes?' The dog's tail wagged furiously, in fact, almost all of his body wagged too and it made Harry laugh. Sykes allowed him to stroke his head and they had a pleasant few minutes making each other's acquaintance. But Harry needed his evening meal, which Marie had kindly started making for him now that he was working. He checked his watch. He mustn't keep Marie waiting, so he set off at a good pace, hoping that Sykes's short little legs wouldn't be able to keep up and he'd go home. But he arrived at Laburnum Cottage with Sykes close at his heels.

He was a jolly little dog, but Harry knew he couldn't keep him so he quietly slammed the door shut behind him and went into the kitchen to greet Marie. He never tired of her cheery face and rosy cheeks. A woman made to be a mother, for certain. 'I'm back, usual time?'

'Ten minutes. I've got WI tonight, and can't be late.'

But Sykes was there when Marie went out to the WI, he was there when Zack went to the Royal Oak intending to escort Marie home when her meeting in the church hall finished, and he was there when they got back.

'Harry! It's Sykes waiting outside. He's been there all evening, did you know?'

'No I didn't. He followed me home, but I thought he'd get bored of waiting. What shall we do?'

'I don't like to offend him, I expect he's missing Jimmy, you see. But Grandmama will be distraught if he doesn't get home soon.'

'If you'll lend me a piece of rope or something, I'll take him back to her. Where does she live?'

'Well,' Marie said, 'there're three very old cottages actually on the green in the centre of the village and she lives in the one with the fancy bright-red door and a brass dolphin for a door knocker.'

'I'll go straight away, she might not want to open the door after dark.'

'You're very kind, very thoughtful. Zack! A piece of rope please.'

But when they reached the three cottages, Sykes had a very different idea of where he lived. He wanted to go to the end one and when he reached it, he whined and scratched at the door with his claws, up on his hind legs. Then he howled loud and long, and it broke Harry's heart. This must be where Jimmy had lived. The poor old dog.

The door of the first cottage burst open and there, standing out in the road, was a well-dressed, well-built lady who he knew immediately had not been brought up in a village at all. She was London and you'd better make no mistake about that.

'Mrs Charter-Plackett?'

'That's me. Come along, Sykes, where have you been? The dear little chap, he's missing Jimmy. And you are?'

The imperious tone of her voice allowed no fibbing, and Harry felt uncommonly like a small boy in the headmistress's office, in trouble for he knew not what. But they had an hilarious hour talking and drinking malt whisky, recounting stories about Jimbo and life in the village, and the fact that she didn't know what to do about Sykes because she really wasn't a doggy person. Of Harry she learned nothing.

Chapter 5

Up on the village noticeboard the following morning was a large, well-designed poster announcing that there would be an organ recital in the church on the Saturday after next at seven-thirty in the evening, given by Tamsin Goodenough, the church organist, in aid of the Organ Restoration Fund. Tickets were five pounds, including wine and nibbles.

Jimbo was providing the refreshments and was one of the main ticket sellers. If it went well, he would set up another recital with Tamsin and a string quartet she knew, in aid of the Church Bells Restoration Fund. Mind you, if some more people didn't volunteeer to ring the blessed bells, they would be restored but silent.

Everyone who went into the store was reminded about the recital and Jimbo was doing brisk business. Well, as brisk as could be in a village the size of Turnham Malpas. The capacity of the church was one hundred, if people sat on the two steps up to the font and they brought in the long bench which provided seating outside in the churchyard for visitors. It would be cleaned, of course. Tamsin's playing was far and away too good for a church the size of St Thomas's, but they were all careful to avoid telling her that in case she decided to up her game and go to the abbey in Culworth – or somewhere even more prestigious.

Jimbo sold two tickets to Valda and Thelma Senior who, much to his surprise, had both longed to be musicians, but whose father had other plans for them. He also sold tickets to Georgie from the Royal Oak, two to the Fitchs and two to

Marcus and Alice March, her being a singer and, to his surprise, one to Paddy Cleary, who looked rather sheepishly at him.

'Didn't know you were musical, Paddy.'

'I'm not, but you have to support things when you live in a village, don't you?'

'Of course. That'll be five pounds, thanks. I'll take that first and then your other stuff, or I'll get mixed up. How's life up at the big house now that you've got your horticulture certificates? Promoted, are you?'

'Earning more money and ... don't tell anyone, but there could be a promotion.'

'Who's leaving, then?'

'I thought you'd have known, you of all people.' Paddy laughed and wagged a finger at Jimbo.

'Well, I don't. Tell me.'

Paddy leaned across the counter and said quietly, 'It's Michelle. She's moving to ...' he paused for effect, then added, 'Kew.'

'Kew Gardens!' Jimbo was stunned. He'd always understood she was excellent at her job, but Kew! 'My word. That's a promotion and a half. What's happening to you?'

'If I play my cards right, I could be Deputy Head Gardener.' Paddy visibly swelled with pride. He couldn't help it, especially when he remembered the thieving rogue he'd been when he first came to the village. Coming here had given him the only chance in the whole of his life to earn an honest crust.

'What a turn round. That's brilliant! You must be proud.'

'I am. All I want now is the joint of beef for our supper tonight.'

'Ah! Yes, of course. I have it in the back, in the chiller. Won't be a tick.'

While Paddy waited for Jimbo, he stood admiring his ticket for the recital. He stroked it as though it was covered in gold leaf. He couldn't wait for Saturday.

Though Jimbo might love gossip and say how much he missed

not working in the store each day since Tom had taken over as manager, he didn't know, and neither did anyone else, that he, Paddy Cleary, had been out with Tamsin three times since that night in the pub. Three wonderful nights! He wondered when he should let Tamsin know how he felt. She was such a bright, jolly person with no edge, even though she was so talented. She was even a very convenient three years younger than himself. He just couldn't believe she hadn't been snapped up by some very eligible man long ago. Classical music had never been of interest to him, ever, but when Tamsin played he was transported to another world. Another beautiful, beautiful ...

'Ah! Thanks, Jimbo! I paid Tom when I ordered it, you remember?'

'Yes, I know. Enjoy!' Jimbo watched Paddy leaving the store and thought, if he didn't know better, he might think that perhaps Paddy had a woman in tow. Still, if he had, he'd have bought two tickets, wouldn't he, so perhaps he was wrong, but he did look livelier than his usual solemn self. Time would tell.

After Paddy, Bel came in to do her stint behind the till, and next his mother popped in for some tinned food for Sykes who patiently waited for her tied to the hook outside provided for that very purpose.

'How's Sykes coping?'

'Don't you mean, how am I coping?'

'Well, yes, the two of you.'

'I suppose it could be said that walking him is doing me good. I'm shattered when I get in but, once I've recovered, I'm absolutely fine. He's a grand little dog, but he does miss Jimmy. We both do.'

'I could never understand how well you got on with Jimmy, Mother. He was all the things you aren't.'

'I know, and never clean enough, but somehow ... Anyway, his blessed dog took a liking to that new chap at Marie Hooper's ... Harry something. He followed him home and Harry brought him back. A thoroughly decent chap is Harry, and he has an appetite for malt whisky of which I always approve. It makes men *real* men in my opinion, liking malt whisky.'

'You don't need the burden of a dog at your age, why don't you find ...'

'*At my age*, what's that supposed to mean?'

'Well, you'll soon be ...'

'Hush up! If you say my age out loud in here it'll be as good as announcing it on the BBC news. There's nothing wrong with having a dog at my age. He's a good companion, I can say what I like to him and he never answers back, he just wags his tail in approval, which is more than you get from a man.' She rooted about in her purse. 'There's the money, Bel. Good morning to you.'

Jimbo watched his mother untying Sykes and admired her vigour. My God, she'd live to be a hundred at this rate. Then he saw her kiss the top of Sykes's head before she set off home across the green, and he was reminded that, despite the tough front she always put up, she was marshmallow inside and always had been.

Damn! He'd forgotten to ask her to buy a ticket for the recital. He'd buy her one as a treat, she deserved it. He placed five pounds, there and then, in his recital money tin, making it seventy-five pounds altogether, and tucked it neatly into the drawer under the till so it was handy for Bel. Then he put his mother's ticket in an envelope with her name on it in his apron pocket.

Later that day, Bel handed Jimbo the tin with the recital money in. 'I'm off, I've got a shift at the pub tonight. Here's the money for the organ thingy. I've sold quite a few actually, more than I anticipated. See you first thing tomorrow.'

'Thanks. Has Tom sold any?'

'Quite a few, he says, and all the money's in there.'

'Wonderful! I'm determined this recital is going to be a roaring success. Bye bye. See you tomorrow, Bel.'

'Bye.'

Eager to see how many tickets he'd sold that day, Jimbo tipped the money out onto the counter and began to count. All he had was fifty pounds. Fifty pounds! In fivers and tens and ten one pound coins. That was ridiculous! Last time he'd counted it was seventy-five pounds. What the hell? A devastating, sinking feeling came over Jimbo as he realised that money had been stolen from the tin. Automatically, out of an instinct born of years of guarding his money, he began to count how many tickets he had left in the drawer under the till.

He had fifty-four tickets left. If that was so, there should have been £230 in the tin. But he had only fifty pounds. He'd lost money before, when someone working the till had mistakenly given too much change to a customer, but this was absolutely deliberate thieving. If he'd sold forty-six tickets, then there should be £230 in the tin.

He double-checked all his locking procedures as he left the store, carefully carrying the till roll, the cash from the till, the recital cash tin, and the box containing the unsold tickets and left for home, feeling badly let down. All his working life he had been completely honest and fair in his dealings with his customers and his staff and he believed that if he was, then they would be honest with him too. He'd only met with dishonesty with that thieving murderer Andy Moorhouse, who'd done his level best to ruin his business with his tales of food gone off. His food gone off! Indeed not! But this ... He had two options when it came to contemplating who the thief was. It was either a member of the public who'd been in after he'd checked the tin, or one of his own staff, in his absence. But his mind shied away from such thoughts, he trusted Bel and Tom as he would one of his own children or Harriet, they were as honest as the day was long.

He flung his front door open shouting, 'Harriet! Harriet?'

'Kitchen. Where else at this time of day?'

'We've been robbed!'

'Robbed?'

'Yes! Robbed. I can't believe it.'

'Robbed? By whom?'

'Exactly. By whom? That is the question.'

'Well, it wouldn't be either Tom or Bel.'

'I agree.'

'So, Jimbo, darling, that leaves the customers. From the till?'

'No. Out of the tin I was keeping the recital ticket money in.'

'How much?'

'It had seventy-five pounds in it before I left the store, and when I opened it before I left just now, there was only fifty pounds. It should have been £230, according to the number of tickets already gone from the drawer.'

'So,' Quickly calculating in her head, Harriet said, 'So that's ... £180 gone! My God! That's someone with the devil of a lot of front.'

'Bel and Tom had already gone by the time I noticed, you see, so I couldn't ask them who'd been in during the afternoon.'

'Then you should get them to write it down while it's still fresh in their minds. Tomorrow will be too late. Do it now, there's time. Supper will be at least another three quarters of an hour, I got held up.'

'I will. You're right. Yes.' Jimbo fled for his office desk, his mind working out how best to approach the matter without making Tom and Bel think they were being accused. It must have happened while they were distracted or away from the till. There was no way that someone could have pinched it if either Tom or Bel had been standing there, using it.

By nine o'clock, the two of them had been round with their lists. Obviously the lists overlapped each other, because Jimbo hadn't asked them who they'd served, just who'd been in. After reassuring the two of them again that they were definitely not on the suspect list, Jimbo suggested that they went home with a photocopy of their own list just in case, on reflection, they remembered someone they'd not put down. Jimbo and Harriet went through them after they'd left.

'They were busy, weren't they?' Harriet observed. 'This boy here is from the foster home on the Culworth Road, isn't he? Mustn't jump to conclusions though, must we? It's not fair.'

'Put a faint cross beside his name. Anyone else, do you think?'

'Not a single one, they're all honest.'

'In that case, someone has been in then and they're not on the list. Someone's been in, drawn either Tom or Bel away from the till with a query, and they've not bought anything ... or ... No, that wouldn't matter because I asked them who'd been in. God, I'm getting all mixed up. They'd have to have been at the till to get hold of the tin.'

Fran had been reading so she was only half listening all the time they'd been talking. 'It could be someone who came in for a special order and either Tom or Bel would need to go in the back to get it for them. Mightn't it?'

'Of course. That could be it. Good thinking, Fran.' Harriet got up to give her a kiss. 'That might very well be it. I'm getting a drink. Whisky, Jimbo?'

He nodded, lost in thought.

'Fran? What would you like to drink?'

'That elderflower thing, please.'

Jimbo rang both Tom and Bel and asked if someone had come in for a special order, but he got no further with that line of enquiry and had to go to bed with the problem unsolved.

In the middle of the night, Jimbo had a flash of insight and said out loud, 'It must have been last thing before we closed, otherwise Tom or Bel would have realised that the money had gone the moment they opened the tin when they sold a ticket. That's the mistake we made, thinking it could have been anyone, right from me leaving to going back in at locking-up time. The net is closing in.'

Jimbo grinned and promptly fell asleep.

But as the days passed the thief was never found, despite Jimbo's herculean efforts with his subtle enquiries and keeping a careful eye out for someone spending more money than normal, or someone coming in and looking shifty. It was all to no avail though, and Jimbo had to stump up for the missing money. The whole episode left a bitter taste in his mouth and his hitherto untainted belief in the basic honesty of everyone who came in his store was left decidedly dented. But life goes on, he thought, and made himself look forward to the recital.

Fortunately, it was a beautiful evening and because every ticket had been sold, it meant one hundred bottoms on seats, much to Jimbo's delight. A programme had been given to them all as they arrived, and no one gave it more attention than Paddy Cleary. He'd got there in good time and was sitting in the front pew, alive with excitement, oblivious to the people filling up the seats. So much so that he hadn't even noticed Caroline and Peter sharing his pew.

Tamsin came in looking utterly superb, wearing her degree gown over a full-length emerald green dress. Tamsin's dress and her flaming red hair made Paddy's heart leap. His face lit up and he longed to catch her eye but knew he musn't, in case he disturbed her concentration.

When her first magical notes flared triumphantly round the church, Paddy trembled with passion. Caroline felt the trembling and, glancing carefully sideways, she saw his face aglow with love. Oh! Poor Paddy, he had got it bad. Did Tamsin know? Maybe not.

Jimbo's pleasure was ruined by the thought of the thief perhaps sitting close by him, possibly even next to him, unless they'd had enough decency to stay away, given the circumtances. By the time he'd sorted the refreshments out in the church hall, the only seat left for him was right at the back, perched on the font steps, but he could see virtually everyone who'd turned up. In his head, instead of listening to the music, he was going through the names he could remember from Tom and Bel's list. Blast it! He musn't let the theft spoil his enjoyment so he concentrated as hard as he could on the music and wished he had that kind of talent. Brilliant! What a treasure!

The recital lasted an hour and a quarter, and the audience were satiated with the sensuous pleasure of Tamsin's music. There were calls of 'Bravo!', 'Encore!', 'More, please!', but Tamsin looked drained and Paddy longed to take her in his arms to give her some of his own strength. He clapped the loudest and didn't care if someone noticed.

Peter stood up and waited for the applause to exhaust itself. 'On behalf of everyone here this evening, I wish to thank Tamsin, our church organist, for the wonderful music she has played for us tonight. We are massively privileged to have, living in our very own village, someone with the superb talent that Tamsin has. Truly privileged. Shall we give Tamsin another sign of our delighted approval before we move across to the church hall for our refreshments?' Peter then raised his hands above his head and began clapping all over again, and everyone willingly followed suit.

The conversation in the church hall was positively bubbling with excitement. As the audience sipped their wine and chose their nibbles, they joyfully discussed the music. Tamsin wasn't there, however. Paddy had helped her collect her music and the two of them had gone to Tamsin's house because she was too exhausted to speak to anyone.

But all the others were there, including Harry with Marie and Zack. To Harry's horror, just as he was halfway down his first glass of wine, Peter came across to speak to him. His bright blue eyes looked down at him, questioning and alert. 'How about that then, Harry? Absolutely splendid, wasn't it?'

Harry accepted Peter's deep gaze as best he could, but it was unnerving him yet again. 'It certainly was, sir. More than good enough for the Albert Hall.'

'We're very lucky to have her. She prefers the quiet ebb and flow of village life, you see. She believes it to be better for her musicality than the cut and thrust of ... say ... London.'

'I can well believe that. She prefers quality of life to adulation, I expect.'

'I'm sure you're absolutely right there. How are *you* finding village life?'

Harry braved Peter's gaze again. 'The ebb and flow suits me well, thanks.'

'I hear you've landed a temporary job with Jimbo?'

Harry smiled. 'I have, inputting his data. You've heard, have you, about Ken Allardyce?'

Peter shook his head.

'He was taken back into hospital and he died. Jimbo's very cut up about it.'

'I had no idea. He lives, or should I say *lived*, in Culworth, you see, so he's not a man I know very well.'

'Neither do I. I'm more sad for Jimbo, he's taken it very badly.'

'That's Jimbo. Tough on the outside, but kindly inside.' Peter smiled. 'I suppose one downside of village life is that everyone knows what one is up to. Everyone knows what everyone's doing, good and bad.' Peter waited for Harry's response but didn't get one so he continued, 'Sometimes it can be very annoying, but at least if you have problems, there's always someone willing to listen and advise you. Many people living lonely lives in a big city would be grateful for that, even if we aren't. Must press on. Can I get you another glass of wine?'

'Thanks, Rector, but no. I'm very abstemious where the vices are concerned.'

'I see.' But Peter's eyebrows were raised in a way that made him look disbelieving and Harry almost shuddered.

'Nice to have had the chance to talk,' Harry forced out in reply.

'Be seeing you, no doubt.' And Peter, much to Harry's relief, walked away. What the hell was he talking about? Fishing? Using an innocent remark, hoping for some kind of revelation? Some nasty revelation which he'd use at some future date? Well, Reverend Peter Harris, I've got your number. I'm not a simple soul like so many of your parishioners, definitely not. Harry decided that he'd avoid him like the plague in future, he could well do without Peter's particular kind of gentle probing. Damn every nosy busybody in Turnham Malpas, he'd do as he liked. And doing as he liked meant seeing Venetia whenever and wherever he wanted. Ah! There she was, accompanied by … presumably Jeremy. Harry threaded his way through the crowd. They certainly knew how to party, judging by the level of conversation and excited laughter. Venetia and Jeremy were talking to Jimbo, so he had a good excuse for joining them.

'Evening, Jimbo. Wonderful recital, wasn't it? Well worth the five pounds.'

Jimbo finished what he was saying to Jeremy and turned to let Harry join their conversation. 'It certainly was. We've made £500 tonight. And a straight profit because Tamsin gave us her services. So, just another £500, and we'll have raised enough for the full overhaul of the organ. I sometimes wish we had an electronic one, then these overhaul jobbies wouldn't be so expensive.'

'But there's something very special about the sound of a genuine organ, isn't there?'

'I agree. There's a quality that the electronic varieties miss out on. I think next time we'll charge ten pounds a ticket.'

'Perhaps seven pounds fifty? In these hard times, ten pounds might be too much for some people.' Harry shifted his foot a little to touch Venetia's sparkling gold sandal. 'What do you think, Jimbo?'

'Perhaps you're right. Venetia here is suggesting that we have a really big do in the abbey in Culworth and charge even more, attract a wider audience.'

'I think you're on to something there, Venetia.' Harry had to get her to talk to him otherwise, in this cloistered community, someone might think it odd.

'Be a big undertaking, though,' Venetia replied, her face deadpan.

Harry looked directly at Jeremy saying, 'You must be Venetia's husband. We haven't met, how do you do?' He reached out to shake Jeremy's hand. 'Harry, Harry Dickinson.'

Jeremy, driven by demons over which he no longer had control, couldn't bear to touch the man who was clearly giving his wife so much pleasure. He ignored the outstretched hand and briefly nodded his head in acknowledgement.

Venetia, for once in her life, was appalled. What did Harry think he was doing? This was not what she wanted. Secret? Yes, that was part of the attraction. Up front and in the open, no. 'Anyone want another glass of wine?' she asked, seeking an exit. Jeremy was apparently frozen to the spot, Jimbo had turned away to speak to someone else, and thus it was only her and Harry capable of speech and movement. 'Harry? I'll get you one.'

'No, thanks. I don't drink much. One's enough.'

So Venetia escaped, leaving Jeremy and Harry to face each other. But Jeremy wasn't having that, he gave another brief nod in the vague direction of Harry, turned on his heel, and clumsily stalked the length of the hall to stand looking out of the window at the night sky. Knowing he'd made a fool of himself, knowing they just might guess he knew what he wasn't suppposed to know, Jeremy stood, incapable of making a decision. Damn it to hell. He decided to drive home right there and then and leave Venetia to struggle home in those ridiculous high-heeled, glittering strappy things she called shoes.

Venetia avoided Harry once she'd got her second glass and chatted to anyone willing to listen. Then she decided that as the crowd was beginning to disperse, she'd find Jeremy and they'd go home. But he had gone. Without her? Alarm bells began to ring. That was most unlike him. No matter what, he always behaved as a gentleman should. Harry spotted her scanning the crowd and quietly made his way towards her. She saw him coming and headed for the main door to escape.

Harry caught up with her as she went through the little wicket gate at the back of the churchyard with the intention of taking the short cut back to the big house. 'Not so fast, Venetia.'

She swung round to confront him. 'You idiot! In public! That's not part of the game.'

'Game?'

'Well, not game, I didn't mean that. It's just that if Jeremy doesn't know, I like it better that way. In public we are two very separate people. Right? No connection whatsoever. Right?'

'I like it either way. But I do see your point. For a start, I wouldn't like that rector to be in the know.'

Venetia shuddered. 'No. And neither would I. So, in future, in public we don't know each other. Right?'

'Right. This your secret way home to avoid the crowds?'

In the darkness Venetia smiled. 'No one uses it any more, but the dark doesn't bother me. After all, who's likely to be wandering across Home Park at this time of night? No one.'

'I am.'

'Ah! Well, you're my lover, that's different.'

'I'm glad you don't think of me as your bit on the side.'

Venetia pretended to be shocked. 'Now that really is a very vulgar expression.'

Harry gripped hold of her hand. 'Is it just a game?'

'Not with you. There's more to it than that. This time.'

They faced each other and, even though it was almost pitch black, they could sense, without seeing, their mutual need. They were standing so close that they could feel each other's breath before they kissed and Venetia knew at that moment that this was different from any other time. Before, it had always been fun, but with this man it was more serious. Then she remembered he could be gone next week, so she clung to him fiercely.

Inside they were both tearing themselves apart. Harry because he was afraid of his feelings, Venetia because she didn't want to get too involved when it was to be so short-lived. She stumbled off in the darkness, shoes in her hand and her bare feet feeling the dampness on the grass left behind by an earlier rainstorm, leaving Harry to find his own way back. He endeavoured to find what he called the country way back to Laburnum Cottage, but got hopelessly lost through unfamiliarity, and ended up being guided by the floodlights of the big house. Then he walked down the drive, down Jack's Lane, and then Shepherd's Hill.

It was a good thing he had a key. But getting in quietly so as not to disturb Marie and Zack was impossible as they were both in the kitchen having a bedtime drink.

'Harry! Want a drink before you go to bed?'

Harry put his head round the door to say no thanks, he was going straight up. And he did, to spend the next two hours fretting about the situation he'd found himself in. He had to pull himself together. Falling in love? Absolutely not. It made life far too complicated and, in any case, he would be leaving in the middle of the week. He'd only promised to work until then.

After all, Jimbo would want someone permanent, and permanent was not his scene. He wouldn't go for a swim tomorrow, he'd stay away, let things cool.

Chapter 6

Harry might not have had a very satisfactory evening, but there were those who had, those for whom love's path ran sweet. Tamsin Goodenough, exhausted by the intensity of her concentration during the recital, was glad to have someone to put the kettle on, get out the cups, those delicate china ones that had belonged to her mother, pull forward a side table to put the tray on, and pour her a life-giving cup of Earl Grey.

Paddy served the tea in such a gentle, considerate manner that Tamsin almost felt revived just watching him. His attention was heaven-sent and yet the man seated beside her on the sofa was not the kind of man she should have been attracted to. She'd grown up in a house where music was prized above rubies. All of them, which included her parents and two sisters, had been more than proficient in at least two instruments, and their greatest joy was to get together to play. They played till the moon shone through the windows, till the clock struck midnight. Passing music exams with distinction was the norm and she'd revelled in it.

Until tragedy struck one bright summer's day. Tamsin was nineteen when her parents and one of her sisters were killed in a horrifying train crash. Happiness fled from her life, for ever, it seemed. Tamsin had won a place at the Manchester School of Music, to begin in the autumn. It gave her a sense of purpose, but her sister, Penny, eighteen months older than her, dug out a rucksack from the loft, filled it with everything she needed for a long adventure, and disappeared to South America. Occasionally, over the next fifteen years, Tamsin got a postcard from her, each place appearing more remote than the last. She kept every one of them in a drawer in her bedroom. About three years ago, a postcard came that gave her an email address and since then it had been emails, not cards, that outlined the latest venture Penny had decided to take up. As for herself ...

'More tea, Tamsin?'

Paddy brought her back to now and, all things considered, she preferred now. 'I don't know why it is I can practise for hours when I'm by myself, but as soon as I have people listening to me, I'm exhausted after an hour.'

'It's because you want to do your best for them, which you do. Your playing is perfect.' Paddy's eyes glistened with approval.

'Thank you. You're a very restful person to be with, you know, and yet they tell me that in the pub you're full of jokes and laughter.'

'It must be you who makes me restful.' Paddy smiled at her and those Irish eyes of his, almost midnight blue with their black lashes, stopped her in her tracks. In all her thirty-four years, Tamsin had never met a man who'd touched her emotions so quickly. One smile, one laugh, and she was captivated. But it wouldn't do. She wasn't the marrying type and neither, she felt sure, was Paddy. Maybe they could be friends and give marriage a kick into touch?

Paddy put down his empty cup. He hated Earl Grey; he only drank it for Tamsin's sake. He said, 'Can I tell you something?'

'Of course.' Tamsin hoped he wasn't going to say anything at all about his feelings. Now wasn't the time, and it never would be.

'I had a very different upbringing from you, sure I did.'

'How different?'

'How long have you got?'

'How old are you, Paddy?'

64

'Forty last birthday.'

'Which is when?'

'November 20th.'

'Is your name really Patrick?'

'No. I was christened Paddy. How much more Irish can you get?'

'You don't sound very Irish.'

'Once I'd left Ireland, I tried to make sure that I didn't sound like an archetypal idiot Irishman.'

Paddy was silent then. It seemed to Tamsin that he had something more to say and suddenly she couldn't bear it another minute. 'I'm all ears if you've something to tell me.'

'I was number three, and the first boy of eight children, not one of whom my parents could afford to have. We were dirt poor. My father never worked, as far as I know. Any money he got to before my mother got her hands on it went on drink. We were frequent visitors to the local convent, begging for food. I felt so ashamed. Everyone knew us for what we were; unclean, ill-mannered, shabby and at the bottom of every pile.'

'I'm sorry.' Tamsin spoke with compassion in every timbre of her voice.

Paddy smiled at her. 'One day I saw the light, as they say, and I realised that life didn't *have* to be like this, that things could be better if only my dad made the effort. So I tried to reason with him, for my mother's sake. I got knocked down for my pains and went to school the next day with a broken arm, in agony. The head teacher insisted that I went to the hospital and, when I turned up at home with my arm in plaster, he knocked me down again. For being soft, he said. That day, iron entered my soul and I vowed that, as soon as I could, I would leave home and damn the lot of 'em. So, just before my seventeenth birthday, I did just that, would you believe?' He laughed, but it was bitter laughter, and it hurt Tamsin dreadfully.

'Paddy! What on earth did you do at your age? How did you live? At sixteen?'

'I stole our neighbour's wage packet. I shouldn't have done it, he was a decent man through and through.'

'Paddy!'

'I struggled on for years, from one job to another, thieving if necessary. I'm sorry, it's not recent behaviour. But when there's no food on the table one has to lower one's standards and get some ... somehow or other. Then I met Anna, the curate from the abbey, and she brought me here when she stood in for the rector. I didn't do right by her but ...' Paddy shrugged his shoulders. 'Then I got lodgings with Greta and Vince, and a job at the big house courtesy of Mr Fitch. But still I couldn't stop stealing.'

'Paddy!'

'Sorry, but I did. I was desperate. However, enough of my life history, it's too sordid for your ears.'

He stood up and looked down at her. At her red hair and green eyes. At the sad, sweet, caring expression on her face. At the light sprinkling of freckles on her forehead and cheeks.

He liked her wholesomeness and the beauty of her spirit. And, at that moment, he lost his heart to her.

But he wasn't worthy of her, not when he thought about his past and the rotten tricks he'd done to stay alive. He'd drag her down, no doubt about it, they weren't in the same class. 'Better go. Thank you for tonight, your playing was beautiful. It goes right to the heart, sure it does, just like you.' He was out of the house and running down the road to his lodgings with Vince and Greta before she could stop him.

Tamsin watched him running away and, to her horror, knew for certain that he must be in love with her. But she must be mistaken, surely. Well, bad luck, Paddy, if you are. I'm not the marrying kind, we're not right for each other. But the moment she thought that she regretted it, because there was a lightness of touch and a sincerity about him that impressed her.

Paddy ached with his love for Tamsin even as he drank the mug of Ovaltine so kindly prepared for him by Greta. 'You're quiet tonight, Paddy. Are you all right?'

Paddy nodded. 'The music was beautiful, wasn't it?'

There was a yearning in his voice which Greta couldn't ignore. 'Yes. Beautiful. It makes you wish you could play like that yourself, it must be wonderful. Neither Vince nor me ever got a chance that way.' As a sly afterthought, she asked, 'Tamsin OK?' Still, she wasn't prepared for the light that glowed in Paddy's eyes.

'Yes, thanks. I made her a cup of tea, she was tired out.'

'I'm not surprised. Playing like that must take it out of her. I'm going up. Turn out the lights, please. Goodnight!' Greta just hoped, as she climbed the stairs, that Paddy hadn't fallen for Tamsin. It would never be right, her a Cambridge music scholar and him dragged out of an Irish bog by his own boot laces, a man of the soil and an ex-thief too; they'd nothing in common.

Paddy acknowledged that too, but there was nothing to stop him dreaming. No one knew he dreamed of her but himself. He'd just have to pine away in his lonely bachelor bed for ever and a day. He sat up in bed with a start. He could buy one of those tapes she'd done in aid of the church funds. That was it! Then he could lie in bed listening and dreaming about her into the night, with his walkman clamped to his ears and no one the wiser. First thing Monday morning, he'd nip into the village store before work, buy the tape and take it with him to the big house! He could listen to it while he worked in the glasshouses, lost in his own world. Excellent.

Tom was having a long weekend so Jimbo was in there first thing. Paddy wished he wasn't, because he knew of Jimbo's predilection for gossip. 'Do you have one of those tapes that

Tamsin did of her playing, you know the ones for the church funds, please? I want one for Greta. Thanks.'

'Just past the stationery, on the top shelf, the special display.' Jimbo had a grin on his face, but the look on Paddy's face when he carried the tape to the till made him hesitate to make a comment, however well meant. 'Lovely Saturday night, wasn't it? Did you enjoy it?'

'I did indeed, and so did Greta. It must be lovely to have a talent like hers. Greta says she never got a chance to learn anything musical and I must say, I certainly didn't. Survival was my priority! Believe me. Here's the money.' Paddy handed his ten-pound note over, whipped the tape into the holdall that held his gardening overalls and his packed lunch, and was out of the shop before Jimbo could come up with a merry quip.

Paddy was in one of the glasshouses, checking the vine, when he surreptitiously got his walkman out of his overall pocket and switched it on. So absorbed was he that he didn't hear Michelle sliding the glasshouse door open.

She had to tap him on his shoulder to catch his attention. 'Morning, Paddy. How're things?'

He swung round, switched off the tape and took the earphones out saying, 'Morning, boss.'

'The name's Michelle. Think it'll need watering?'

'Just finding out. It's not been all that hot this weekend, has it? We don't want to drown it.'

'No, that's right. You're doing a good job with these vines, the best chap I've had looking after 'em. Remember last year's crop? I thought they'd never end. Let's hope it's the same this year.'

'You won't be here to see.'

'No, I won't.'

Before he knew it, he was saying, 'If you need someone when you get to Kew, you know I'm reliable.'

'Come on, Paddy. You can't leave Turnham Malpas, you've put roots down.'

'A chance to work at Kew can't be turned down for the love of Turnham Malpas.'

'I turned down several jobs till Kew came on the scene but somehow, this time, I can't say no.'

'You'd be a fool if you did.'

'Do you mean it about going to Kew if the opportunity arises?'

There came a brief pause while Paddy stared out of the window and then he replied, 'I do, indeed I do.' But his tone wasn't entirely convincing.

'Well, in that case, I'll let you know. At least I'd know I could rely on you, one hundred per cent.'

'Thanks. Thanks too for getting me this promotion, by the way.'

'You deserved it. When you've checked the glasshouses, that piece there is looking a bit sick. It needs snipping off. Come and see me in the office later, to talk about things a bit over a coffee. OK?'

'Righto.' Paddy was surprised by his spontaneous request for a chance to work at Kew Gardens. Whatever had made him say it? He was the biggest fool, how could he separate himself from Tamsin? He couldn't. He closed his eyes for a moment to think, without distraction, about how beautiful she was. Those clear, green eyes of hers, so unusual. The red hair she wore without any restraint, like a hairclip or a ribbon. It must be the very devil to dry he thought, then he imagined himself helping her to dry it in front of a big roaring fire and taking her up to bed … Ouch! Snipping off the piece Michelle had said needed snipping off, he'd cut his finger. Blast. It had gone deep. Blood poured. He'd nearly cut the end of his finger off! Oh, God, not hospital. He was terrified of hospitals. Perhaps a bandage would do the trick. Anything rather than white coats and needles. The piece of flesh was hanging by a thread. Hospital? Hell! He was scared. He sped with the speed of light to the staffroom, a handkerchief wrapped tightly round his finger doing nothing to stem the blood. It dripped with every step he took. Once bandaged up by the official First Aider, Paddy fainted. Out cold.

When he came round, Paddy couldn't believe what a fool he'd made of himself. Three of the groundsmen were in there having their morning tea so they were crowded round, along with the First Aider and, to add to his feeling of foolishness, there was Michelle. 'Honestly, Paddy, there was me thinking you were a man. I got the message to come ASAP imagining that at least your arm was hanging by a thread, and all it was was your finger! Get him some hot tea, somebody, with sugar in it, right now.'

The First Aider, in a huff about Michelle's interference and her mockery of the first patient she'd had in days, snapped, 'Here it is, waiting for him. Blood takes people that way sometimes. It could have been very serious. Here, sit up, Paddy. Mind, it's hot.'

'It's bleeding a lot still. We'd better get you to the hospital to have it stitched.'

This advice from Michelle made Paddy go as white as a sheet again. He was going to resist that idea. He simply was not going, no matter what she said.

'You work with soil, Paddy, so you can't work with it bleeding so much. If nothing else, it could get infected. That would be dangerous for you, not the plants. Right, Mrs First Aider, take him to hospital.'

'I'm the one qualified to say whether or not he goes to hospital, not you.'

'And I'm manager here, and I say he has to go. Get galvanised, woman, I don't want him passing out. *Again.*'

Muttering furiously under her breath, the First Aider escorted Paddy out, to find, halfway across the staff car park, that her car keys were in the staff room. Unfortunately for her, Michelle came out into the car park at full speed at that precise moment, shouting, 'You might find these useful!' This was her final humiliation.

Paddy was given the rest of the day off by Michelle when he finally got back to the big house. 'You look as white as a ghost, Paddy. We can't have you working with equipment in that state, else that First Aider will think it's Christmas and her birthday rolled into one. Home you go. Can you walk there OK? Or perhaps you'd like me to give you a lift?'

'Of course I can, the fresh air'll do me good. Thanks.'

Greta wasn't working that afternoon and she was horrified when she saw the size of the bandage Paddy's finger was swathed in. 'Oh, Paddy! I'm glad I can't see it. Oh! Look! There's blood coming through. It must be bad.'

'It is, but ...' Paddy said, more cheerfully than he felt, 'I'll survive.'

'Do you want a lie down?'

'No, but I'll sit in the lounge for a bit.'

'Cup of tea and a biscuit. Plenty of sugar, that's what you need.'

Greta bustled away and fussed over him all afternoon till about four o'clock when he said he'd have a lie down. She agreed it would do him good and told him she'd give him a shout when his supper was ready, if he hadn't put in an appearance.

Paddy fell asleep soothed into unconsciousness by Tasmin's music. My, she could play ...

When Vince came in and Marie had told him the story about Paddy, he went upstairs to see how Paddy was. He tapped on the door and, getting no reply, decided for safety's sake, he'd better walk in, just in case Paddy had taken a turn for the worse.

71

The door creaked a little and the noise woke Paddy. Vince was convinced he needed an evening in the pub, but Paddy didn't want to go. 'Go on, Paddy. You need something to take your mind off it. Eat a good supper and you'll feel a new man. Go on.'

Paddy allowed himself to be persuaded, mainly because he hoped doing something positive might take his mind off his throbbing finger.

They joined Don and Vera at the same time as Willie and Sylvia. As always, they were all careful not to sit in Jimmy's old chair. Somehow they'd developed a kind of dark wariness about that chair, as though, if they sat in it, a sudden, unwelcome visit by the Grim Reaper would inevitably occur. They told each other it was all nonsense, but still no one sat in it.

Consternation was the order of the day when they saw Paddy's heavily bandaged finger. 'My, Paddy, that looks bad. How did you do it?' This was Vera, looking terribly concerned.

Greta said, 'It's terrible, he fainted.'

Willie was scornful. 'Paddy, you never did! I thought you were a real man.'

Greta spoke up in his defence. 'It's real bad. The First Aider took him to hospital. Stitches, tetanus injection, the whole works. Michelle insisted.'

'You can't work then? All that soil and funny germs.'

Paddy rubbed his hand to relieve the throbbing. 'It's a bit difficult. Michelle's very particular about tetanus and that, but I'll go mad if I don't work. It's my life blood, is gardening.'

'Perhaps you could do some office work to broaden your experience. There's bound to be office work in running gardening projects. Bills and things to pay. Seed catalogues to study.' Sylvia suggested.

'I'm right-handed so I couldn't hold a pen.'

'Oh! Of course not.'

Don leaned across to speak confidentially to Paddy. 'A little bird tells me that a bit of experience in the office could stand you in good stead, seeing as Michelle's off to Kew at the end of the month.'

They all heard, even though he was only speaking to Paddy.

'No!' They said in unison.

'Who's going to be Head Gardener then? You? You'd better get the drinks in to celebrate,' suggested Willie.

'I'm telling you here and now, I'm not going to be Head Gardener. I haven't been there long enough. And I don't have enough experience yet.'

'No, I should think not, considering what a thief you were some years back.' Don picked up his glass of home-brew and drank from it as his comment sank in.

Greta, who'd taken Paddy into her heart right from him first coming to lodge with her at Sir Ralph's request, was genuinely horrified. 'How dare you, Don Wright. What a cruel, unkind thing to say. You know full well Mr Fitch has complete faith in Paddy, otherwise he wouldn't have paid for him to go to college, now would he?'

Vera nudged Don and said, 'That's enough, Don, you've gone too far.'

Don retaliated with, 'Maggie told me that she saw him steal in the railway station once. So yes, he was. And well you know it. I shan't apologise.'

Vera was mortified and Sylvia was full of sadness at the hurt Don had caused and, as for Willie, he plunged in with, 'What about the milk of human kindness, Don? There's no need to rake all that up.' He looked at Paddy and saw how hurt he was.

Paddy was ashen-faced. His throbbing finger didn't help either. It just didn't seem to be his night. 'I'd better go. Goodnight.' He pushed his chair back and stood up, preparing to leave.

'No, don't go. Finish your drink. Go on. Take no notice.'

'I'd rather go. Goodnight.' Paddy left, speaking to no one as he weaved his way between the tables.

'I can't believe it of you, Don, that was cruel.'

'It was the truth and well you know it.'

Vince, a man of few words, chimed in with the final comment on the matter. 'It would have been better left unsaid and the next time you see him I shall want to hear that you've apologised. It was unforgivable and, if you've nothing better to say, you'd better shut up.'

'Right then, I will. 'Cept if anyone's interested, they've started.'

Vera, Vince, Greta and Willie sat waiting for further enlightenment, but it didn't come. Impatiently Vera asked Don what he was talking about.

'Ralph's old house. They've started renovating it after the fire, you know. It'll take some doing, it was a fire and a half. Must be nigh on a year since it burned down. Poor Ralph, he loved that house.'

'Poor Muriel too, burned alive. She didn't deserve for that to happen.'

'Someone's bought it then?' asked Vince.

'Couldn't say.'

Vera began huffing in exasperation. 'For heaven's sake, Don, tell us what you learned.'

'I learned nothing. This chap was coming out the door and locking it behind him, though heaven knows why seeing as there's nothing in it and no roof on it. When I asked him, he shut up like a clam.'

'So,' said Vera, 'we're no wiser.'

'Well he said he'd been asked by a solicitor in London to take over restoring it. That was all he knew. Just that this solicitor in London was in charge of it. But it's being completely restored on the instructions of the new owner and they're starting next week, scaffolding and that. Apparently they've been a few times making plans and now they're really starting work on it.'

'Not before time. It's a right eyesore, and that tarpaulin flaps in the wind all the time. It can't half be annoying if you live nearby I should imagine,' remarked Greta.

'Grandmama Charter-Plackett said that the other night, when that gale got up, it was flapping and banging all night.'

'I wonder who's bought it?'

'Maybe it's been inherited by the so-called possible long-lost nephew or whatever of Ralph's they've been searching for. There must be someone, somewhere who's inherited it.'

'Well, all I can say is, if they're half as nice as Ralph, they'll do all right. It'll be a long job.'

'Well, time will tell,' said Willie. 'Anyone ready for another drink? Sylvia, Vera?'

'What about me, don't I count?' Don angrily pushed his glass along the table towards Willie.

'Only if you remember about that apology. You've really hurt Paddy's feelings, you have, Don.'

Paddy sat outside the Royal Oak on the seat they all called Saul's seat, named after the old soldier who was banned from the pub two centuries or so ago, and who sat there waiting for the pub customers to take pity on him and bring him a drink out.

He was devastated about what Don had said about him. Normally comments like that he simply shrugged off, but to-night somehow he couldn't. It was so unfair of Don when he'd been honest ever since Mr Fitch gave him his chance to reform. Thieving never crossed his mind now, not since he'd felt so secure in the friendship he'd been given by Vince and Greta. Moving in with them had been the icing on the cake of his new life and he'd foolishly hoped that everyone he knew would allow him to leave the bad times well behind him. Life could be so unfair. Even his finger was throbbing something terrible.

Paddy sat there knee-deep in self-pity. One person entered the pub without even glancing at him; so much for friendly villagers. Two cars hastened by, and what he hoped would happen but didn't, was that someone from the table he had been sitting at would come out and beg him to return. He wouldn't have gone back in if they had, but it would have been good to have the opportunity to refuse their offer. Another car slowed up, went by, then reversed and stopped alongside Saul's seat.

And there she stood, the love of his life. Now he really felt foolish. Wallowing in deep self-pity! What a fool he was.

Tamsin walked round the bonnet of her car and stood in front of him. 'Been banned? For fighting?' She pointed at his finger and her face broke into a wide smile. When he didn't reply, she tapped his shoulder gently and, still getting no response, sat down beside him. 'In the dumps? What's brought that on? Where's the laughter and the jokes in the pub I hear about?'

'You see, you try so hard to leave your wrong-doings behind you. You turn over a new leaf, become ambitious, an optimist instead of a pessimist, hard-working instead of an idle good-for-nothing at the bottom of the pile, and then someone kicks you in the teeth and reminds you of the past.'

'Who?'

'Don Wright.'

Tamsin smiled to herself. 'Oh, Paddy! Don't take it to heart. Don's a great chap but since he had that bad fall when he was repairing the guttering at the nursing home in Penny Fawcett, he's never been that good.' She tapped her head to indicate where Don's problem was. 'Looks all right, but he forgets to be thoughtful sometimes.'

'Who told you that?'

'Peter did. He told me to remember not to take offence at strange things he might say.'

'I see.'

But she didn't seem to have been any comfort to him. 'So don't let it upset you.'

Paddy sighed, then looked up so he wasn't staring at his feet and said, 'Right.'

'That's better. Now, as I see it, you have two options. We go in the pub for a drink or we go home to my house and have a drink there. I think the pub, in the long run, would be the better option, don't you? Show them you're proud of what you've achieved, which you've a right to be.'

Curiously, Paddy's self-pity lifted and he could bear to look her in the face. 'OK then. With you, I will.'

'Wait there. I'll go and park my car, then we'll go in together.'

Chapter 7

Harry had been in the pub and observed the incident with Paddy and he was left to wonder what Paddy had done. Thieving? Thieving what? He'd ask Marie and Zack when they joined him. He checked his watch. They were late, in fact, twenty minutes late, and that wasn't like them. On the dot, or ten minutes early, was more their style. So he was still waiting when Paddy came back in with the church organist. What the blazes was her name? Surname was Goodenough or something. And her first name? Harry was saved from the struggle to remember when Georgie spoke to her by name. 'Now, Tamsin, what can I get you? Not often we see you in here so you're very welcome indeed.'

Harry heard Tamsin ask in her sweet voice for a Martini and lemonade.

'And what for you tonight, Paddy?' Georgie asked as she leaned over the bar counter and said something sotto voce to Paddy. She must have said something encouraging because Paddy smiled a little. The two of them carried their drinks to a table just the other side of where Harry was sitting and he was able to keep them in his sights by slightly adjusting the angle of his chair. There was a little awkwardness about their being together and he guessed this wasn't the first time, but that they were still new enough not to be absolutely comfortable with each other. Now, if it had been him and Venetia, they'd have been possibly holding hands and laughing together, their heads close so others couldn't hear what was said.

The promise he'd made to himself about keeping cool, treating her a bit off-hand, had failed miserably. He was quite simply fascinated by her. Well, perhaps there was more to it than that. He went swimming almost every evening after work now. It was so easy, just a stroll across Home Park and there he was, stripping off, and there she was already stripped off and they could swim and tease and tempt and then … He'd made up his mind that they couldn't meet at the maisonette she and Jeremy shared though, not when he was likely to meet Jeremy at any time and have to look him in the eye. But there was no doubt about it. He, Harry Dickinson, was enslaved. Even so, he recognised her for what she was, free-living and enjoying it, and he knew that if he walked away tomorrow, in a few days she'd be looking for someone to replace him. Though he did get an inkling sometimes, just briefly, that this time she was more serious about him than was usual for her.

Tamsin went to the bar again. There was a burst of laughter from one of the tables and from the table with the settle down one side, there was an angry exchange. Then the outer door opened and in came Venetia, alone. Dressed outrageously. The light of battle in her eyes. Conversation died immediately.

It was a summer's evening, but it wasn't warm enough for the outfit Venetia was wearing. It was a pansy purple dress held up by shoestring shoulder straps, a clinging bodice that left nothing whatsoever to the imagination, a skin-tight skirt just to the knee that emphasised every curve, and her face was made up as though she was just about to go on stage. The outfit was finished off with a huge, metallic gold bag with matching shoes. Briefly, Harry was disappointed. He liked smart clothes and the women who loved them, but this … in a country pub, was on the verge of embarrassing. She paused for a moment as the outer door slammed behind her, saw Harry and, without hesitation, headed straight for his table. It was obvious to everyone it was him she'd come to see.

Venetia leaned over Harry, clearly intending to kiss him, but he quickly leaped to his feet. 'Sit down. Your usual?'

He made for the bar. 'Gin and tonic, please.'

Dicky winked at him. 'My word, she's looking great tonight.' He nodded in Venetia's direction.

'Yes. And a whisky, neat. How much?' Harry slid the money across the counter, picked up the drinks and went back to his table.

Everyone began talking again. No doubt, about the two of them. 'I thought we were keeping us under wraps.'

She giggled helplessly and Harry realised she had been drinking before she came. 'Careful, Venetia, please.'

'Why?' She raised her glass to him and toasted him with her eyes. Harry fell instantly under her spell all over again. What the hell? She had a right to dress how she wished, and he didn't care that she'd made it so plain to them all. It would be round the village by the next morning, on that he knew he could rely. And if Jeremy couldn't keep her to himself, why should he worry? Under the table Venetia rubbed her bare leg very gently against him, and that put an end to his embarrassment completely. Was there ever such a woman as Venetia? Sitting here, in the full public gaze, teasing him like this. He sneaked a look round the bar while taking a sip of his whisky and saw the disapproval, the eyes raised to the ceiling in disgust, and the heads brought close together as the villagers gossiped.

Tamsin and Paddy noticed what was going on, but had no interest in it because they had eyes only for each other. Tamsin was telling him about an invitation she'd received to play the violin at a concert in Smith Square.

'Play the violin? I thought the organ was your instrument?'

'Well, yes, but I also play the piano and the violin.'

Paddy had no answer to that. He might as well just pack it in right now. Three instruments, and he couldn't play a penny whistle. What was the point in hoping? They were totally mismatched. He was so disheartened by her casual statement that he was on the verge of leaving. But then she said something that left him speechless.

'I could teach you the piano? Or maybe you can play it already, I don't know. Can you?'

Tamsin saw a light come on in Paddy's eyes which was quickly switched off. 'No. No, I couldn't. I don't have a musical background, far from it. It wouldn't be any use trying.'

'You haven't tried then. I'm a good teacher, even though I say it myself.'

Paddy's eyes looked cautiously into hers and, for a moment, he was lost in thought. Then he said, 'Greta hasn't a piano. So I can't.' He was both relieved and disappointed.

'You could use my piano. Or there's one in the village hall. I'd love to teach you.'

Paddy shook his head. 'No. No. I couldn't.'

'It wouldn't be any good thinking you'd master it in two or three weeks, it would be hard work, believe me. But think about it. You see ...' Tamsin then stopped talking, as she found herself to be the only person speaking at that moment because someone had walked in and everyone was suddenly busy looking at no one in particular while awaiting events. Only Harry and Venetia were unaware of the new arrival because they were gazing into each other's eyes, oblivious to their surroundings.

It was Jeremy Mayer.

He surveyed the bar, looking at every table in turn and, when his eyes came to rest on Dicky and Georgie waiting to serve drinks, he walked across to them saying in a loud, confident voice, 'Double whisky, please, landlord.'

He withdrew his wallet from his back pocket, took out a twenty-pound note with a flourish, and laid it on the bar top. He tipped the whisky down his throat in one magnificent gesture, and asked for a second, then a third. When he was obviously going to order again, Dicky was about to say, 'Is this wise?' Then

Jeremy ordered a gin and tonic and another double whisky. He then walked majestically over to Venetia and Harry's table and handed their drinks to them.

Jeremy wasn't the huge, impressive figure he had been in the past, but he had enormous dignity in every inch of his bearing. He nodded to one or two people he recognised, then turned his attention to Harry. 'Good evening, Harry. Beautiful evening, isn't it? Full of promise for a wonderful summer, they say. Are you enjoying village life?'

Harry looked Jeremy straight in the eye, deciding to answer him in the same casual way. 'Yes, I am actually. Really enjoying it. Thanks, Jeremy.'

'Nice people, aren't they?'

'Indeed. I'm living at the B&B down Shepherd's Hill. I've been made very welcome.'

'I know you are. Marie and Zack are very friendly. You'll not lack for friends here. Venetia, darling, another G and T?'

Venetia couldn't help but think: What's this all about, the conniving beggar? What's he up to? The first gin and tonic had gone in a moment, her thirst being somewhat excessive due to panic. She didn't normally panic about Jeremy, but somehow there was a threat present and, for once, she was flummoxed.

'Yes, please. I'm terribly thirsty.'

Harry was about to offer to buy her a drink, but he was too late. Jeremy had instantly sprung up from his chair and gone to buy it for her. Conversation had begun again all round the bar, muted for fear of missing anything, but conversation nonetheless. Tamsin was still trying to persuade Paddy to have piano lessons.

'It's no good. I can't, really I can't.'

'I know! I'm quite good at playing the flute, how about that? I could teach you the rudiments and I have a flute that I could lend you. Then you could practise at home in your bedroom. Please, Paddy?' Those green eyes of hers pleading with him turned opposition into agreement in Paddy's mind. At the very least, it would mean seeing her regularly. That could be his opportunity!

'Very well. You win. I can't afford much in the way of paying, I'm afraid.' He had to say it, but dreaded her reply.

'Pay? I don't want money, not from a friend. I know it's something completely alien from anything you've ever done before, but you never know what it might lead to. Playing a musical instrument might turn into something you have been waiting for all your life, and you just didn't know it.'

Tamsin was so full of missionary zeal that Paddy simply couldn't resist her. So he agreed, and when she said it would be a good idea to make an immediate start, then drained her glass and got ready to go, he meekly followed her out of the door, ignoring the winks he got from several punters still happily awaiting the turn of events with Jeremy, Harry and Venetia.

Half an hour later, they were still waiting for a piece of action from the three of them, but it had all got rather boring as Jeremy was obviously carrying the whole of the conversation on his shoulders and was apparently enjoying himself. Then they spotted him glancing at the clock over the bar. Ah! Was this the moment they'd all been waiting for? Would she go home with Harry or Jeremy?

Rather unexpectedly, Jeremy stood up, saying loudly, 'Time we went home, Venetia. I've not brought the car so we'll have to walk. It's a lovely evening and it'll do us good. They've forecast rain for tonight and I've no umbrella so let's hurry up, just in case.'

Venetia ignored him while she made up her mind. She'd had every intention of going home with Harry. She'd tried ringing him on his mobile but there'd been no answer. She'd rung him at the B&B and there was no reply there either. So she had come to the pub as a last, desperate measure. Now Jeremy had ruined the whole escapade. Spending the evening incarcerated with him, listening to his pointless, trivial conversation, had tried her temper to the limit. Should she make a stand here and now and declare ...

'I'm waiting, darling.'

Since when had he persisted in calling her darling? It was all a front. A hidden challenge to Harry, who now appeared dumbstruck by Jeremy's fluent performance. Stuff it. She wasn't having any of it. 'You go home, I'll follow on. I won't be long.' She half turned away from Jeremy and began talking to Harry, who looked to be in shock. 'So, next Thursday night we've organised a gala night for the students and I was wondering if ...'

'Venetia!'

Harry's response to Jeremy's anger was a muttered, 'I think you'd better go.'

If he'd stabbed her through the heart, she couldn't have been more upset. For one terrible moment, she almost began to cry, but then she swallowed hard and bent down to pick up her bag. She got to her feet. How to leave the pub with her dignity intact? She'd kill him the next time she saw him. How could he let it happen like this? Giving in to Jeremy when all she'd wanted was him? But if she felt so upset about him, then he must mean more to her than she'd acknowledged to herself. So, head held high, she twinkled her fingers at a couple of the punters who knew her, and followed Jeremy out. The sound of their argument as they tramped across Home Park to their maisonette echoed far and wide.

Marie and Zack had arrived while Jeremy had been sitting with Harry, but he hadn't noticed so he was surprised when they suddenly materialised at his table, drinks in hand.

Marie put a hand on his shoulder. 'Sorry we're late. We ran out of petrol. Stupid thing to do. It's only the second time in our lives we've done it. Zack thought I'd filled it up and I thought he had, so there we are. You all right if we sit here?'

'Of course.'

She had to say it. 'I didn't know you knew Venetia.'

'I don't, not really, Marie. Her husband's a bit overpowering, isn't he? Keeps her on a tight rein, does he?'

Marie exploded into laughter. 'Oh, Harry! You are an innocent! I do like you for it! Zack calls her ... Well, anyway, never mind that. No, he doesn't. I doubt anyone could keep Venetia in order.'

Zack spoke up, feeling the need to warn a nice chap like Harry. 'You need to keep away from her, Harry. For a decent chap like you, she's bad news.'

'Ah! Right. Thanks for the advice.' Harry stared into his drink and wished himself anywhere but where he was. She'd been so full of promise earlier, before the arrival of the dreaded Jeremy.

Drinks finished, Marie and Zack, with Harry in tow, got into their car. They'd parked in Stocks Row because the pub car park was full, and they were passing the church when Marie said, 'Zack! Stop! There's a light on in the church. In the vestry!'

Zack stamped on the brakes and came to a sudden, alarming stop. 'My God! Who could that be? Right, wait there, Marie. Don't you follow me.'

'Go with him, Harry. Take care. Here's a torch.' She fumbled in the glove compartment and handed him a thumping great torch, big enough to light a football ground.

Harry followed Zack down the path to the main door. Zack quietly tried the door, only to find it had already been unlocked. He turned the heavy iron latch and softly stepped inside. Had the door been left open by the flower ladies or was it someone with illicit access to the key?

Harry followed closely behind him, sniffing the unaccustomed smell of an old church: the slight perfume of flowers, the definite aroma of furniture polish, and the strange, almost sad, smell of a very old stone building. Zack could have found his way without the torch, but Harry switched it on for fear he should stumble over something or other.

Zack turned to look at Harry and put his finger to his lips. Harry nodded. The vestry door was very slightly ajar, just enough for Zack to slip his fingers inside to push it open and surprise the intruder. There stood Peter.

'Heavens above, sir, you've given me a shock! We saw the light and came for a look-see. Everything OK, is it?'

Peter, equally shocked by their silent arrival, agreed that yes it was. 'I came in for some papers I needed and, for the life of me, when I got home I couldn't remember turning the lights off so I came back to check. Then I stood looking at the safe, thinking about our church silver and I wondered if, in fact, we should sell it. We do need the money.'

Harry swore that Zack's hair stood on end, he was so horrified. The safe was big and newish-looking, and thoroughly out of place in such an old building.

'Sell the silver! My word, they'll never agree to that! Never. Over my dead body. We all love it. No, no. That won't do. Not at all.'

'But you tell me, what does it contribute to the worship of God in real terms? It only comes out four times a year and then we lock it away. Think what we could do with the money. It's almost akin to vanity to keep it.'

'It's too precious to us all. I love getting it out, polishing it, seeing it shine, and knowing some of it's over three hundred years old. What other church as small as ours is as lucky as us? Eh? None, I bet. I swear some of 'em come special on the days when they know it's on display. No, sir, it won't do. It will not do. The village will go mad. I can't begin to imagine what they'll all say when this comes out. I wouldn't like to be in your shoes, not for anything.'

'Think of the insurance money we would save every year. It's so costly to keep it.'

Peter asked Harry what he thought. 'Well, sir, I haven't got an opinion on it, being someone just passing through, so to speak. I can see your point, that it contributes nothing to God, but if it's something special to the village ...' Hell's bells! What was he doing giving opinions on church silver? He must be going mad. Harry then wondered just how special it really was in money terms.

Peter took Harry's comment very seriously indeed. 'I'll think about that.'

Their conversation was interrupted by Marie's arrival in the vestry. 'My word! I thought you'd all been murdered. It's late. Are we going home now?'

So Peter switched off the lights and they trailed out into the night. Peter said, 'You're probably right to be horrified, Zack. It's a silly idea, I suppose. God bless the three of you. Goodnight.'

Harry got back in the car thinking Peter's blessing was a first for him, Marie was looking forward to her favourite bedtime drink, and Zack was still seething about Peter's plans for the old silver. There'd be hell to pay.

Harry was still pondering on the church silver. Three hundred years old. The village up in arms. It must be something special. But then he shrugged his shoulders. Only another week and he'd be gone, driving into the sunset, never to be seen again. It wasn't in his nature to put down roots and three weeks was quite long enough for him. Then he thought about Venetia. It was all purely physical, of course. Not the real thing, he knew that, but my God she fascinated him. Even so, he'd still break the bonds and be gone.

But fate had other plans for Harry, of which he was blissfully unaware.

Chapter 8

Jimbo had made plans, long before the unexpected demise of Ken Allardyce the accountant, to take Harriet on holiday. Tom was to do extra days as Jimbo wouldn't be there to relieve him, and Tom would be in charge of making sure all the money from the store and from the internet sales would be carefully counted and recorded before taking it to the bank in Culworth every day. They hadn't had a holiday together for years, Harriet and himself, so Jimbo had decided that, damn it all, they deserved it. Now he was in a fix.

He knew Harriet was fretting about the holiday, though she hadn't mentioned it to him. One morning he made up his mind. What could go wrong? If Tom counted and recorded the takings from the store, and Harry did the same for the internet sales and bookings for the events he had organised, and he made sure that there was nothing important in the catering department at the Old Barn while they were away, and Harry took responsibility for taking the money to the bank each day because it was easier for him to take the time out to get into Culworth rather than Tom, it would all go like clockwork. Then he remembered the signing of cheques because bills always had to be paid and ... Blast it. The wages had to be done every week. It wasn't easy because of the catering staff like Pat Jones, who worked odd hours here and there. He drove straight round to the Old Barn to see Harry, bursting in through the door as though his and Harriet's plane was about to taxi down the runway.

'Now, see here, Harry.' Jimbo outlined his plans, asking what Harry thought as he finished.

'Well now, Jimbo. I am almighty flattered that you feel so confident in my ability to manage all this, but you don't know me from Adam. I could be the biggest rogue under the sun and you did say you always handled the money ...'

'I know all that.'

'Well, how about sleeping on it and then asking me again? Don't get me wrong, I am more than willing to do it, and capable of doing it too. After all, you know what I think about figures and how they deserve to be accurate. I don't mind working extra hours to make sure it all goes smoothly—'

'Oh shut up, Harry! Sometimes you have to take the bull by the horns and now's your moment. If I don't get off on this holiday, it could be divorce in capital letters ten feet high and I'm not having that. Desperate problems need desperate solutions, and this is it. I shall spend one whole afternoon working it all out. You're a bright chap, look how you got the whole system under your belt inside a couple of hours. Will you do it? Please?'

Harry fiddled with his pen, adjusted a few papers on the desk, looked out of the window, and said, 'It would please me more than anything for you to go home to think about all this overnight and then tell me tomorrow if you are of the same mind. I *know* I'm capable of doing it all, and I'll be glad to get my teeth into something more challenging, but I want you to be sure. After all, I'm leaving Turnham Malpas next week, because I can't afford the B&B much longer. I've got to find somewhere else, you see. Somewhere cheaper.'

'Ah! Right, I might have the answer to that. I'll be back tomorrow morning to see you. I'll think about it overnight, like you said. I know Harriet will be delighted. I've sorted Fran. She's going to live with my mother while we're away. They get on really well. See you!' And Jimbo hurtled out of the door, heading straight to his mother's cottage on the green.

'Jimbo, dear! How nice, and in the middle of the day, too. You look as though you have something on your mind. What is it?'

'Sit down. I've a proposition to put to you.'

'A proposition! You're not going to ask me to take over the business while you and Harriet are away? Because frankly, I can't. I hate to admit it, but I'm past such jollifications.'

'Oh! Right. No, it isn't that. It's Jimmy's cottage. You know, next door but one.'

'What about it?'

'Is it ready for occupation by a normal person?'

'I resent that remark. He was his own man, was Jimmy Glover, I do admit. But he was a dear friend of mine, and I don't like to hear you speak about the dead like that. You know he handed his cottage over to me about a year before he died. All official, through the solicitor and such—'

'You never said.'

'I don't tell you everything, just like you don't tell me everything. Anyway, what about it?'

'So you're not waiting for probate because it's already yours?'

Katherine nodded. 'Well?'

'So I could rent it out for a while, if you were happy with that?'

'Who's going to live there?'

'Well, it's Harry Dickinson.'

'Oh, him. He's a nice chap, very much the gentleman. Why?'

So Jimbo told her the whole story, emphasising how much it would help him to go away thoroughly relaxed about everything being in good hands while he was absent.

His mother didn't answer him immediately. When she did, he was a mite surprised. 'You're leaving all the money side in Tom and Harry's care? Tom, yes, you've known him for years and can rely on his honesty. But Harry? Have you got references for him?'

'No. But I know he's as honest as the day is long. I'm convinced of it. Believe me, I know. He's astute with business matters and so far he hasn't given me one moment of doubt. In fact, he's told me to think about it overnight and make sure I'm sure. He's OK, Mother. Believe me.'

'I shall want rent. I've put a new bathroom in and a new kitchen for Jimmy, and I'm glad I did. After all, he hadn't the money to do it himself after he got too old to run his car as a taxi. We sat laughing about his taxi adventures for hours, believe me. Such fun he was.'

Briefly Jimbo thought she was going to cry and he'd never seen her cry in his life.

'We all know you did. It caused some scandalous remarks, you know. I never could see why you got on with him so well.'

'I don't know either. But we did. We were both lonely, you see, and I put up with his untidy, careless ways, and he put up with me being bossy. Which I was. Which I am. So if Harry's wanting somewhere more permanent, he can rent Jimmy's Cottage. In fact, I think I'll have a plaque made and call it Jimmy's Cottage. They'll all like that.'

'They will. I'll tell Harry tomorrow that the cottage is his to rent and that he can move in as soon as he's finished at Marie's. Will he be short of anything for the cottage?'

'No. It's all been cleaned out. I got a firm in Culworth to come and do it. There's even bed linen. He can move in when he likes. In fact I shall also present him with master Sykes as a gift until he leaves Turnham Malpas. It'll save me having to look after him. This walking lark might be a good idea, but it's too much for me. He runs for miles, and won't come back to me when I call him. I just hope to God your trust in Harry will not be abused.'

'Do you know something I don't?'

'No. It's just not like you to be so trusting with someone you barely know.'

'I'm in a fix. Harriet and I need this holiday together. It's all right being in business but there comes a time ... Well, anyway, I mustn't let her down. Thanks for helping me out. Good night, Mother.'

'Give me a kiss, you dear boy. Go away and have a wonderful time. That wife of yours certainly deserves it.'

'I know she does, and has for some time. I feel sorry, Mother, that you weren't able to have such a loving marriage as Harriet and I. I expect Dad regrets his itchy feet and having three sons the wrong side of the blanket. How you both kept that from me when I was growing up, I shall never know. But thank you anyway.'

As Jimbo left he turned and smiled at her. He reminded her so much of the husband she'd loved that she had to force herself to smile back at him.

After he'd closed her front door, his mother couldn't hold back her tears of gratitude for having the lifelong delight of a son she'd adored since the first moment she laid eyes on him. 'I'm turning into a daft old woman and it's got to stop. I loved his father no matter what he did to hurt me, and I shall love him till my dying day, the damned, cheating liar that he was.' She had two gin and tonics before she went to bed to make sure she slept and didn't waste any more tears on that wastrel she'd called a husband.

So Harry told Marie the following night that he would be leaving, how sad he was, and how he'd miss her lovely breakfasts. 'You see, Marie, I honestly can't afford to stay here any longer. No, no, I don't *want* to move. It's so lovely here with you and Zack, but I must. Jimbo has offered me a cottage at a low rent so you can see it's a good opportunity to save some money and I need to do that. Cars don't run on hot air. So I'm going to be living in the cottage next but one to Grandmama Charter-Plackett. I'm told there's a virtually brand-new bathroom and kitchen and it's all furnished properly so I will have really fallen on my feet. I hope I'm not leaving you in the lurch.'

Marie dabbed her eyes. 'That's Jimmy's old cottage, it's very nice. I'm being silly, you only promised two weeks when you first came and it's been longer than that. It's been lovely having you, but you can't turn down such a good offer. Low rent and more work. Good for you. When will you move?'

'I'll pack up tonight and move after work tomorrow. If that's all right with you?'

Marie wagged her finger at him. 'You'll have to behave yourself, living near to Mrs Charter-Plackett. She's a bit of a stickler. She won't stand any nonsense and says what she thinks. So watch it with Venetia ...'

Harry looked horrified.

'Don't look so horrified, we all know what's going on. Just take care, that's all.'

'Sorry.'

'What is there to be sorry about? Jeremy seems to take it all in his stride.'

Harry looked crestfallen. 'It embarrasses me.'

'Well, don't let it. You've a right to some fun in your life and, if she's willing, which she is ... Anyway, there's been more than you, believe me. There was this chap who came to the village and—'

Harry backed away from her.'No, Marie, don't! I don't wish to know.'

'Ah! Well, perhaps you're right. Best not.'

That was the part of Venetia he couldn't bear. That he wasn't the first. Mind you, he knew that the first time, so it was no good deluding himself. There was just that something about her, the freedom she felt to do anything she wanted. He liked that, it gave him such a feeling of liberation when he was with her. She answered something in him he'd never known he possessed.

Now he had a cottage all to himself, Venetia, the pub, and a job. What more could a man ask for?

So the following night, Harry moved to his new home, which was fully equipped. It even included Sykes the dog, who'd appeared accompanied by Grandmama Charter-Plackett with his basket, his food bowls, a cardboard box full of his toys and a few days' supply of dog food.

'I know you didn't know you were getting a dog too, but you would be doing me a great favour if you took him on. He's too much for me. I only took him in because of my friendship with Jimmy. You know, this is primarily a business arrangement which helps Jimbo and also helps you. So I shall expect the rent every Friday morning through my letter box or you can pay monthly, first of the month, if you prefer.' Grandmama Charter-Plackett was trying to weigh him up as she cocked her head to wait for the answer. Yes, like Jimbo, she was sure he was OK. Maybe Jimbo *had* made the right decision. He'd also taken the idea of the dog very well indeed.

'Every Friday morning would be best for me. And I quite like the idea of the dog.'

'If there's anything missing, like a vital chair or something, let me know. I don't think there is. I've thrown out masses of Jimmy's rubbish. He was a terrible hoarder, but lovely with it.' Her smile was sad and Harry felt sad for her though he knew, being the woman she was, he mustn't allow her to see his sympathy.

Harry looked round the living room and felt as though he'd come home at last. 'It all looks lovely, you've done a great job clearing it out. I'm sure I shall be very happy here. Thank you for your kindness.'

'Not at all. Malcolm the milkman calls every day, but I've put a pint in the fridge to tide you over. Just leave a note in the empty bottle and he'll leave whatever you need. He comes by at about eight o'clock nowadays. It used to be six, but there's been a big new estate built and he arrives here later because he goes there first.' She left swiftly, as though standing in Jimmy's old cottage was becoming too much for her. Harry finished unloading his belongings from his car, parked it at the end of the garden where Jimmy had made a hard standing for his taxi all those years ago, and went inside to settle himself in.

The TV was terrible, but he didn't watch it much, although it would be nice to have a decent one to look at. The kitchen was marvellous. It was small, but absolutely everything he needed was packed in it. Even a tumble drier. The bathroom was minute too, but bang up to date, and the bedroom had obviously been newly kitted out because the bed linen, carpet, walls and pictures all toned with each other. It was definitely not the stuff an old bachelor would have had. Altogether it was wonderful. As for Sykes, he ambled into his basket as though he'd never been away, surveyed the living room, then curled into a comfortable ball and fell asleep. It was as if he was glad to be home.

It was almost dark when there was a knock at the door. A visitor already? Harry didn't answer for a moment, but as he got up from the depths of the easy chair and went towards the door, the flap of the letterbox was pushed open and a voice whispered, 'It's me, Harry.'

And there she stood, laughing at him. He opened his arms wide and she rushed into them, kicking the door closed behind her as she grabbed him.

Sykes, startled awake by the knocking on the door, observed them kissing as though they hadn't seen each other for weeks. Breathless, they broke apart and grinned at each other. 'Thank you, Jimbo!' said Venetia.

'Thank you, Grandmama Charter-Plackett.'

'It's very cosy. It used to be a dump when Jimmy lived here. What's the kitchen like?' Venetia was hugely impressed. 'You've landed on your feet, haven't you, Harry? I'm going upstairs to see the bathroom. I'm very particular about bathrooms.' Harry followed her upstairs, guessing it wouldn't only be the bathroom she'd want to see.

He was right. The bedroom got a gold star, as did the bathroom. 'You have to admit, Grandmama has taste. This is all her doing.'

The mention of her name reminded Harry that he needed to be a little circumspect. 'Did you walk here?'

'Walk? Of course not. My car's in the pub car park so no one knows where I am. Don't worry.' She kicked off her shoes on the landing and began undressing slowly, her eyes fixed on Harry. She made an elaborate performance of removing her clothes and Harry watched, totally fascinated.

'We can't waste a lovely bedroom like this, can we, Harry darling?' She took his hand and led him in, undoing his shirt buttons as they walked. Finally, Venetia began ... Then the doorbell rang.

Venetia put a finger to her lips and they stood, skin to skin, waiting. But the doorbell rang again and then someone shouted through the letterbox, just as Venetia had done.

'Harry, it's us! We've brought a pack of beer for a house-warming. Open up!'

Harry rapidly threw his clothes back on again and raced down the narrow, twisting stairs. 'Just coming,' he shouted.

On the doorstep stood Willie and Sylvia, Don and Vera, Maggie from next door, Paddy Cleary and Zack.

Paddy said, 'Oh! Your shirt's unbuttoned, you were getting ready for bed. Well, hard cheese. It's still early and we're coming in.' And they did, and they didn't leave till a quarter to eleven. They got through the twelve cans of beer with ease and did lots of laughing and leg pulling. Altogether, they had a riotous time.

Twice, Venetia decided to go down but changed her mind. By half past ten, she had all her clothes back on again as she was feeling so cold and, by the time the ones downstairs decided they really must leave, all appetite for Harry had withered away and passion had turned to a steaming temper.

She stormed downstairs once she'd given them all a chance to disperse and said, 'You could have got rid of them sooner.'

'How could I? They'd have known something was up.'

'I doubt it, they're all thick.'

'Not so thick as to not be suspicious of me going to bed at half past nine. I felt such a fool.'

'*You* felt a fool, what about *me*? Anyway, in another ten minutes, when the car park's cleared, I'm going too.'

Harry ran a finger along her well-tanned forearm. 'There's time?'

'Sorry, but no.'

Harry was incredibly tempted to laugh at the thought of how they'd almost been caught, but Venetia in a temper was an unknown quantity to him and he couldn't risk it. She might never want him again and that would never do. After all, the only reason he'd taken the job with Jimbo was Venetia and how he felt about her. 'Goodnight, then. Shall I come for a swim tomorrow after work?'

'Can you possibly spare the time?'

'Anything is possible where you're concerned.' He smiled and, ever so slightly, she began to melt. But no. She wasn't staying.

'See you tomorrow then.' Venetia didn't want to kiss him so he had to let her go.

So the following morning, Harry left on foot for the office, his swimming things in his rucksack and Sykes by his side. The morning was clear, and promised to be bright and Sykes delighted him by racing about once they'd gone through the little wicket gate in the churchyard and were crossing the estate. He was very willing to sleep under Harry's computer desk and only occasionally went to keep an eye on the estate through the enormous window that was Harry's delight. The day sped by until, at two forty-five, Harry got ready to collect the money from the store and drive into Culworth to bank it. Today was his dummy run day and he had decided that, when he got back to Turnham Malpas, he'd report to Jimbo, just to make sure he'd got everything right. There was yesterday's takings, cheques to do with events booked for the Old Barn, and cash to be taken out for paying the casual staff who weren't included on the pay roll.

Sykes went with him to the bank and, as he behaved so impeccably, Harry decided he would take him every day. He meticulously reported back to Jimbo, going through everything to such an extent that Jimbo almost lost his rag. 'Look, you don't need to prove anything to me. I know what you're doing and you know what you're doing so it's all OK. Go!'

Then, next on the agenda was his swim with Venetia, something he'd been looking forward to since first light. What to do about Sykes? Leave him in the car or let him run about Home Park? He decided on letting him run about. A risk, but not too much of one.

Venetia had recovered her eagerness for him. All her bad temper at last night's disaster had obviously gone and she was as thrilling and satisfying as ever. When it was time to leave, Harry went outside to call Sykes but he didn't appear. So he put his wet things in the car and walked about a little, calling Sykes and enjoying a closer view of the estate.

Barry, the estate joiner, met up with him down by the Old Barn. 'Barry, you don't happen to have seen Sykes, do you? Old Jimmy's dog? He's living with me in Jimmy's cottage and I let him run about for a while but he isn't coming when I call.'

'We all heard about your stroke of luck. Nice little cottage for a *bachelor*. No, I haven't seen him. Sorry.' Barry noticed the wet hair. 'Walk up to the big house for a swim after work, do you?' There was a leering kind of grin on Barry's face and instantly Harry knew that Barry knew what was happening after the swim, and probably half the village did, too.

He decided to laugh it off by saying, 'Sitting at a desk all day, I need to keep fit.'

'Oh, naturally. You're lucky to have permission. Old Fitch, who owns the estate, is very careful who he lets have the run of the place.'

Barry's short speech was loaded with unsaid inferences but Harry ignored them and said, 'So, you don't happen to know any of Sykes's favourite places, do you?'

'Sorry, no. You'll be all right just so long as old Fitch doesn't see him. He doesn't like dogs. In fact, he'd have all pet dogs annihilated if he had his way. Working dogs are OK but not pet ones. Be seeing you.' Barry climbed into his old van with a wicked grin on his face. What he'd said about dogs was true, but he had rather exaggerated the matter. He put his foot down and powered off to the Garden House where he'd lived with Pat, her Dad and Michelle, ever since their marriage. He was bursting to tell Pat they were right in what they suspected about Venetia and her latest fella. Eventually Harry gave up the search for Sykes, deciding that perhaps he had actually gone home, having grown tired of waiting.

But Sykes wasn't there. He knocked on Grandmama's door but she hadn't seen him all day. 'He does sit in the church some-times, he always has done. He used to belong to a vicar before Jimmy adopted him so he might have gone there. Let me know if you don't find him, he doesn't normally go AWOL.'

So Harry wandered across to the church, reluctant to say the least. He walked in cautiously, his sandals making not a sound on the stone floor. And there was Sykes. He was curled up asleep on a flat bit of a tomb which, apparently, was the last resting place for two long-gone members of the Templeton family. Seeing as there was no one but himself in the church, Harry decided to have a look round. He looked upwards to the high-timbered roof and took in the regimental banners hanging tattered and torn in the roof space. He studied the wonderful stained glass window behind the altar, then stood in the pulpit pretending to be addressing a congregation until he thought he heard a noise in a side chapel. He rushed down the three steps leading up to the pulpit and went to see who was there. Peering through the rood screen he could just see Peter kneeling before the small altar making the sign of the cross and then rising to his feet.

Not him. He must avoid him at all costs. Out. Out. Out. But he was too late.

'Hello there, Harry! Looking for Sykes? He's been here half an hour or so, sleeping in his favourite spot.'

Harry pretended to be surprised. 'Oh! Sorry, I didn't realise anyone was around. He's been in the Old Barn with me all day and then, when I wanted to come home, he'd disappeared. I've taken him on for Mrs Charter-Plackett.'

'So I've heard. How's the job going, Harry?'

'Absolutely fine. I'd never meant to stay, but somehow I am. I've been lucky.'

'Jimbo's a good employer. He's been very upset about poor Ken Allardyce, as you know. Of course you never met him, but I understand that he was a lovely chap. He wouldn't say boo to a goose but he was a genius when it came to figures.'

'I must say, I haven't found any mistakes in anything that he's done. I just hope I'm as good.' So far he'd managed not to look Peter straight in the eye but this couldn't go on.

'The trouble with Turnham Malpas is that it gets to you, it makes you content and you can't get away. It happened to me.'

Harry laughed but he couldn't think of a satisfactory response. 'Well, better be off, get Sykes out of your way. Funny him liking to sit in church, he must enjoy the peace and quiet.'

Peter's reply was too frank for Harry's liking. 'You don't want

to sit in church though do you, Harry? Anything but, I'd guess.'
He studied Harry's face while he waited for his reply.

Harry decided to speak the truth because he knew Peter
would know if he lied. 'Never gone to church and not likely to.
No use for it. Sorry.'

'One day, perhaps, you won't be able to help yourself because you'll need the church, desperately. What is it soldiers say?
"There are no atheists in foxholes." If you do need a church one
day, it will be here for you, Harry.' Peter smiled, then stroked
Sykes as he passed him and left.

Harry, furious at what Peter had said, pushed Sykes off the
tomb and, before he'd got his balance, gave him a shove with
his foot to hurry him up. 'Let me get out of here. Don't you get
lost in here again. Come on.'

Mrs Charter-Plackett must have been watching from her
window because as Harry passed she opened her door. 'I was
right then, he was in church.'

'Yes, he was. Can't stop. Got lots of things to do.'

'I didn't intend keeping you, believe me. Good afternoon.'
She couldn't imagine why he'd thrown his toys out of the pram,
it was most unlike him.

Chapter 9

That evening in the bar, heads were bent together around the table. They were discussing the house-warming party over at Harry's. They couldn't help it because they all had opinions on the matter and needed to air them.

Maggie started the discussion off by saying, 'I don't care what you say, I smelled her perfume. I know I'm right.'

'Well,' whispered Sylvia, 'I didn't. What's it smell like?'

'Oriental, like. Musk or sandalwood or something. I definitely smelled it, say what you like.'

'But we were there for well over an hour. Surely she couldn't have been hiding all that time.'

'Maybe she'd already been and gone?' Sylvia said.

Paddy declared that they must have interrupted something, him with his shirt buttons undone and it being only half past nine. Well, maybe nearly a quarter to ten.

Zack spoke for the first time and, of course, he spoke in defence of Harry. 'I think it's disgusting, you all talking like this about him. It's absolutely thoughtless. For a start, he's got the right to do what he wants under his own roof and secondly, he wouldn't, he's not that kind of person.'

Maggie patted his hand. 'I know you're very fond of him, but I walked down Shepherd's Hill with him when he lived with you and he admitted he'd been swimming. I knew he had because his hair was wet.'

'What does that mean?' asked Zack.

'Well, like I said, he'd been swimming.'

'Just because he went swimming didn't mean he'd been ... you know ... with that Venetia. He's too nice a chap to be interested in a tart like her.'

'Now who's being thoughtless? Calling her a tart?' Willie commented. The outside door banged in the wind and Willie looked up. 'Eh up! Here he comes. Watch out.'

Zack shouted across to Harry, 'Get your drink and come and sit with us. Tell us what it's like living in your own cottage. Managing all right, are you, Harry?'

Harry gave him a thumbs up and nodded. He lingered a while talking to Alan Crimble the barman, hoping against hope that someone he knew would be in besides the gossiping crowd who'd ruined his first evening in Jimmy's Cottage. Then he turned as though he was going over to sit with Zack when he spotted Peter and presumably his wife. He froze. No, no, that wouldn't do. No more of him. Then he saw Tom sitting on his own and he decided he would be his target.

'Evening, Tom. May I sit with you? Good day in the store today?'

'Indeed you may.' Tom pulled the other chair out for Harry and passed a beer mat to him. 'Yes, a very good day. How are you feeling about being in charge of the money while Jimbo's away? It's only the second time since I've known him that he's left and gone on holiday with Harriet. Usually they go away in turns. My Evie offered to have Fran but she'd already planned to stay with Grandmama. Get on with her all right, do you?'

'I don't really know, I've been there barely twenty-four hours. But she seems all right. For heaven's sake, Tom, don't forget to put the daily takings in the safe overnight, will you? I couldn't bear it if we had a burglary.'

'I cash up every night before I shut up shop, fill in the banking slip and put the lot in the safe. The keys go in my jacket pocket and home with me, along with the shop key. I always put the alarm on. I never forget.'

'I've been thinking that perhaps it might be better if I banked the money in Culworth first thing the following morning rather than waiting until the afternoon. Otherwise, going just before the bank closes in the afternoon means that my afternoon is fragmented and I get nothing done. What do you think? The danger of theft would then be even less, wouldn't it?'

'You have a point. I wouldn't alter the regime without speaking to Jimbo about it, though. But either he or I will let you know before he leaves. There's got to be a complete understanding between you and I while he's away otherwise ....' Tom looked Harry straight in the face to make sure he understood and Harry nodded his agreement.

Tom downed the last of his drink and offered to get Harry another.

'Thanks, that's kind of you. Whisky, neat please.'

When Tom came back with their drinks, Harry commented, 'It seems to me that everyone in the village knows exactly what everyone else is doing before they even know it themselves.'

'Very well observed, that. On the other hand, if you're in a fix they all turn their hand to doing something about it for you. Taken ill, out of work, and you're inundated with offers of food and the like. Sykes OK with you, is he?'

'Matter of fact, I told him I was going to the pub and he insisted on coming with me. At the moment he's under the settle over there. He's his own man is Sykes.'

'Jimmy always sat at that table and Sykes used to hide under the settle, still as still, waiting for Jimmy to pass his pint down for him to have a drink.'

'Dogs are all right in here then?'

'Not really. Sykes is the exception because he's so well behaved. He was in here with Jimmy the night he died. Sad that. Laughable though, looking at it another way. They were all shouting at Jimmy, telling him it was his turn to get the drinks in, only to find that he didn't move. Sitting bolt upright in his chair he was. Willie said, "Stop kidding us, you're not asleep. You're just trying to avoid paying for the drinks." Then Sylvia screamed and pointed at Jimmy, who had begun to slowly keel over to one side. She went into a faint and they realised that Jimmy was as dead as a dodo. Anyway, Dr Harris was in with the rector and she went to examine him. She went white and said, "I'm sorry, but Jimmy has ... Well, he's ... He's died." You should have heard the uproar. Out of respect, we all trooped out leaving, as you'd expect, poor Jimmy, Dr Harris and the rector waiting for the ambulance. Poor Georgie was in a right state. She didn't work in the bar for three whole days, so upset she was.'

'I see. It all happens here, doesn't it?'

'You're right there. The tales I could tell, and I've lived here only what, ten years? Them what's lived here all their lives could tell you a thing or two. Must go, Evie will be wondering where I am. A word of warning.'

Harry looked puzzled. 'A word of warning about Evie, you mean?'

'No, of course not. About that Venetia. Fickle she is. Very fickle.'

'I don't know why you're telling me.'

'Don't pretend you don't understand. We all know, even if you don't. Which you must do. I'm just advising you to watch your step. Right?' Tom tapped the side of his nose with his forefinger and winked at him. Then he waved goodnight to Dicky and left.

Harry fumed, downed his drink, and was about to leave when his mobile rang.

They all surreptitiously watched him nod his head once or twice and then switch it off. He leaped to his feet and called, 'Sykes!' To their surprise, Sykes popped out from under the settle, which was decidedly spooky and made them glance nervously at the empty chair they now called Jimmy's chair.

Then the two of them went out the door without so much as a goodnight.

All thoughts of Tom's warning about Venetia went out of Harry's head the moment he saw her arriving on foot at his front door the same time as he did. He quickly whisked her in, pushed Sykes out into the back garden, and went to sit beside her on the old sofa in the living room.

'So?'

'Jeremy's gone on a business trip with Craddock Fitch so here I am.'

She took hold of his hand and gripped it tightly. 'They decided tonight at about five o'clock to go to Heathrow and catch a plane to Ireland. They're gone for three whole days. I gladly packed a case for him and thought about you. Are you glad?'

'You walked?'

'Yes, I thought the exercise might do me good.' Venetia giggled and snuggled up to him, and he sensed her perfume was having its usual effect on him. She certainly knew how to tempt a man. 'So, is there a drink going? It's like an Alcoholics Anonymous meeting at the big house at the moment. Fitch has still forbidden drink. There'll soon be a mass migration to the Royal Oak. I wonder if it's legal to ban it, something to do with contravening their human rights perhaps? Anyway, damn him. Drink? Darling? Please?' Getting no response, Venetia grew irritable. 'Have I done something wrong? What is it?' She nudged him. 'Mmm?'

'To me you're such a lovely person, and I'm so glad I met you, so very glad.' Harry kissed her on her temple. 'But everyone I see warns me about you. Why?'

'Jealous, that's what. Sheer jealousy. Nothing more. Believe me. Because I dress well, I'm well groomed, and men can't take their eyes off me. I have masses of sex appeal and I don't belong in the village. I haven't changed in order to try to belong either, because I don't care a fig for what they say and neither should you. We're as free as air, you and I.' She looked appealingly into his eyes. 'OK?'

Harry was so relieved by Venetia's reply that he pulled her to him and showered her with kisses. He brushed aside the fact that he didn't completely believe her.

'Can I stay the night? I'll leave very early. Promise.'

'I could drive you up there when I go to the office? I start work at eight-thirty, so we'll leave at eight? Would that be OK?'

'Wonderful! Let's have that drink.'

By the next morning, Harry didn't care what people thought or said about him and Venetia. It was his business and no one else's and they could say what they liked. With Jeremy away, he felt rather more comfortable about being with her and he'd decided to enjoy the next couple of days as best he could. Having some agreeable female company meant a lot to him because he'd been without it for far too long so he'd do all he could to keep it that way. He was tempted to suggest that she came to live with him while Jeremy was away, but decided against that. It would be going much too far, especially with the old dragon living in the next house but one. Then there really would be a scandal, and he didn't want the bother of that.

So Venetia sneaked into his car at eight and he dropped her off down the side of the big house so that she could dash into the maisonette without anyone seeing her. Then he took his car round to his alloted parking space, got Sykes out, and left him to wander about for a while, with strict instructions not to go back to the church if he got bored. Then he pulled himself up sharply: what was he doing thinking a dog would understand what he said? But there was something in the angle of Sykes's head and the alert expression in his sharp terrier eyes as he listened that convinced Harry that maybe Sykes did understand. Coming to the village had definitely softened his brain; falling so seriously for Venetia, someone who in his right mind he would never have fancied, and now talking to a dog! And what was much worse, being convinced the dog understood.

But their attempt to keep their love life secret was in vain. Grandmama Charter-Plackett had witnessed the whole episode and hastened round to Harriet's for advice.

'Harriet! There you are! I'm furious! Absolutely furious! I've never had a tenant before, and never will again. I know we don't worry about these things like we would have done fifty years ago, but there is a limit. I suspected things weren't right but then I saw them with my own eyes. I hasten to add that I was bringing the milk in, not just peeking. I saw Venetia jump in his car, he'd pulled it right up to the front door, but they didn't escape me! And Sykes having to put up with it! He's not used to it. Jimmy might have been a widower for years but there was none of that going on. What should I do, Harriet?' Grandmama flung herself down in Jimbo's chair and waited for sympathy from her one and only daughter-in-law.

'My advice would be to ignore it. At least you can't hear them at it through the wall.'

'That really is vulgar of you, Harriet. But he's such a nice young man. I just can't believe it. He's so polite and so caring about Sykes. I've half a mind to take him back.'

'Well, don't. He's too much for you. In any case, dogs don't have morals so he won't care.'

'You may be right.'

'Coffee, or would brandy be more appropriate?'

'Both.'

'Right.'

'I would offer to look after the business while you're away instead of that Harry but I won't.'

'Absolutely not, but thanks all the same, Katherine.'

'I do think I should, maybe.'

'Just because Harry fancies Venetia that doesn't mean that

he's dishonest. In any case, Jimbo has the finance side so well structured that Harry'd have to be a genius to steal from him. Don't worry. I'll get the coffee.'

So Harriet managed to soothe her mother-in-law's ruffled feathers and they spent a good half an hour discussing Jimbo's plans for the long-awaited holiday.

'My dear, I must be going. You've better things to do without spending hours calming me down. How are all my grandchildren doing? We really don't see enough of them, do we?'

'No, but that's what children are supposed to do; go away to lead their own lives. They are all doing brilliantly and don't cause me a moment's anxiety, thank goodness. But you can enjoy Fran's company when she stays with you. Now, off you go and *don't say a word* about what's going on in Jimmy's cottage.'

'I've made up my mind I won't, it's easier that way. I'll see you before you go. Take care, you're my favourite daughter-in-law you know.'

They grinned at each other and Harriet gave her a peck on the cheek before watching her march away across the green, but not without misgivings. Should they really be taking this holiday? Were they being selfish? Was she doing a prima donna act by demanding they went? Of course they should, and they'd deal with everything when they got back. Whatever it was. Possibly there'd be nothing to deal with. She fervently hoped that there wouldn't.

That evening in the bar, everyone forgot about Venetia and Harry because it faded into insignificance compared to the devastating news they heard that night.

It was a normal evening, and Dicky was with Alan Crimble, helping him behind the bar. The usual table with the settle was full with at least five people of assorted relationships, but all from old village families. The windows were wide open, letting out the heat that had built up during the day, and pleasant conversations were going on, interspersed with bursts of laughter. There was a couple of solitary drinkers standing by the bar conversing with Dicky, and two or three others from Little Derehams were at a table beside the open fireplace, its massive logs replaced with a flower arrangement put together by Georgie. They no longer had a pub of their own in Little Derehams village and had adopted the Royal Oak rather than the Jug and Bottle in Penny Fawcett. That, everyone acknowledged, was too rough for gentle folk like themselves.

It was Zack who burst in through the door, went straight to the bar, and demanded a double whisky in breathless tones. This was so contrary to his usual drinking patterns that everyone noticed.

'Double whisky coming up,' replied Dicky. 'You're looking a bit flushed, Zack, everything all right?'

'No, and it never will be ever again.' He drank the double in big gulps and it hit his stomach at such a pace that he had to steady himself by clinging to the bar top.

Before another word was said, Marie rushed in, also breathless. 'You silly fool, going up the hill at that speed. It's a wonder you haven't had a heart attack.'

'Another double whisky please, Dicky.'

Marie protested. 'Serve him if you dare, and you'll have me to reckon with. He's not having another.'

'Oh yes I am.'

'Oh no you're not.'

Willie called, 'What's up, Marie?'

'He can tell you when he gets his breath back, the idiot that he is. He *ran* up Shepherd's Hill and here he is, drinking whisky like a mad man.'

'Come and sit with us, Zack, there's a good chap. Whatever it is.' Don patted the seat next to him.

They were all bursting to know, even the people from Little Derehams, but Zack's breathlessness, his deep-red face and the sweat on his forehead warned them not to press matters too far. They didn't fancy another fatality in the pub so soon after the last one or it'd be getting a bad name.

Marie ordered her lemonade and lime, being of an abstemious nature, and a pint of Dicky's famed home-brew for Zack.

Zack stormed across to the table with the old settle and sat in Jimmy's favourite chair. No one dared object. Marie squeezed on the settle and sipped her lemonade and lime in silence.

Eventually Zack mumbled, 'I love it you know. I polish it with tender, loving care, I do. I can't bear the thought.'

Sylvia whispered, 'Is he talking about that special copper kettle of yours, Marie? The one that was your great-grandma's?'

'No.'

'Oh! What then?'

But Marie didn't get a chance to answer her because Zack said, loudly gasping between the words, 'The church silver, that's what.' Zack fell silent while they all waited for his explanation. But it wasn't forthcoming.

'He's very upset,' said Marie gently. 'It's come as a terrible blow.'

Willie was scandalised, thinking he might be landed with the job of verger all over again if Zack went. 'The rector hasn't *sacked* 'im, 'as he?'

'He might as well have. In fact, I could give my notice in right now.'

Sylvia, anxious to know the truth, said, 'A clear explanation of what we're talking about would be helpful. If he hasn't been sacked, what is it that's happened?'

With his index finger tapping the old table at every syllable to emphasise his point Zack said, 'The rector informed me, to-night, sitting bold as brass in our house in that chair of my dad's that he likes that ...' Zack stopped to blow his nose. Tension mounted significantly while they waited for him to speak again.

'He is proposing to the bishop that he gets permission to *sell* the ... church' ... he gulped. 'Silver.'

If he had said the Third World War had broken out and a nuclear bomb was about to be dropped on Culworth, they couldn't have been more shocked.

Chapter 10

It was fully a minute before anyone managed to get a word out.

'The church silver?'

'What's the matter with 'im?'

'Has he lost his mind?'

'He must have. It's sheer madness.'

'Whatever for?'

This last question Zack could answer. 'Money to pay for the roof repairs and decorate the inside. He also wants a bit of a clear out of the pews at the back to make a space for small group meetings. That's what. I don't know what he thinks the church hall is for. That's what he said, true as I'm sitting here in this pub with a pint of home-brew in my hand. Honest. Ask Marie.'

Marie nodded. 'Oh, it's true all right. I was there. He meant every word. He knows there'll be opposition. Imagine if Sir Ralph was still here.'

'Well,' said Vera, 'I guess if he was, the rector would never dare to suggest it.'

'My very words,' said Marie. 'He loved that church, did Sir Ralph. I bet he's spinning in his grave at the very thought. It's just dreadful.'

Willie, shaken to the core by this news, said, 'We'll have to get a petition up. No, better still, a demonstration.'

There was not much enthusiasm for that because they all remembered him organising a mass turnout in opposition to the market on the village green and what a fiasco that had been. No, they didn't want to be connected with a disappointing flop like last time.

'I think ...' said Don, very slowly, as though his brain processes were being severely tested, 'that we should select someone to go to the rectory and talk about it. It'll be more subtle, like, than a big shouting match. He's like that. Subtle and educated, and he'll respond better. Give him a reasonable argument, you know. See what I mean?' As an afterthought, he added, 'Just one person, not a crowd.'

Sylvia thought Don's idea was a good one, but when she made a stab at who would best fit the bill, the only one she could come up with was Sir Ralph, and what good was that? Him being dead and all.

Very commendable, thought Maggie, but who exactly fitted the bill for this subtle approach? 'Mr Fitch?'

Don shook his head. 'No, not 'im. Never. Remember they hid the silver in that room at the big house and boarded it up so that the Germans couldn't find it when they thought we'd be invaded in 1940? Old Fitch found it hidden in 1997 when he was doing some alterations after he'd bought it, and he said it belonged to him. My, what a fight we had to keep it. Don't you remember? He was for sending it all off to London to sell at one of them big auction houses. He said it belonged to him because he'd bought the house as it stood. It all came about because ...'

Willie interrupted Don when he realised that they were in for one of his long ramblings and, still very disgruntled at his idea for a demonstration being dismissed without even the smallest comment, said sharply, 'Jimbo's best.'

There was a wholehearted, 'Yes! Yes!' from everyone at the table and everyone else within hearing.

'Well? Has he gone on his holidays yet?' asked Willie, his confidence remarkably restored by their enthusiasm.

'No he hasn't. He goes Wednesday, ever so early.'

'Then we've got time, haven't we?'

They all nodded. Willie glanced at his watch. 'They'll have finished eating now. So who's going across to broach the subject? We can't let the grass grow under our feet, it's essential to make the first move. *Now.*' He finished the last dregs of his home-brew and got to his feet. 'Well? Are you coming?' And he set off for the door.

Jimbo was not best pleased when he found a crowd standing on his doorstep. With his mind racing through what to pack ... and had he told Tom about ... and ... had he left that list for Greta ... and did Harry need any more final instructions ... had he actually done the staff rotas for the fortnight he was away ... he found it hard to smile and look welcoming. 'Yes, how can I help?'

'Can we come in? Just for a minute?'

Jimbo opened the door wider and said, 'Of course.' While under his breath he was cursing them for coming. Consequently, he was not in the best of moods when they burst out with their request.

'What? I don't believe this. Are you sure you're right?'

Zack spoke, telling him the tale word for word as it had happened and Jimbo felt the shockwaves. 'Has he taken leave of his senses? How can he be so thoughtless? This is ridiculous. Absolutely ridiculous. I'll go straight across there this very minute. Are you coming?'

'Well, no. We thought a more reasoned person on their own might make more of an impression. Not a crowd, all shouting.'

'Right. Well, it'll be one man shouting then. Do we know if he's in?'

'No,' said Zack. 'There're no meetings in the church hall though, apart from Scouts. We just hoped he'd be in.'

Jimbo pushed his way through the crowd. 'Out of my way. See you in the Royal Oak when I've finished with him. Harriet! Won't be long.'

They trailed after him, anxious and afraid that their idea might go badly wrong. What had happened to 'subtle and educated'? It appeared that Jimbo was going to the rectory more like a mad bull than anything. So they all scuttled back to their table in the bar and nervously toyed with their drinks, hoping against hope that Jimbo would calm down once he got into Peter's study.

Conversation was desultory for a while and more than one of them was considering other approaches than Jimbo going headlong into a row. Peter could be remarkably stubborn when he chose and, what was worse, make you feel like a worm for suggesting whatever it was that had brought about his ire. Even so, they had to stand firm on this.

Beth answered the door. 'Hello, Uncle Jimbo. Have you come to see Dad?'

'Is he in?'

'He's in his study on the telephone.'

'I'll wait here in the hall. You get on with whatever you're doing, I'll be OK.'

Beth couldn't understand why she appeared to be in trouble and was relieved when she recognised the sound of Peter's receiver being put down. 'Oh! He's just finished, I'll tell him you're here.'

'No need to bother. Thanks.' And Jimbo marched in and shut the door behind him with a bang. The temptation for Beth to put her ear to the study door was almost overwhelming, but it had been drummed into her as a small child that what went on in the study was sacrosanct, so she didn't listen. She could hear her Uncle Jimbo raising his voice though and she wondered what on earth could have happened.

'I've just had a deputation at my door and I'm not best pleased.'

Peter looked up at Jimbo and gestured for him to take a seat on the sofa.

'No thanks. I'm too angry. What is all this about selling the church silver? Is it true?'

'It is true that I have broached the idea of selling it. The church needs the money.'

'Have you gone out of your mind?'

'No.'

'Have you a good reason for doing so? Though what on earth it could be, I have not the faintest idea. I do know that I'm very angry.'

'To pay for the pointing, the new arrangement of the pews at the back near the font, and to paint the walls of the church. Even you must know they need it.'

'Peter! Peter! It's our pride and joy.'

'More important than the church falling down? Oh, yes, I can hear them say. They had silver worth a small fortune locked up in the church safe but unfortunately the church has fallen down so ...' Peter shrugged his shoulders and gave Jimbo a hopeful half-smile.

'Fallen down! That is ridiculous. It's nowhere near falling down, and you know it. That silver is *ours,* not yours. Well, it is, but as custodian on our behalf you have no right to even suggest that we sell it. No right whatsoever, and when I get back from ... wherever it is we're going ... I sincerely hope there will be no more of this nonsense. I have been deputed by a group from the village to convince you it is not *right* to sell it, and you mustn't. Do you hear me?'

'Jimbo!' Peter got to his feet and looked down at him. 'I want to do the best for the church and keeping a church available for three villages is of primary importance, we can't let it dilapidate. We *must not* let it dilapidate. Don't you see?'

'You must not sell the silver. Absolutely not. That's my final word. So think about it and don't do anything official till I get back. Right? Ralph Templeton would go mad if he were here, God rest his soul. Absolutely mad. He'd have had you hung, drawn and quartered in earlier times and I for one, would stand by and watch. With relish.' He prodded Peter's chest with a vicious forefinger, 'And don't you forget what I've said. The whole village will be up in arms otherwise. Believe me.'

Jimbo slammed the rectory door shut behind him and marched across to the Royal Oak steaming with temper. He couldn't really understand *why* he was so angry, but angry he was, and he charged into the bar still seething.

'I've been to see him.'

'What did he say?'

'Some ridiculous story about how if we let the church fall down through neglect there won't be any point to the silver anyway. I've warned him that nothing must be done. The silver must not be sold and I've told him that the whole village will be up in arms if he goes ahead with this ridiculous scheme. OK. I'm leaving you all responsible till I get back. Right?' Jimbo glowered at everyone in the bar, then left in an angry flurry. But more than one person had avoided his eye. It seemed like a blinking good idea to some, and why not? Better the silver got sold and the church was still standing. After all, where would they all get buried or married, come to that. Or the grandchildren christened? Just exactly where? Definitely not in that grim barn of a church they politely called Culworth Abbey. They shuddered at the prospect.

After the initial silence while the shock wore off, a great hubbub of noise broke out of conflicting opinions and at the table where the old settle was, a distinct feeling that 'subtle and educated' had completely gone out of the equation. They trembled at what they had begun.

Sitting at the table close to the hearth where Georgie's flower arrangement sat, Tamsin and Paddy were far too engrossed in each other's company to worry about the anger swilling around the bar. 'Tamsin, did you know about this?'

'Paddy, I've known a while, but I thought it would all blow

over. Apparently it hasn't, but I'm keeping out of it. Right out of it.'

Paddy nodded his head. 'That's for the best, let it all flow over your head. There'll be a big dust up and then everything will settle down. Peter will change his mind, the bishop will say no, or the village will get their way. I've practised that piece you gave me, by the way. I think I'm sending Greta mad with it but I can't stop.'

Tamsin grinned at him. 'Good. I'm so pleased. Do you enjoy it though? Because that's what music is for.'

'If I don't enjoy something, I don't do it. I got a craze on fishing once and, being a bit flush at the time, I bought all the gear, fished every day for two weeks, then gave it up. I haven't fished since. It's an idiotic sport is fishing. In fact it doesn't even earn the name sport. Waste of time.'

Paddy didn't notice the amused grin on Tamsin's face until she replied, 'I love it, to be honest.'

'Oh! Sorry. I didn't ...'

'Only teasing, Paddy! For heaven's sake, you try too hard, you know.'

'Try too hard?'

'Yes. I'm well aware you think your education and your life before you came here is beneath mine. It isn't. Honest. Your origins don't matter at all, it's what you are now that counts.'

Paddy was mortified. She'd understood what he'd wanted to keep hidden and he felt a fool. An uncomfortable silence followed this statement of Tamsin's and Paddy couldn't find the words to fill the gap. But then the outside door opened and in came Gilbert Johns.

It was very chilly for a summer's evening, but that didn't faze Gilbert at all. He was wearing his usual year-round outfit; a shirt with the sleeves rolled up to the elbow and open almost to his navel, crumpled cotton trousers, hefty sandals on his bare feet, and his hair was wild and unkempt-looking. He was tanned the year round and, although men never noticed, he did have tremendous sex appeal. It must have been the combination of deep-set nut-brown eyes, hollowed cheeks, and a strong jaw that emphasised his attraction. He spotted Tamsin as soon as he walked in and he raised a hand and gave her a nod of his head before going to the bar to buy a drink.

Paddy knew Gilbert was no competition where Tamsin was concerned, as he was happily married with five children, but it seemed to him that it would be easier just to disappear and leave them together. He wouldn't even finish his drink.

Gilbert came over, nodded at the spare chair, and Tamsin agreed that he could sit down.

'Good evening, Paddy. How's the flute going?'

So he knew. 'Fine, thank you.'

'Enjoying it? Tamsin said you were learning. Nothing like music for healing the soul, it lifts you away from the mundane tasks. Well, anyway, I find it does.'

'That's right.' Paddy nodded and sat awkwardly, wondering how he could escape.

'I've come having heard about the sale of the church silver. Where do you stand on it, Tamsin?'

'Not got an opinion either way, actually. We hardly ever see it, so what's the point?'

'Ah! Right. And you, Paddy?'

'Don't have a say, I never go.'

'Well, that's honest anyway. So at this table, I'm the only one who's going to fight for it? To keep it, I mean.' Gilbert nodded his head in the direction of the table in front of the old settle. 'Bet they object to selling it.'

'They do. From what we can hear from this table, they've sent Jimbo across to see Peter. Jimbo came back here afterwards and told them straight from the shoulder that nothing was to be done while he was on holiday. Well, he told all of us nothing had to be done and was he in a temper? He was. Wasn't he, Paddy?'

Paddy agreed he was by nodding his head and saying nothing. Why Gilbert made him feel so useless he couldn't explain, because he was the most kind and understanding man you could ever hope to meet, but he did. Gilbert and Tamsin could converse but Paddy, Gilbert and Tamsin couldn't. It struck Paddy very forcibly that they all spoke the same language, but theirs was on a different level from his, it was even a different vocabulary. He guessed that if they began speaking about music, it would be double Dutch to him. He wouldn't know the composers, nor the music, nor the musicians, nor the places they spoke of. What a fool he'd been, dreaming of him and Tamsin being ... He got to his feet and interrupted them by saying, 'Sorry, got a few things to do, must go. Goodnight.' Then he left.

Gilbert half stood up, intending to encourage him to stay, but there was a determination in Paddy's stride that changed his mind. 'I'm sorry, I didn't mean to interrupt.'

'That's Paddy for you. He has this inferiority complex. It's very sad really, he's a lovely chap.'

Gilbert raised an eyebrow at Tamsin, but she wasn't going to be tempted into any confessions and quickly asked him if he had any ideas for thwarting Peter's plans for the church silver. 'I shall write to the bishop first. No demonstrations, no confrontations, no protests for Gilbert Johns. A letter written and posted tomorrow, explaining very succinctly that the wishes of the village will brook no opposition. As church choirmaster, I feel I have a right to say how I feel.'

'You sound very confident.'

'I am. He's a great chap is Bishop Simeon Julian Thomas Cartwright, a man after my own heart. We understand where each other is coming from and I shall trade on that.'

'Does Louise feel the same?'

'My beloved and I are of the same mind, yes.'

'Good. Well, I'm off down Shepherd's Hill to Greta Jones's to see Paddy. Good luck with your campaign.'

'Not a word. OK?

'Promise. See you Sunday, Gilbert. I've got your music list.'

Gilbert nodded. He was very aware he'd interrupted a happy tête-à-tête and he said softly, 'Hope I haven't ... upset the apple cart.'

'There's nothing to upset.' Tamsin grabbed her bag and disappeared.

She arrived at Greta and Vince's cottage in a state of turmoil. She'd no idea what her interest in Paddy amounted to, but she did know she didn't want him hurt. She knocked on the door and waited. Slow footsteps could be heard approaching the door and when it opened, there stood Paddy.

They looked long and hard at each other until Tamsin felt foolish. 'Is it possible I could come in?'

He opened the door a little wider. 'Look,' she said. 'Have I upset you? If I have, it's the last thing in the world I want to do.'

He ignored her question. 'Greta's just making a cup of tea.'

'Oh! Right. Another time then.'

Greta shouted from the kitchen. 'I'll make one for you if you like, Tamsin. It is Tamsin, isn't it?'

'Yes. Thank you.'

Paddy jerked his head in the direction of Greta's voice so Tamsin followed him into the kitchen. Greta had her back to them as she was filling the teapot with boiling water. Paddy pulled out a kitchen chair, but Greta said, 'For heaven's sake, Paddy. Company goes in the lounge. Vince has gone to bed and I'm about to. Come on, Tamsin, follow me, Paddy seems to be dumbstruck.' She collected a third cup and saucer, put them on the tray, and bustled past the two of them, leading the way into her lounge.

'Sit down, dear. Strong, medium or weak?'

'Medium, no sugar. Just milk.'

'Right you are.'

Paddy still hadn't spoken. He accepted a cup of tea and began to drink it. 'Manners, Paddy. That was for Tamsin.'

'Oh! Sorry, here you are.'

'Not that one, Paddy, you've been drinking from it.'

'Oh! Right.'

'Honestly, you've had one too many, you have.'

'He hasn't, Greta, he's only had one tonight.'

'Oh! Right. Sorry.' Greta picked up the third cup and said, 'I'm off to bed, don't forget to put the lights out and lock up.' She left, closing the door firmly behind her.

All Paddy wanted to do was lie in his bed feeling sorry for himself.

Conscious her hair was blown all over the place, Tamsin tried to bring some order to it. Paddy noted the long artistic fingers and the beautifully kept nails and longed to have her hand touching his hair in exactly the same way. Unaware Tamsin had seen the longing in his eyes he muttered, 'Sorry for leaving so suddenly, but I can't ... I couldn't.' His lips closed tightly. He couldn't finish his sentence.

'Look. I know you feel you can't talk about music like Gilbert and I can, but you seem to forget I can't talk about gardens like you can. I know nothing. I don't even know the difference between weeds and real plants. Nor their names, nor where they belong for the best in the garden. I couldn't look after a vine successfully, nor grow peaches like you can, not for anything. So both of us have our own expertise. Mine is music. Yours is gardens. They're both beautiful passions.'

He didn't answer.

'So what's the difference? We both make a contribution to beauty in the world. Don't we? In our own way?'

Paddy still didn't answer.

'I'd better be going.' She put her cup down on Greta's tray, picked up her bag, and said, 'Goodnight, Paddy. Sleep tight.' As she passed close to him, she bent her head and gently kissed his lips. Then she saw herself out. She didn't see him reach out to touch her as she passed, nor did she see his hand touch his lips where her lips had touched, nor the smile that flooded his face with joy.

Chapter 11

It felt very odd for everyone who worked for Jimbo that neither he nor Harriet were there to refer to for two whole weeks. He'd deliberately not allowed any big catering event to be booked at the Old Barn so that was one worry off their minds, but they still had the day-to-day running of everything else to deal with. Greta, in the Mail Order office, scurried about wishing she had extra help because, since Jimbo had set up his website, her workload had doubled. In fact, some weeks she did extra hours just to keep up with the orders, never mind any extra chores like checking her stock. In fact, she was working hand to mouth with the stock, as Tom had to go out to collect all the jams and chutneys and things from the people who made them in their own kitchens now that Harriet wasn't doing her usual collection rounds.

'Tom, you'll have to go round tomorrow, else I shall be out of all the popular lines by lunchtime. I need all the pickles, chutney, and the new season strawberry jam from Hazel Whitehouse in Penny Fawcett. Can you go?'

'I might be able to. I've everything to do you know.'

'I know, but I can't go to collect it, can I? I don't drive.'

'I'll try to squeeze it in.'

'Could Harry go? He'd be willing, I'm sure. Or could he do something for you while you go?'

'Greta! I'm serving. Leave it with me.'

'Well, when Jimbo comes home and sees my sales have slumped, I shall tell him why. It's not part of *my* responsibilities to be collecting the supplies.'

Greta turned on her heel and went back to the Mail Order office in high dudgeon. But Tom came up with the best idea yet. He'd ask Harry to cash up and prepare the banking while he took the opportunity to go round the farms to collect Greta's stock. That would be best. He was sure Harry wouldn't mind. After all, he couldn't be in two places at once, even Jimbo couldn't do that. Relieved he'd found a solution, he rang Harry when he had a lull and they agreed that he would come to the store early tomorrow morning and sort out the banking himself before going with it to the bank first thing. That would allow Tom to do Harriet's collection round tonight instead of staying on to add up the cash. 'I open up at seven-thirty, Harry, so you can come as soon as you like after that.'

'Right. I'll do that. Don't forget to put the contents of the till in the safe tonight will you, before you set off? I'll come round at eight-thirty tomorrow morning instead of going to the office, do the banking, and then take it straight to the bank. Then I'll drive back and begin work. Glad to be of help. Bye.'

So that was one problem solved satisfactorily. Others were not so easily solved, but they struggled on. Twice the deliveries didn't arrive on time, then the deep freeze in the front of the store packed up. They lost a lot of food as it had almost completely defrosted during the night and Tom daren't refreeze it, just in case. Then some boys playing football out in the street close to the store put a ball clean through a side window that had to be boarded up before Tom could lock up for the night. All in all, Tom would be glad when Jimbo returned.

Jimbo's return was eagerly awaited by others besides Tom, in particular the ones who had taken exception to Peter wanting to sell the silver.

The news about selling the church silver had flown far and wide. In Penny Fawcett and Little Derehams they had heard almost as soon as Turnham Malpas, and they were furious. 'Sell it? Over my dead body' was a frequent remark and Tom was inundated with queries and questions all the time in the store. But where else could they grumble? No one fancied facing Peter head-on over it. It needed saying, but they all kept their heads below the parapet for fear of his wrath. In truth, Peter was not wrathful at all, merely amazed at the trouble he'd stirred up with a mild suggestion of a possibility.

Caroline had warned him, but he'd felt sure he could carry them all with him.

'It's no good,' she said for the umpteenth time, 'you'll have to drop the whole idea.'

'I don't want to. It's a very simple solution at no cost to anyone at all. They won't have to lift a finger, all the jobs can be done and the church fabric will be kept in good order.'

Caroline had to laugh at Peter's attempt at common sense. 'Wait until Jimbo gets back, like he said. You'll have to hope a holiday has done his temper some good and he comes back in a better mood!'

'I have never seen him so angry about anything at all.'

'Overworked, I suppose.'

'He's got some good workers though. Tom, Harry, Bel and Greta. They all worship the ground he walks on.'

'Everyone worships the ground *you* walk on, except maybe not so much as they used to!' Caroline couldn't help but laugh a little.

'It's not funny, Caroline. Not funny at all. Bishop Simeon says he's had a letter from Gilbert putting the case for not selling. I'm surprised, he's never opposed me before, not once in all the years I've been here.'

'Is that telling you something? Telling you it's time to step away from your suggestion and let it be, perhaps?'

'Or I could always suggest that we have a big fundraising effort and raise the money for the repairs ourselves?'

'They've done a lot of fundraising lately, they've only just finished fundraising for the Organ Fund and, before that, there was the money for your New Hope Mission. That was a whacking great effort, you have to admit. Maybe you've reached a kind of saturation point with fundraising.'

'All the more reason for selling the silver.'

Caroline had to laugh but, at the same time, she was worried that Peter was in danger of overstepping the mark with his congregation and undoing all his years of patient, loving work.

Word of Peter's tentative plans reached the big house and Mr Fitch's secretary thought he would have an apoplectic fit when he heard, so she secretly looked up details of how to deal with it in her First Aid manual, just in case. He stormed round his office and at one stage, swept a pile of papers awaiting his attention clean off the desk. She wanted to go and pick them up immediately, before he walked on them, but decided that would not be politic at the moment.

Instead she escaped to her office and brewed a pot of coffee for him, waiting until he'd finished fuming over by the window before she entered with the silver tray and all the accoutrements he so loved. She crept towards him, cup in hand, served just how he liked it, and tentatively mentioned the word coffee.

'Thanks. Find out if the rector is home at the moment.'

She hesitated, thinking about his first appointment in fifteen minutes.

'Now. If you please.'

'You have that appoin—'

'That can wait. Phone them and delay them till later in the day.'

She still didn't move.

But Mr Fitch swung round and confronted her, his temper rising again. 'I said *now*.'

Accepting defeat, she replied, 'Very well, Mr Fitch.'

★

'He's in,' was the answer.

'Back in an hour.'

'Very well, Mr Fitch.'

Craddock Fitch roared up to the rectory in his Rolls, braked harshly, leaped out, and forgot to trigger the remote control lock, a very real sign of how angry he was.

Peter answered the door saying, 'I could have come up to see you, I know how busy you are. Coffee?'

'No, thank you.' He marched into Peter's study without waiting for an invitation, dropped down onto the sofa, and held back from speaking until Peter had closed the door.

'I am angry.'

'Yes.'

'Very angry. In fact, so angry I could punch you right on the nose for this stupidity.'

'Right, I see. About ... ?'

'You know full well what about.'

'Ah! The silver, you mean.'

'The proposed selling of the silver. I won't have it.'

'Something like fifteen years ago, could be more, you were more than willing to sell it to your own advantage. I'm thinking of selling it for the benefit of the church, a very different matter.'

Mr Fitch looked momentarily contrite, but the jibe at the end of Peter's speech really got to him. 'I've ... I've had a change of mind since then. That silver belongs to the church and the people of the three villages, and I'm defending their rights. Not mine.'

Peter fiddled about with his desk, straightening the pens and tidying his papers while he waited for Mr Fitch to dig deep for some more reasons to not sell the silver.

'Have you heard me?'

'I have.'

'Well?'

'We get the silver out for display only on high days and holy

131

days, perhaps four times in a year. The rest of the time it is out of sight in the safe. Surely it would be more useful to sell it and use the money wisely. Let's face it, Craddock, how many times this year have *you* actually *seen* the silver? Mmmm?'

A long silence fell. Eventually, Mr Fitch muttered, 'Not once.'

'There we are then. There's your answer. It hardly counts that you have decided that you have a right to dictate to me what I do with the silver, because fifty-two Sundays in the year you don't give a damn about it.' Peter snapped his middle finger against his thumb and the sharp click made Mr Fitch jump. Peter turned as though he was about to continue what he had been doing before he was interrupted.

Mr Fitch, sitting silently on the sofa, wondered how he'd arrived at this insurmountable situation. On three counts really. One, it was so unlike Peter to be so hard, so confrontational; two, Peter was absolutely right, he didn't give the silver a single thought from one year to the next; and three, why did he feel so strongly about it when what Peter had said was absolutely right?

But he did feel strongly about it. He didn't want it sold. He remembered the thrill of handling the plates and the candlesticks and that magnificent floor-standing candlestick, especially.

'Very well then. I hear what you're saying, but I will oppose you selling it if I never do another thing. I'm deeply upset by the idea of it leaving the village, I don't know why, but I am. But let's part friends. I can't be at odds with you, not after all these years. I've always had respect for you, Peter. A man of the cloth and all that.' He held out his hand in friendship and of course Peter shook it. 'Still friends then, Peter?'

'Of course.'

As Mr Fitch closed the heavy rectory door behind him, he muttered, 'But it will be me who wins.'

Chapter 12

The summer turned very hot indeed, and some of the enthusiasm for action drained away. Lethargic clapping at the cricket
matches on Saturday afternoons was about the most energetic
activity any of them could muster. Ninety degrees some days,
made most people disinclined to take any positive action until
Jimbo returned.

Tom couldn't wait for Jimbo's return, but only from the
point of view that control of the business was just beginning
to slip away from his grasp. Harry seemed to be taking charge,
and that wasn't what had been intended. Tom didn't like it.
Greta found herself stewing in the Mail Order office because the
very necessary air-conditioning seemed to be overcome by the
excessive temperature. Everyone, customers as well as staff, were
inclined to be edgy. Sharp exchanges of temper occurred all too
regularly in the store and Tom was beginning to grow weary of
keeping his temper when he felt like turning everyone out and
locking the door.

But only five more days to go and Jimbo would be back.
Several emails had come through to the store and it appeared
that Jimbo and Harriet were the only ones enjoying this brilliant
weather, allowing for two notable exceptions. Namely Harry
and Venetia.

Harry was loving the heat. His office was cool as the sun
didn't creep in through the vast window until late in the afternoon, by which time he was on his way to his swim. Well,
more accurately, on his way to his beloved. His fascination for

Venetia had not waned; if anything, it had increased. He looked at the office clock only to count how many minutes it would be before she was in his arms. Frankly he felt her to be the most delightfully tempting woman he had ever met, and he couldn't get enough of her. The feeling appeared to be mutual and the two of them had cast aside almost all attempts at keeping their affair secret. So long as Jeremy didn't know, and he never gave a hint that he did, they simply didn't worry who saw them, who raised a questioning eyebrow, who looked disapprovingly in their direction. Well, until the evening in Home Park. That sweltering evening when they escaped outside to lie underneath the trees enjoying the shade and somehow they'd been embracing and progressing towards the inevitability of the outcome of their actions when Peter, of all people, had come walking by. He never spoke a word of recrimination, simply paused for a moment, and then walked on. Harry recollected the anger Venetia had felt, and expressed, in loud terms once Peter was out of hearing. She'd slipped her bra straps back in place, tidied her skirt and stormed off home in a blazing temper.

Occasionally Harry's conscience switched on and he had uncomfortable moments about the whole matter, but one second in Venetia's arms and all the pricks of conscience in the world bothered him no longer. All that mattered was their passion for each other. Harry had even been planning to stay on in Turnham Malpas and not disappear over the horizon as soon as Jimbo came back. In fact, not seeing Venetia every day brought him out in a cold sweat and he had to get a grip on himself. They couldn't stay as they were, because Jeremy wasn't going to just disappear into thin air, not now that he and Mr Fitch seemed to have come to an understanding and got on tolerably well. In any case, Jeremy was reaching that point in his career when, agewise, applying for another job would not be a good move. So if he wanted to keep Venetia, then he and Venetia would be leaving together. Harry's fingers were poised over the computer keyboard but he was gazing out of the window seeing nothing but Venetia's lithe figure coming towards him, arms outstretched in an all-encompassing, loving welcome. He questioned whether it was love or lust that kept him by her side, but seeing as he'd never known the kind of passion poets wrote about, he didn't know. Whatever it was, he wanted to keep it. But how long could it last?

At the very same time, Venetia was planning a visit for the students to a massive building project seventy-five miles away that Craddock Fitch was also involved with. She also sat gazing out of the window, the end of her pen tapping against her front teeth while she pondered exactly the same question as Harry. There was no doubt in her mind that her feelings for Harry could be for life. He never left her mind and any hours spent not in his company were wasted ones. Ten times a day she decided that going to live with Harry would be the most wonderful thing to happen to her. And why not, she'd spent years chained to Jeremy and for what? He neither charmed her, nor excited her. Nothing at all, he was a void ... someone who slept in her bed, someone who aggravated her beyond all reason every day of his life. But Jeremy's job kept her housed in the big house, which she loved. It gave her the chance to flirt with the students, organise their free time, and give parties, which she loved doing. Being surrounded as she was by all these young, smart, go-getting students, female as well as male, gave her a fillip no other job could ever do. And seeing as Jeremy didn't appear to know about Harry, why should she worry? Enjoy it while she could, was her motto.

But the third person in the triangle was totally aware of the situation and sometimes he writhed with the agony of it all. Despite everything she had done he still loved her. Someone less loving than himself would have demanded divorce at the very least, but he still loved her. He tried not to, but he always took her back as though nothing had happened. He never discussed the whys and wherefores with her. She'd been unfaithful to him more times than he could remember, and still she reinstalled herself and carried on as though nothing was wrong between them. Jeremy couldn't understand why he was so tolerant and the idea that this time would be the last time he'd tolerate her bad behaviour filled him with dread. She was so wonderfully full of life and shining with a love that she was incapable of hiding that he had reached the point where he might have to, for once in his life, stand tall and put an end to her dilly-dallying once and for all. Quite how he'd do that, he'd no idea.

Chapter 13

At last! Jimbo and Harriet were back! No one greeted them with more enthusiasm than Tom. They got back about half past eight in the morning, just as the pre-school rush was beginning, and he could have handed the business over to them then and there; the keys, the till, the post office, the whole blessed lot, he was so exhausted.

Glad though he was to see them, he couldn't drum up the enthusiasm to show them his delight and so both Jimbo and Harriet independently thought that things must have gone terribly wrong while they'd been away.

Jimbo nodded his head towards the stock room and Tom followed him. 'Well. How's things been? Mmm?'

'Absolutely fine, but I'm exhausted to be honest. When you go away together next time we'll have to organise more help, it's too much for one person to handle.'

'Look here, Tom. Hand me the keys and you go home. You look shattered. Come back tomorrow rested and recharged.'

'I can't do that, it's not fair. You must have jet lag, and you can't possibly do a full—'

'We spent the night at an airport hotel and drove here this morning. Believe me, I shall be glad to get back into harness. You've obviously done a brilliant job and I insist, on threat of dismissal, that you go *home*. At once.'

'The greetings cards need revitalising, I haven't done those for days, and I was going to—'

Jimbo took Tom by the shoulders and propelled him towards

the door. 'Out! This minute!' Then he gave him a final push through the open door.

'Well, I must say I shall ...'

'Out!' Jimbo then turned, smiling, towards the customers waiting at the till. 'Now, who's first?' He rubbed his hands together in anticipation and got down to work.

His customers were delighted to see him too and for the next hour Jimbo immersed himself in the day-to-day nitty-gritty of running a village store. It was only when Zack came in for a snack lunch for himself in his shed in the churchyard that Jimbo cleared his head for a moment and asked him the state of play on the church silver.

Zack leaned his forearms on the counter. 'Well, now. Nothing has happened while you've been away. The weather's been that extreme we've none of us given it a thought, except ...' Zack glanced round to make sure he wasn't being overheard, then continued, 'I have heard that Gilbert has sent a letter to Bishop whatever his name is, to say that the whole village and the two other villages are dead against selling the silver. Now that's all I know. Whether or not he's had a reply, I do not know.'

'Gilbert? Eh! My word. I'm surprised by that. I thought maybe lots of people wouldn't care a button.'

'He's written without asking anyone their opinion. He's said in his letter that they think like he does, without asking 'em, but I can tell you that there's them who wouldn't mind it being sold. They're thinking along the lines of if the church falls down, then where would they be when they want burying or something similar.'

Briefly Jimbo hesitated while he thought about what on earth could be 'similar' to being buried. Half-buried? Three-quarters buried? Or burned on a pyre on the village green? He shook his head to clear it and said, 'I'll go and see him as soon as I have a minute.'

'That won't be easy.'

'What won't?'

'He's in York, you see. He's been called in as a specialist on an excavation problem at the minster. He could be there for weeks.'

'Right. Must press on. One sausage roll, one prawn cocktail crisps, one bottle of orange and one Chelsea bun. Right?'

Zack nodded. 'Glad you're back, things just don't seem right when you and your Harriet aren't here in the village. There's nobody to take charge, except for the rector, and he's not flavour of the month, believe me.' He beamed at Jimbo as he handed him his change and bounded out of the door, but returned to shout, 'Harry's dead set up with Jimmy's Cottage and old Sykes is as happy as a sandboy, off to work every morning with him. They make a right pair. See you.'

However, Greta, who'd finally emerged from the Mail Order office, had a different slant on village life from Zack. 'Glad you're back, and Harriet. Did you have a good time?'

'Excellent. Thank you, Greta. I'm longing to get back in the groove.'

'Mmm?'

'And what does "Mmm" mean?'

Greta leaned against the counter, glad for a moment's peace in the store so she could tell him. 'Mail order is doing well. I'm glad Harriet'll be doing her round again. I've almost run out of stuff to complete my orders 'cos Tom was so busy. But the big thing is Harry and Venetia. Everyone knows, they can't help but know.'

'What?

'Don't tell me you don't know, because you do.'

Jimbo spread his hands as though he had no knowledge of what she was talking about. 'How can I? I've been away two whole weeks.'

'You know what I mean. They don't care who knows. They even go in the pub together, holding hands and kissing. Georgie told them off one night. She said they shouldn't kiss and cuddle like that in public, not in her pub anyway.'

'I see. Has he been working? You know, doing his job?'

'Oh, yes. Cashing up for Tom each morning and then off to the bank, regular as clockwork.'

'I see. Poor Tom, I'll see he gets extra help the next time we go away. I didn't realise how much there is to do once I'm not here, nor Harriet. What you're saying is that they're having a love affair?'

Greta nodded her head. 'Absolutely, no doubt about it. What Jeremy must think, I do not know. Poor chap, I never really liked him, but you can't 'elp but feel sorry for him. All that going on in such a brazen fashion. Must press on, you do keep me talking when you shouldn't.' But she smiled and patted his arm saying, 'So glad you're back, it's not been the same without you.'

Greta shot back to the Mail Order office, leaving Jimbo feeling slightly worried about Harry. It was when Greta said 'cashing up for Tom' that he felt alarm bells begin to ring. He had not intended for Harry to actually cash up and make out the banking slips. Tom, yes. Harry, or anyone else for that matter, definitely not. In particular, he remembered his mother's doubts about Harry not giving references and he wondered ... but he had to rush into the post office 'cage' to deal with some parcels so he didn't do anything about it. Nor did he give it another thought until he finally closed the store at seven and staggered home to find out what Harriet had been up to and to give Fran a good welcome back after her sojourn at his mother's.

She was full of what had happened while they'd been away. 'The talk is all about Venetia and Harry. They're out and about together all the time.'

'In working hours?'

'Oh no! They all say that they are both diligent about their work, it's their extra-curricular activities that are fascinating everyone.' Fran leaned forward confidentially, as though making sure they heard every word of her spectacular news. 'They got caught one night in Home Park. It was a very hot night. By the way, we've had brilliantly hot weather while you've been away. In flagrante delicto is what they're all saying. Well, not those exact words, but we all *know* ...' She rolled her eyes and Jimbo looked appalled.

'Harriet! Is this right for Fran to ...'

'For goodness sake, Jimbo, she's almost fifteen ...'

'Still.'

'Oh, Dad! Grow up. I know what life's about.'

Harriet had hardly dared ask who found them, but she did.

'Well, you'll never guess, so I'll tell you.' Fran paused for effect. 'Peter.'

This statement left Harriet and Jimbo stunned.

'We missed all the fun then?' commented Harriet, unable to take in the almighty explosion there must have been when this piece of news got out.

'Absolutely. Grandmama said she wasn't surprised, considering what was going on in Jimmy's Cottage. She's got the sign up, by the way. Jimmy's Cottage it is, for eternity.'

'Has Harry paid his rent, do you know?' Jimbo enquired.

'Each Friday morning in cash in an envelope through her letterbox.'

This greatly stilled Jimbo's alarm at what he'd heard from Greta. Obviously jet lag was making him unreasonable and the sooner he got to bed and got over it, the better it would be for him. But he still had this niggling feeling deep inside and he almost wished they'd never gone away. But then he looked at Harriet and how glowing with health she was. He thought about the wonderful evenings they'd had sitting out on the palm-fringed shores sipping their drinks and languidly chatting and he changed his mind.

'So ... Apparently Peter stalked away and never spoke to

either of them, but he turned up at the Old Barn office the following day and spoke to Harry. Now what was said is all speculation, but ...'

'Well?' asked Jimbo, a little too eagerly.

'There are those who say that Harry gave him a "none of your business" reply. But I find that hard to believe. Anyone who can say that to Peter ... Well ... takes their life in their hands, I would have thought. He's so compelling and brilliant at making you feel a complete worm for not matching up to his standards.'

'Agreed.' Jimbo helped himself to another portion of date and rhubarb crumble and pondered on what had happened between Peter and Harry up there in that lovely office. Would Harry be completely honest about other people's money when he was behaving like that with Venetia?

That night in bed, desperate for sleep and with no time for really talking, Harriet said, 'Are you very bothered about what you've heard? About Harry's fundamental honesty?'

'Yes, but I'm too tired to think about it. I'll keep it till morning.' Jimbo then fell asleep.

But it was his first thought the moment he woke.

He was not expected to be in the store first thing that morning, but he was. He told Tom what he was doing and Tom, too busy to talk, nodded to him and carried on serving his early morning customers. Jimbo took out all the banking slips filled in while he was away, the box with the cash rolls from the till, downloaded the current bank statements, and sat down in his office behind the store with the door firmly shut.

He emerged, two hours later, grey-faced, and immediately disappeared home.

'Harriet!'

'In the utility room, Jimbo.'

She appeared to be running a Chinese laundry because the entire floor of the utility room was piled with washing. 'My God! Have you started taking in washing?'

'No. It's washing we left behind, washing we brought home, and Fran's washing as I forbade her to let your mother do it for her and Fran doesn't know one end of the washing machine from the other. Now?' It was only when she looked him full in the face that she saw how upset he was. 'Darling!'

'Something has gone terribly wrong while we've been away.'

Harriet propped herself against the washing machine, arms folded, waiting to hear the worst.

'We've taken over three thousand pounds less than we would have expected to. Some days it's so bad it would have been cheaper to keep the shop closed because the takings didn't cover the wages.'

'Now, look here. You've still got jet lag, you've feared the worst, and now you think it's happened. I'm sure there's a simple explanation.'

'Such as a new supermarket having opened in Culworth? All our food has gone off and no one wants to buy it? They let the customers help themselves? In the dim and distant past, I qualified as a chartered accountant, as you know, and I haven't forgotten *all* I learned. It's true. When I say three thousand pounds, I mean it.' Jimbo stood absolutely still, staring at Harriet, not knowing what to say next.

'What the blazes?'

'How do I say to Tom, "where's the money?" Mmm? Or Bel? Or the part-timers, eh? Or Greta?'

'Very difficult.'

'Exactly. Having their honesty put under the microscope, they'll leave en masse.'

'Jimbo! I hate to say this, but your mother did query with me about ...'

'Who? As if I need to ask. Harry Dickinson.'

Harriet nodded.

'But everyone has trusted him right from him first coming. He comes across as being so honest and straightforward. He even told me to think about it overnight when I asked him about taking the money to the bank for me while we were away. "Sleep on it," he said. "I'd feel happier if you did." So I did. What if it isn't simply a downturn in trade due to the extreme weather? What if it's the start of the business going downhill because people can't afford us? What if that damned cheapo place on the bypass has persuaded everyone to buy there? We're done for.'

'Look! We've had crises before and weathered them. We'll weather this one too, believe me. We'll have to have order quality food at budget prices. You know, essential food but slightly less good quality.'

'That's my ideals down the pan. You know how I like to rely on quality.'

'Hard times make for hard decisions. Anyway, it may not be as bad as you think.'

'No?'

Having put the wind up Harriet, Jimbo then decided to face a few unpleasant facts and went to the Old Barn to see Harry Dickinson. Since he'd known him, he'd always been Harry, but somehow he'd changed into Harry Dickinson today, in a kind of withdrawal of friendship until Jimbo had made sense of his predicament.

At the Old Barn, Jimbo drew a blank. No Harry. No sign of Harry having been to the office at all. So he drove, post-haste, round to Jimmy's Cottage. Maybe the chap was too ill to get to work or ... There was no reply to Jimbo's loud knocking at his front door. But Jimbo's mother heard the banging and came out to see what the matter was.

'Can't help there, I haven't seen him since the day before

yesterday when I saw him leaving for work. I'll see if Maggie's in, she might have seen him.'

But Maggie hadn't. But what about Sykes? If he'd gone, had he taken him with him?

'I have the spare key. We'll go in and see for ourselves. I'll kill that Harry Dickinson if he's abandoned him.'

So together, followed by a very curious Maggie Dobbs, they went inside. No dog. No Harry, and everywhere clean and tidy. Grandmama went upstairs. The bed was made, and the drawers and wardrobe still had a few clothes in them. Out of the bathroom window, she saw there was no car on the hard standing at the bottom of the garden. He'd gone! Sykes' water bowl and food! They were downstairs, where they stood forlornly side by side in the living room where they'd always been when the cottage was Jimmy's. The fridge had food in it, and milk. Even today's milk was still standing by the front door.

He'd cleared off. Jimbo and Grandmama stood, staring at one another. The dreadful truth was written on both their faces. Maggie put it into words, 'He's gone then. Too good to be true Harry.'

Jimbo swung round and asked her pointedly, 'What do you mean "too good to be true"?'

'Well, he was. In a village like this, new people aren't usually accepted with open arms, we take the time to assess them, find out what they're like, and if they'll fit in. He was in and accepted straight off. Funny, don't you think?'

The three of them stood together, their minds racing, unable to think what to do next. Then Maggie added, 'Venetia, she might know.'

'Of course. Of course. That'll be my next port of call.' Jimbo raced off, leaving Grandmama to lock up.

Maggie, always rather wary of Grandmama's sharp tongue said rather tentatively, 'Jimbo seems very worried.'

'Indeed he does.' But nothing more was said between them.

Grandmama went home to await Jimbo's news and Maggie went to start her school dinner obligations, her head filling by the minute with yet more reasons for Harry's disappearance.

There was no reply at the maisonette. Even though he knocked hard enough to wake the dead, Jimbo could hear no response.

Jeremy! Of course. He raced round to the front door of the big house where he found the receptionist sitting in the hall on the telephone with obviously no intention of interrupting her phone call to find out what he wanted. So he set out to find him. First he tried Mr Fitch's office.

'He's not here,' his secretary replied. 'Mr Fitch and Jeremy have gone this very morning to Ireland and won't be back for about three days. Sorry. Can I help at all?'

'I'm looking for Mr Harry Dickinson, he—'

'Ah! The infamous Mr Dickinson.' She wagged a finger at him. 'Now, we haven't seen him at all since ... Let's see, this is Thursday ... So, the last time he was round here was Tuesday evening. He'd come for his usual swim with ... Well, we all know, don't we?' She grinned at him.

'So no one has seen him for certain since Tuesday evening. Right. And Venetia?'

'Nowhere to be seen.'

'Not since Tuesday?'

'She was supposed to be organising a race meeting for the students on Wednesday evening and it had to be cancelled. Not a vestige of her could be found. Her car has gone and so has she. We all assumed she and Harry had gone walkabout.'

'In two cars? But what about Jeremy? Surely he's said something?'

'Nothing at all. He went off this morning with Mr Fitch to the airport and we're not expecting to see him till Sunday at the earliest. Sorry.'

'What do *you* think has happened?'

'I can leave that to your imagination, surely. Good luck to them, I say.'

Jimbo found her attitude disquieting. By her manner, he could tell that the staff liked neither Venetia nor Harry.

But the dog? What had happened to Sykes? Had they taken him with them?

Then Jimbo had the inspiration to go and see Kate Fitch. He glanced at his watch. Yes, he'd try her. She might have an inkling.

The joyful sound of children happily playing together greeted Jimbo as he pulled up outside the school. The playground was buzzing with activity and there was the very person he needed to see. She was wearing a sun hat, supervising the break.

'Mrs Fitch!'

She turned to see who had called her name and beamed with delight when she saw it was Jimbo.

'Mr Charter-Plackett! What a pleasure. How can I help?'

'I won't keep you a minute. I'm looking for Harry Dickinson. I'm just back from my holiday and I was expecting to find him in the office at the Old Barn doing my accounts, but he isn't.'

'Jeremy hasn't mentioned anything. Craddock nothing whatsoever as far as I am aware. They must have gone off together. There's no other explanation for it. I doubt Craddock would be prepared to ask Jeremy. After all, it is shaming for the chap if that's what has happened. My dear husband understandably tries not to get involved in the private life of his staff. Apart from that, I'm afraid I can't help at all.'

'Right. Maybe Craddock might know something more when he gets back from Ireland.'

'Maybe. Sorry I can't help, but they were having a rather frantic, very public, affair, you know. It must have made Jeremy very upset. I don't like the man, but somehow you can't help feeling sorry for him in the circumstances.'

'Exactly, I think we all do. I can't understand why he's put up with her all these years.'

'It's time I rang the bell. I caught a look on Jeremy's face once and I saw how much he loves her. It must have been hard-going for him all these years. Bye!' She rang the bell so close to his ear that Jimbo wondered if he'd be deaf for life and hastily fled.

So Harry's whereabouts remained a mystery until early Monday morning, when he arrived most unexpectedly in the store.

Greta crept away to make a quiet phone call to Jimbo, who was working at home that day, and he came bounding in, hoping he wasn't too late to catch Harry.

'Harry! You've had us all worried to death. You should have said you were going away for a few days.'

Harry looked wound up and tense, not quite the upright military man he'd always appeared to be. 'Sorry. Like the Resistance woman in that TV show, *'Allo 'Allo*, I shall say this only once. I've been to a family funeral and now I'm back. I don't wish to discuss it right now. Sorry to have made you worried.'

Jimbo felt a heel. After all his suspicions! 'Sorry to hear that. We're glad you're back.'

'I'll catch up, don't worry. Have a good holiday? You look well. Very sun-tanned.'

'Yes. Thanks, Harry. I'm fully restored to abundant health and ready for anything.'

Jimbo still didn't feel that he'd gauged Harry's mood correctly, but the chap appeared genuine enough. 'You're in the office today?'

'That's right. I might see you?'

'Very probably.'

Harry left. He'd parked his car outside and Jimbo noticed Sykes peering from the back window on the lookout for Harry returning. He was glad to see him there. The place wouldn't feel the same without Sykes. It was only then that it struck him that Harry's return didn't in any way solve the mystery of the takings being three thousand pounds short.

Chapter 14

Harry kept an eye on the clock all day, waiting for the magical half past four. Jimbo hadn't put in an appearance, but that didn't matter because he was struggling to catch up with his work. He didn't even go downstairs for his lunch. His only company was Sykes, who popped in and out occasionally to make sure that Harry was still there. He was such a comfortable dog to be around that Harry felt quite sad at the thought of leaving him behind. He knew that Sykes belonged to the village though, rather than to a particular person, and it would be wrong to remove him from his familiar surroundings.

Four-thirty! Just finished. Everything was done. Venetia would have received his messages and would be expecting him. He'd missed her almost beyond endurance.

Sykes walked across with him to the big house. From habit, he'd learned to remember where Harry would be, and now he entertained himself hunting for rabbits in the huge warren that ran along the edge of the wood on the slope going down to the lake. He always seemed to know exactly when Harry would be leaving.

But Venetia didn't appear. Harry waited for half an hour, fully clothed, sitting on a lounger thinking about her lithe figure and the beauty of her vibrant body as she dived into the pool. Today its surface lay undisturbed, still as still, blue as blue, with no mistress to ruffle its calm. He wouldn't swim by himself. He'd ring her on his mobile. Her number was at the very top of his list. But though the phone rang and rang, there was no reply.

He left a message for her, put his mobile away, and went home disconsolate. Should he ask Jeremy? No, he mustn't. Mr Fitch? No, because the blasted man angered him with his arrogance and his wealth, and he suspected that Venetia had been one of his 'women' at some time, an idea he gleaned from half a sentence she had said once and then quickly abandoned. Why he should feel jealous about that, he didn't know, but he did. Basically he'd stayed in the village not because he had a regular job, but because of her. If he went, would she want to go with him? He was sure she would, because one night they'd both admitted that what they felt for each other went deeper than they'd ever felt for anyone else. But why hadn't she left him a note or a message on his mobile? Where was she? He'd told her he'd be away for a few days, back by the weekend, he'd said. So she knew. She definitely *knew*.

Harry had no appetite for his supper and eventually he went to bed, hoping against hope that he'd hear from her before he went to sleep. But sleep eluded him. He could hear Sykes shuffling about in his basket downstairs, heard him stand up and shake himself a couple of times, then silence, so at least someone was getting some sleep. One thing was for certain, he wasn't. Who could he ask about her without feeling a fool? Then the thought struck him that she'd been taken ill. His insides seized up and he felt sick. He longed for morning so he could figure out her whereabouts.

So he called in at the store before going to his office and asked Greta Jones. She was already working away on her mail order parcels and really had no time for visitors but, when he asked her if she knew anything at all about Venetia, she instantly put down her sticky tape and turned to face him.

'Why are you asking me? We all assumed she was with you.'

'With me?' Harry was astounded. 'Well, no. I've been ... to a family funeral.'

'Oh! I see, we've got it all wrong then. No, I don't know where she is. Gone off in her car she has. Somewhere. No car. No Venetia.' Greta was rather moved by the horror showing on Harry's face. 'Tried her mobile?'

'Yes.'

'Ask Jeremy. He'll know, won't he. But you might not ...'

But Harry didn't stay to hear what she had to say, he went in a flash, leaving Greta to contemplate what might take place between husband and lover.

The receptionist tried to stop him from speaking to Jeremy, but Harry would have none of it. He found a door with Estate Manager written on it and opened it to find Jeremy reading his post.

'Got a minute?'

'No. Get out.'

'Where is Venetia?'

'None of your business.'

Harry rested both his hands on the edge of Jeremy's desk, leaned forward and, with his face less than a metre away from Jeremy's and looking menacing to boot, asked, 'Where's Venetia? I need an answer.'

Jeremy got to his feet. 'Where Venetia is, is none of your business. She isn't here and that's that. Right. Now. *Get out.*'

'I asked you where she is. I have a right to ...'

'You have no right. Now, get out.' His voice was so loud it ricocheted off the walls and brought his secretary in.

'Who are you? What's this all about?' she demanded.

Harry ignored her and persisted with his request. 'Where is she? Tell me. That's all I want to know. She wouldn't just disappear and not tell *me*.'

Jeremy sat down to calm things, endeavouring to bring some common sense to the situation. Very quietly he said, 'She needed some breathing space so she's gone to see her mother. Satisfied?'

He calmly began sorting his post again but Harry wasn't satisfied.

'She hasn't got a mother.'

'Now you are being ridiculous. You must be unhinged. Everyone has a mother and if I say she has, she has.'

'She said she hadn't. She said she was dead.'

Jeremy sighed at Harry's stupidity and made an effort to placate him. 'When she feels more like herself, she'll be in touch, I'm sure. Now, just go, there's a good chap.'

Harry stood in front of the desk looking down at his feet, feeling beaten. It was then that he realised just how much Venetia meant to him, and how bereft he felt at not being able to either see her or speak to her. He'd never known, until this minute, how much in love he was with her; that kind of honest-to-God love you can't escape, no matter how senseless or inconvenient it is. He allowed the secretary to take his arm and show him out. Sykes appeared, as if from nowhere, and scuttered about his feet in greeting. Harry leaned down to stroke him and got some comfort from Sykes's pleasure. At least someone still cared about him, even if he was only a dog.

But what nagged him all evening was: Why hadn't Venetia been in contact? About nine o'clock, Zack banged on the door and walked in. 'We've been waiting for you, Harry, are you not coming? Are you not well?'

'Sorry, I didn't realise the time. Yes, of course.' He grabbed his keys and followed Zack out, with Sykes weaving between his legs, desperate not to be left behind.

As they entered the bar, a sudden silence fell which embarrassed Harry, but Zack saved him by saying, 'He's back! You see, I told you he would be. What you having, Harry? A whisky as usual?'

Harry braced himself. 'Yes, please. Good evening, Marie.'

'Good evening, Harry. We were getting worried about you.'

'A family funeral. I had to go rather suddenly.'

Marie patted his arm and then, in a rush of sympathy, kissed his cheek. 'Sorry about that. It's very difficult sometimes, isn't it?'

Harry nodded. 'Yes.' The whisky didn't help. In fact, it made him more morose than ever. He hadn't a thought in his head except about Venetia, and self-preservation made him realise that he simply mustn't mention her.

'Is Venetia back yet?' asked Marie, still feeling sympathetic.

'She's gone to visit her mother.'

'Oh! Right. I see.' Everyone else sitting at the table had waited with bated breath for his reply and were mightily let down by it. 'Gone to visit her mother.' Now, that was disappointing. The very least they'd expected was for Harry to come up with a really mind-boggling explanation. It was a load of twaddle that reply of his. She hadn't got a mother. Well at least, she'd never mentioned a mother. It was a cover-up. Where was she? Their minds ranged over many solutions to her disappearance but none of them had any basis in fact.

The weather was a more interesting subject than Venetia at the moment, and that took some doing because she'd been a compelling subject of conversation since the first day she'd arrived in the village when she and Jeremy had tried to set up the health club that simply didn't flourish. It was just when they were sinking under massive debts that Craddock Fitch had arrived, bought the whole lot, and saved their bacon.

'When is it ever going to rain, can anyone tell me?' asked Zack. 'I'm sick to death of watering everything day after day, just when I got all my new bedding plants in too. I've filled the churchyard flowerbeds with plants, I 'ave, and it's 'ard work keeping 'em going.'

Willie offered no hope to Zack. 'No sign of rain, I'm afraid. They were saying on the news this teatime that some reservoirs are already well below what they should be for this time of year.'

'Rain when you don't want it, but not when you do,' moaned Zack.

'Cheer up,' said Sylvia. 'It'll stop eventually. It always does, you wait and see. Has Peter said any more about selling the church silver?'

Zack shook his head. 'No. Now that Jimbo's back, I hoping for something to happen. But Gilbert's now in York and you know what it's like with this digging for old pots and skeletons and that, they have no understanding of time. Another three weeks or three months is all the same to them.'

'Ask him. Ask Peter. You see him more than we do. After all, you're all friendly in your shed, aren't you?'

'Maggie, I'm not going to ask him. I'm hoping that if no one says anything, he might go off the whole idea.'

'That's not very likely now, is it? He's tenacious, he is. Is that the right word?'

Zack admitted he wasn't quite sure, but if it meant stubborn, then it was.

Someone burst into the bar full of news. It was Dottie Foskett. 'Zack! The notice has gone up.'

Zack spluttered his beer back into his glass. He wiped his chin dry and said, 'You're not talking about what I've just been talking about, are you?'

'How do I know? It's the notice about a meeting asking for the villagers' opinions about the church silver!'

'What did I say? I knew something was brewing. When is it?'

'Tuesday next week, at seven-thirty in the church hall.'

'Ha! Can't be! That's the Girl Guides night.' Zack chuckled at the thought of the rector having made such a foolish mistake. That would teach him. Providence, that was.

'No it isn't though. They've got that big area rally in Culworth, remember. They're not meeting here next week.'

Zack muttered, 'Blast it!' under his breath.

Dottie said, 'I know I'm right because the rector was talking about it this morning when I took him his coffee.'

Sylvia wagged her finger at Dottie. 'I thought you had a

golden rule about not letting on what you learned when you worked in the rectory.'

'For heaven's sake, it's not as if it's a secret, like letting on where Venetia is.'

There was an instant of breathtaking stillness as they realised what she'd said, their eyes wide with anticipation.

'You know then?' asked Sylvia.

Dottie admitted she didn't. 'I was only using her as an example of what not to let on about. Why? Do you all know where she is? Harry? Do you?'

It was painful enough having her used as an example but then, to be asked if he knew where Venetia was ... 'Jeremy says she's gone to her mother's for some breathing space.'

'Well,' said Sylvia, with a wicked grin on her face, 'you can have too much of a good thing, I suppose.'

It was the undisguised sniggering after that comment which finally drove Harry to leave, with Sykes hard on his heels. Why did they find what was so close to his heart, in fact his whole being, so amusing? It was deadly serious to him, not a matter to laugh at. He plunged his key in the keyhole, hoping against hope that Venetia would be there waiting for him. She wasn't. Maybe it hadn't been quite honest to have a key made for her, but it suited him and he was paying the rent after all. But she wasn't there, and he knew at the bottom of his heart that she wouldn't be. But gone to see her mother? That didn't ring true at all. Not Venetia. She would have left him a message somehow. A text. A voicemail. A note in the letterbox. He flung himself down on the sofa and saw Sykes was studying his face. Suddenly Sykes leaped up on the sofa and snuggled against him, his chin resting on Harry's thigh, his eyes gazing up at him as though offering comfort.

Harry ruffled Sykes's ears. 'You're too wise for a dog, do you know that? Far too wise. She'll be back, won't she? Of course she will. We'll just have to be patient, you and I.'

★

But the day of the big village meeting about the selling of the silver dawned bright and clear with no sign that Venetia was even in the country, let alone about to return. Her disappearance was no longer the big topic of conversation it had been though. It seemed that the only person giving her even a single thought was Harry, and he thought about her every day. Every day he looked for emails from her, any kind of message at all that would provide comfort, but it never happened. In fact, he began to wonder if he'd dreamed about his affair with her; had she actually existed, or was she wholly imagined? Jimbo said nothing about getting a permanent accounts person, so Harry said nothing about leaving either. He struggled along from day to day, barely functioning as a normal human being.

The church hall was almost full fifteen minutes before the meeting was to begin. People from Little Derehams and Penny Fawcett were all squeezed in and Zack was kept busy bringing in more chairs. Even the bench that stayed outside in the churchyard for people to rest on when they came to visit graves was to be used. He'd cleaned the bird dirt off earlier in the day in case it might be needed, and by seven-twenty he'd dragged it in. It was promptly filled with people. Three people were standing and five had hunkered down, leaning against the back wall. Obviously, thought Zack, they all felt as keenly as he did about not selling. But he was wrong. By seven fifty-five he was of the opinion that well over half the people who'd taken the trouble to attend were in favour of selling. He was horrified.

Peter had begun the meeting by explaining his reasons for selling their precious silver. 'Yes, we own it, or rather the church does, and yes, it is beautiful and precious and yes we use it. But how often? Only three, or at most, four times a year. What good does it do? We love to see it gleaming there on the altar, the floor-standing candle beside it, it fills all our hearts with joy at its beauty, but – and it is a big but – what good does it do for the spiritual life of the three villages? I can tell you, though you may not agree with me, it does *nothing*. It pleases us, yes. It gives us pride that our church owns such beautiful ornaments, but *ornamental* is *all* they are. A far, far better use of them would be to sell them and use the money to improve the church. The tower needs attention, the interior desperately needs redecorating, and that is just two of the major things that need doing to preserve the building.'

'The question is, rector, 'ow much will we get for 'em? It might not be enough and then where would we be?' This was the publican, Bill Montgomery from the Jug and Bottle in Penny Fawcett.

'These beautiful ornaments, as you call them, rector, are ours and have been for more than two hundred years. That must count for something, surely?' This was Gilbert Johns, back from York especially for the meeting.

'We could raise the money for doing the improvements and keep the silver as well?' said a woman from down Shepherd's Hill who only ever entered the church at Christmas. A woman Zack knew put only ten pence in the collection plate once a year.

This brought on a rumble of low mutterings from the back row, mainly occupied by the crowd from Penny Fawcett. One of them stood up. 'I've had an idea. If everyone put an extra one hundred pounds in the collection plate this Sunday, that would help, wouldn't it?'

Someone who preferred to stay well hidden behind the over-large wife of the publican said, 'And how many Sundays would we have to do that to make up the amount? I know, how about if you set the ball rolling right now? That's it. Pass the collection plate round right away. Cheques and credit cards accepted.'

The whole atmosphere of the meeting became very uncomfortable and Peter did wonder if he'd better drop the idea before murder was done.

'If ... If ... we had a go at raising the funds like you did so wonderfully when you raised all that money for my New Hope Mission, we could manage it, but it would be a herculean task, believe me. Would anyone be in favour of raising the money ourselves?'

About one third of the meeting put up their hands, but many were very tentative.

'It's the ideas that's the trouble, isn't it? I mean, the WI were inspirational that time, truly inspirational they were, and it was all such fun. I don't suppose ...' said a person from Little Derehams, who ought to have had more sense.

Sheila Bissett, speaking as the newly installed president of the WI yet again, shook her head. 'Absolutely not. I'm sorry. It all got too much.'

'But Sheila, you were excellent at it, with your clipboard and all that.'

'I cannot possibly agree to it, not for myself, nor for the committee. Sorry. That's my final word and I shall resign if there is any more pressure brought to bear on us. It's not fair. We, as a committee, *are not taking it on.*' Sheila quickly sat down, trembling with shock at how adamant she'd been. She whispered to Ron, 'We're not, you know. Definitely not, and don't let them persuade me.'

Ron took her hand in his and gripped it tightly. 'Absolutely not. I agree.'

Peter suggested that he got someone from a London auction house to value the silver and then hold another meeting. That, he found out too late, was the very last thing that should have been suggested.

'I disagree. Forget it.'

'So do I.'

'And me. If it's pots of money we'll get tempted and it's not right. I won't vote for it.'

Gilbert Johns stood up. 'Neither will I. It would be sacrilege to do any such thing as sell it. In my job I see far too much of this country's heritage being destroyed, adapted, moved, built over, all for some pathetic reason or another. Some council that makes hasty decisions in a moment of weakness, some idiot industrialist who wants to build a block of offices right on top of ancient artefacts to create more jobs, when all the time it's our heritage, our *children's* heritage and our *grandchildren's* heritage that is being defiled. It's not right. And I, for one, shall vote against selling them, no matter how much they are valued at. People like us have to stand firm or, in fifty years' time, England will be full of appalling office blocks and dozens of spaghetti junctions and all that beauty that is *ours* will be lost. Sorry, Peter.'

'Hear! Hear!' someone shouted.

'Absolutely right,' someone else said.

'I vote we don't sell it.' This was shouted out very loudly by Willie.

'This is all very well, but what if the church falls down. Then what?' said someone from Little Derehams whose grandson was being christened next Sunday, so consequently was full of self-interest.

'And what about my great-grandad, buried in the churchyard? What about him, eh?' No one had an answer to that.

'It's stood for nearly eight centuries or so, why should it suddenly begin falling down? Eh? I ask you?' This from Zack, feeling deeply caught up in this passionate discourse.

Finally, Peter called for silence. 'I shall wind up this meeting now, this very minute, and go home to pray for a benefactor, because that's all that's left for me to do. I'm deeply disappointed. But if this is your will, then so be it.' He stormed out of the church hall more angry than he could ever remember being with these stubborn people, each one of whom he loved and respected. But what love and respect had they for him, to say nothing of their church?

Chapter 15

Tamsin had been at the meeting and had agreed to meet Paddy in the Royal Oak when it finished, but she got there ahead of everyone else as most of them had stayed behind to state opinions they hadn't dared say outright in front of Peter.

Paddy was already seated at their favourite table with her drink on a mat beside his own. The bar was almost empty, with Georgie and Dicky standing idly behind the bar waiting for the explosion that would ensue when all the villagers came out of the meeting and poured into the bar to continue it in a more relaxing atmosphere.

'Meeting finished, is it, Tamsin?' Dicky called across to her.

'It is. Thank goodness.'

'Trouble?'

'You can say that again. Yes, there was trouble.'

'Is the rector going ahead with it?'

'No he is not. Not for the moment anyway.'

She sat down and she and Paddy smiled at each other. In these last weeks, the two of them had become very close. He took care to touch her hand very circumspectly so that no one would suspect that they were becoming more than just good friends.

'Well?' asked Paddy. 'How did it go?'

'An awful lot of people were against it. It got quite nasty at one point. You know how Sheila Bissett always supports Peter? Well, she most definitely didn't, not tonight. I am so ready for this drink.'

She picked up her Martini and lemonade and as Paddy watched her take a long drink of it, he knew he'd never tire of her company.

'You didn't want to come then?'

Paddy shook his head. 'No. I'm not interested.'

'I have to be, being the organist. I ought to have supported Peter, but I couldn't.'

'Did he ask you if you would?'

'No, not Peter. He wouldn't. Even if he tried to persuade me to, I wouldn't agree to sell. They wouldn't even agree to a valuation. I've never known him lose a battle.'

'I've got going on that piece we tried.'

Tamsin smiled at him, grateful that he was changing the subject. 'Good. Like it?'

'I love it. Greta thinks I'm improving by the minute. She's really very tolerant. Even though I shut my bedroom door, she must still be able to hear me.'

'Well, I suppose she feels like your Mum.'

'Hmm. Greta's more of a mum than mine ever was. More than mine ever got the chance to be, I should say. That's why I don't go to church. My mum would have coped if she hadn't felt she should obey the church's rules and have lots of kids.'

'Where is she now?'

'Same address, I understand.'

'You should write. I would if she was mine.'

'Not after the life I led as a child, you wouldn't.'

'Yes, I would. Nothing that you can do in this world will *ever* make her *not* your mother. And you will always be her son, whatever—'

The door burst open and the crowd from the church hall poured in, all demanding to be served at the same time, so worked up were they about what had been said.

'Paddy? Let's finish our drinks and we'll go to my place. OK?'

'That's fine by me. Are you sure?'

'I wouldn't ask you if I wasn't.'

'No, of course not.'

'I'll go first and then you come. I'll leave the door ajar, then you won't have to knock.'

Paddy nodded. As he watched her leave, he did think that maybe tonight was the night to admit to the world they were as people say, 'an item'. Why not? They were and, the more they saw of each other, the more convinced he became. But then the frightening thought that really they were not suited entered his head. Her with her education and her musical background and the people she knew and the marvellously wonderful things she did to earn her living bore no relationship to his past life, nor his present. He was trying to bring them together through music but, in his darker moments he knew he was merely on the foothills while she had already reached the pinnacle. He knew he would never catch up with her musically.

Had he but known it, while he was saying goodnight to Dicky and Georgie, Tamsin was at home thinking similar thoughts. It was no good them thinking no one knew they were seeing each other. She'd noticed the elbow nudge Marie gave Zack as she said goodnight to them as she left the pub. But what would Paddy think about it? Maybe he preferred the secrecy because he'd no intention of it being anything other than a casual friendship. But she'd found that that wasn't what she wanted at all.

She heard the soft click of the door as Paddy came in. She decided to go for it.

Paddy, as he clicked the door shut, thought: Tonight's the night to come clean about how he felt. He could hear her in the kitchen filling the kettle, and he went straight in there. One look was all it took and they were in each other's arms, kissing and hugging as though this would be their very last chance ever.

Five minutes it took before they broke apart and began to laugh with a surging, overwhelming happiness, the like of which neither of them had experienced before.

Breathless, Paddy said, 'It's no good, we'll have to admit it.'

'We can't pussyfoot about any longer, can we?'

'Absolutely not. I love you.'

'And I, Tamsin Verity Goodenough, love you. Very, very much indeed. There. I've never said that before, but I can't help myself. I'm not supposed to love anybody, but I do love you.'

'Not supposed to?' Paddy thought she meant he wasn't right for her, that he didn't match up to her aspirations for a lover.

'I mean, I have always said I would never marry … Sorry, we haven't said we want to marry, have we? I do apologise.'

'But that's what I want. Don't you? Do you?' Paddy trembled at the thought of his temerity to say such a thing to such a wonderful woman. How dare he? She'd probably turn him out.

Tamsin placed her hand in his and held it tight. 'Is that a proposal?'

Paddy had to admit she was right about that. 'Well, yes it is. Yes, it is.'

'Better say it right then. I, Patrick Callum Cleary, bachelor of this parish, request that you …'

He had to laugh. Life was going to be such fun! So he said his line and she, Tamsin Verity Goodenough, said hers, and they kissed solemnly to seal their agreement.

'I've got champagne in the fridge.'

'You planned this?'

Tamsin nodded.

Paddy laughed. 'But I want it understood, for my part, that I don't want any shenanigans beforehand. You understand me? I want our first night together to be the very first. The very best, ever. A new, fresh start. A new beginning, like it should be. I feel very strongly about that.'

Tamsin was surprised by this outburst of Paddy's, to the point of amazement. This wasn't something she'd expected, nor had she wanted it this way, but if he wanted it then so be it.

Somehow this decision of his made their future plans very much more special than she had expected.

'Except I won't want us to wait for months to get married, like some people do. You know, getting married August of next year, or something.'

'No, neither would I. Open the champagne, Paddy.' Tamsin got out the two glasses from her kitchen cupboard that came the nearest to champagne flutes, and placed them on her best tray. The cork flew out, hit the ceiling, and left a dent in it.

'I shall never get rid of that dent! It will always remind us of tonight.'

'To the two of us!' Paddy raised his glass, then tapped his gently against hers. They each took a sip and laughed.

'To the two of us! Oh, Paddy! I'm so thrilled! I'm so glad that we've decided.'

'So am I! When shall it be?'

'Let's make it a month from today. We've got banns and things to do, so it can't be any earlier than that. Here in the church? Oh! No, perhaps you'll want it in a Catholic church? I don't mind if you do.'

'No, here is where I'd like it best. Where we both belong.'

'Greta and Vince will be glad. Shall we go down there right now and take the rest of the champagne with us?'

Paddy nodded. It was so wonderful how she knew what would make him, and the people he cared about, happy.

The front door of Greta and Vince's house was open to allow some fresh air in so they knocked and shouted at the same time, to find them in the kitchen sitting by the back door to catch the best of the through draught.

'Hello! What's this?' Greta stood up, a broad grin beginning to spread across her face. 'Something special? It is. You've got champagne!'

Paddy put the champagne down on the table so his hands

were free and, taking hold of Tamsin's hand, he announced in grave tones but with delight written all over his face, 'I am a very lucky man. Tamsin has agreed to marry me.'

Vince was deeply affected by the news, having grown to think of Paddy as his son. Greta had tears brimming in her eyes. 'Oh! That's the most wonderful news! When did you decide this?'

'Just now, after the meeting. So we've come down here to share it with you. Champagne to celebrate?' Tamsin held up the bottle, her face a picture of love and delighted surprise.

'Vince! Come on! Get some glasses out.'

After the first flush of excitement it dawned on Greta what this would mean. She hated the idea of losing him. 'I expect you'll be going to live with Tamsin in her house right now then, Paddy?'

'I most certainly will not. We haven't decided on anything at all, but we have decided we're doing it right. I shall stay here, if that's all right with you, until the wedding day and when we come back from our honeymoon,' he glanced at Tamsin for approval and she nodded, 'I shall move to Tamsin's.'

Greta flung her arms round Paddy and hugged him close, whispering in his ear that she was delighted for him. 'It's the best thing that could have happened to you. We've been waiting and watching, hoping for the best.'

'You knew?'

Vince, slightly heady with the champagne, declared, 'Honestly, Paddy. How could you imagine no one knew? You must still be wet behind the ears.'

Tamsin asked, 'Are you pleased, Greta? Because I am.'

'I'll give you a hug too! He couldn't have found a lovelier person in all the world, he couldn't. We're delighted, Vince and me. Here, let me give you a kiss.'

So Greta hugged Tamsin and looked from one to the other with such delight that it almost brought tears to Tamsin's eyes. 'I'm so pleased you're so pleased at our news.'

'We definitely are. He's been playing that flute morning, noon and night, he's been that determined to please you. What with you and your musical unstruments and Paddy with his, there'll be no time for conversation in your house. It'll be a white wedding then?' Greta looked hopefully between the two of them.

'Of course. But simple, not all lace, frothy net and sparkles. Something kind of dignified.'

'That would be lovely. You know, when our Barry married Pat, her being a widow, they didn't have a white wedding and they had just the one bridesmaid, that being Michelle of course. It'll be lovely all done proper. I like a fresh flower head-dress, do you, Tamsin? They looks so … Well, I don't know what exactly, but lovely anyway.'

'We haven't got as far as that yet, Greta, but you will come, won't you? You must sit on the top table because both my parents died a long time ago and Paddy …'

Greta promptly stepped in with a remark she thought important to make. 'You'll be asking your mother, won't you, Paddy?'

'Well …'

'You must. Write to her and warn her. She'll want to come, I'm sure of that. If one of my other boys was getting married, I'd want to be there. Wouldn't we, Vince?'

Vince nodded, but not very convincingly. 'We'll see. Except we don't know where they are, either of 'em.'

Greta snapped, with bitterness in her voice, 'Don't bring that up right now, if you don't mind. Does Peter know yet?'

'No, we only decided tonight!'

Paddy walked Tamsin home and they stood on her doorstep to say goodnight.

'Paddy! I want you to know that I shall do my very best to be the best wife in all the world.'

'And it's the same for me.' Paddy turned to leave, decided

he needed another kiss, and turned back for one more. Just as he was leaving for the second time, Tamsin said, 'I shall want children, you know. Shall you?'

'Children? Children? I hadn't thought of that. My God! I hadn't.' Paddy smote his forehead with the flat of his hand. 'I don't know if I'm clever enough to be a father.'

'I don't know if I'm clever enough to be a mother, but we could try together, couldn't we? We're not complete idiots.'

'But what about your music?'

Tamsin's lovely green eyes sparkled with laughter. 'I shall have to let it play second fiddle for a few years.'

They both burst out laughing. Then Paddy sobered up and said hesitantly, 'I'm not sure about what Greta said.'

'About your mother? I should love her to come, for your sake, but it's up to you. Only you can decide.'

'Would you *really* like her to come?'

'Yes.'

'Then I'll think about it. Goodnight, and thank you for making me the happiest man alive tonight. I never thought you felt the same.' Paddy kissed his index finger and placed it on her lips as a goodnight salute, then he went off home doing the Sailor's Hornpipe with his heart full of joy.

While Paddy was dancing down Shepherd's Hill, Greta was saying. 'Isn't it lovely? Paddy and Tamsin, I'm so pleased.' She dashed a tear away from her eye, 'It's lovely. We'll have to give them a right royal send-off. And I'm proud of them for not living together, it shows how much they care about each other. I know everyone does it nowadays, but somehow their decision feels good through and through.'

'Exactly,' said Vince, shaking the last drops of champagne out of the bottle into his glass. 'Better than those other two, Venetia and Harry. I mean, fancy Peter, of all people, finding them at it! At least our two know how to behave decent, like.'

'It is funny though, her disappearing like she has. Harry says he hasn't heard from her, which is odd, don't you think? He confronted Jeremy, would you believe, and all he'll say is that she's gone to stay with her mother. I didn't even know she had a mother.'

'That's plain daft, she must have. Venetia didn't just materialise!'

'No, I know, but you see what I mean? It is funny. Harry being mad about her and her disappearing without any warning, and him not hearing from her, what with all this text business and mobiles and that, to say nothing of emails.'

Vince answered by saying, 'He'll have murdered 'er.'

Greta asked, 'Who will have?'

'Harry. He's been away to get rid of the body somewhere.'

'Sometimes you can be absolutely daft. Talk about way off the mark. Listen, that's Paddy back. Perhaps he'll want to talk about wedding plans. We're in the kitchen, Paddy!'

Vince wasn't the only one who had macabre thoughts about Venetia's disappearance. It did seem very odd. Harry disappears without a word to anyone and then, the very next day, everyone finds out that Venetia has also disappeared. But, and this was the big but, if they had gone away together, they wouldn't have taken both their cars, now would they? It didn't make sense. So … Maybe it was right what Jeremy had said. Venetia really had gone to see her mother. But considering the way her and Harry had carried on before they both disappeared, why had she not communicated? On the other hand, *he* hadn't communicated to anyone either, except he'd come back with this tale about a family funeral. But don't forget that he'd never said whose funeral it was. And what was wrong with saying, 'Shan't be here for a few days, I've got a funeral to go to.'

These and dozens of other explanations were being discussed everywhere anyone met. In the store, in the church hall at the embroidery group meeting on Monday afternoons, in the bar, after church, and even eventually at the school, when the mothers collected together at going-home time. The more they all talked about it, the more mysterious the whole matter became.

Even Kate Fitch discussed the matter that week over dinner. 'The mothers are all talking about it. It really is odd. How does Jeremy seem?'

'Honestly, Kate! As if I know how he's coping. He's probably glad to have her off his back for a while. You know I don't get involved in my employees' private affairs. He certainly doesn't appear upset, not like I'd be if you'd gone off.'

'Ask him. And if you won't, I will.'

'It's none of our business.'

'She is one of your employees.'

'One of *our* employees, you mean.'

'Put like that, then I shall ask. After school tomorrow, as soon as I get back.'

As good as her word, Kate went straight to Jeremy's office after school. She knew immediately he was upset because he was just finishing a Mars bar, and he hadn't munched Mars bars since he'd had that heart attack and made a big effort to lose his excess weight.

Jeremy hastily popped the wrapper in his bin. 'Hello, Kate, what can I do for you?'

Kate thought, he might sound jolly and welcoming, but he didn't look it, anything but. 'Just thought I'd pop in and see how you were faring with Venetia still away. I'm assuming she isn't home yet?'

'No. Another week, she thinks. Her mother's not at all well.'

'I see. How about if you come for dinner one night, it must be lonely without her.'

Jeremy hesitated. 'Well ... most kind, but I won't intrude. Mr Fitch sees enough of me during working hours.'

'No, please come if you wish, we'd be delighted.'

Jeremy got up and wandered over to the window and she

noticed his hands were trembling as he clasped them behind his back. 'Thank you all the same, but no. Very kind.'

'If you're sure?'

'Absolutely.'

'She'll be back soon then, you think?'

He nodded and Kate left, bewildered. She'd noticed his trembling hands; maybe he missed her more than any of them could possibly imagine. Love could affect people in very different ways. So she reported back to Craddock that Jeremy was expecting her back in about a week. Rather sceptically, Craddock replied, 'Mmm. Only time will tell.'

'Are you thinking she's left him for good?'

'Frankly, I don't care.'

'You should. You've known him for a long time, you've finally knocked him into shape, and he is very useful to you. You've said so yourself.'

Craddock blew a circle of cigar smoke into the air and remarked very coldly, 'He's a fool to care for her. She's worthless. Not worth anyone's devotion.'

'Harry must think a lot of her.'

'He's equally worthless.'

'Harry? But everybody likes him, what makes you say that?'

'It seems to me that there's a lot more to Harry Dickinson than meets the eye.'

'Yes. He's a nice, decent, friendly chap doing a good job for Jimbo.'

'Believe that if you wish.'

'Is there something I don't know, and you do? Something Jimbo should know?'

'To be honest, Kate, my darling, I know nothing. It's simply my gut instinct. That's absolutely all.'

'I see.' Kate decided to let the subject drop for the moment, but the whole matter of the Harry, Venetia and Jeremy triangle would not go away. But at least her conversation with Craddock had confirmed, once and for all, that at one time, long before she and Craddock married, there had been something going on between Venetia and him. Otherwise why should his voice sound so venomous when he spoke of her?

Chapter 16

From his front window, if he glanced across to his left, Harry had a full view of the daily improvements to Sir Ralph's old house. The work progressed slowly, but provided an interesting object for contemplation. Imagine having so much money that one owned a house of that size and could also afford to live somewhere else while the fire damage was repaired. Never in the whole of his life had he had money on that scale. He stopped once or twice and talked to the builder, who was there every day, but he found out absolutely nothing about the current owner from him. The same story was told to anyone who enquired. The house was being restored under instructions from a solicitor in London.

Everyone in the village was curious to know and no one more so than Harry. He knew he was curious simply because he had nothing else to do, his life had suddenly become a complete blank filled with pointless drinking in the pub and doing Jimbo's accounts while he waited. Waited? For what? For whom? Venetia Mayer, that was what. Another week and he would be gone because he could not wait any longer. He missed her in a way he'd never, in all his life, missed anyone. When he'd been turned out by his family for his thieving ways he'd thought good riddance to his mother, his father, and his two sisters. But Venetia, she was different, he'd found out he needed her. As a last, desperate measure, he'd taken great pains to compose a letter to her, talking of his love for her, how much he missed her, and asking for her to reply. No, begging her to reply would be more accurate, and he'd taken it to Jeremy's office yesterday to ask him to let her have it. Not having her address, he'd simply written *Mrs V. Mayer* on the envelope.

He'd forced his way into Jeremy's office. 'She hasn't phoned me, texted me or emailed me and I don't know why. Is she all right? Have you spoken to her?'

'Yes.'

'Please, for the sake of my peace of mind, will you send this letter to her?'

'You're only one of a string of men she's had, you know. I can't imagine why you think you are any different from the others.' Jeremy pushed the letter to one side and ignored Harry.

'But I am, and so is she for me. You just don't understand how much we love each other. It's for real, believe me.'

'How can you stand there and ask me, her husband, for help? Just get out and don't darken my door again.' Again, Jeremy ignored Harry and carried on tapping briskly on his computer, making scores of typographical errors which he didn't bother to correct.

'Please.' Getting no response, Harry had suggested that he'd post it himself if Jeremy would give him the address. It was as if Harry had not spoken.

So he leaned across the desk and grabbed Jeremy's tie in one tight fist and put pressure on his jaw with the other. 'Answer me! Do as I say. Answer me. Or else ...'

Jeremy sat completely still, which enraged Harry. The tight rein he'd had on his temper these last weeks snapped and he landed a solid punch on his victim's jaw.

Jeremy's head shot back and then forward again, but he didn't protest. He did nothing to retaliate, simply sat there, immobile, a heavy sweat gleaming on his ashen face.

'Send it to her. Please. Even if you don't care about her, I do. She loves me and I love her, and we want to be together.' Appalled by his foolish outburst, Harry stood back. He was being an idiot. What did Jeremy care? Not one iota and, what was worse, he was shaken by how pathetic he sounded, like some feeble teenager with his first love. But she was his first love, that was why he felt so deeply about her, why he was so bold.

Jeremy straightened his tie and his jacket. 'Love? She doesn't know the meaning of it. I feel nothing but pity for you, loving her. She's not worth it. Believe me, Harry, I know. She's not worth your anguish. I'll send the letter for you, but don't expect too much from her, she's more than likely gone to her mother's to escape you.'

Totally defeated by Jeremy's intransigence, Harry could see no further point in pleading with him and he'd gone home, his heart shattered, his whole being defeated.

So he didn't see Jeremy drop Venetia's envelope in the bin where the words *Mrs V. Mayer* stuck to the wrapper of the last Mars bar Jeremy had consumed. Harry didn't see Jeremy wipe the sweat from his face, nor see him drink a whole glass of water because fear had made him desperately thirsty.

Chapter 17

The news of Paddy and Tamsin deciding to get married spread round Turnham Malpas like wildfire. The store, in particular, was the main distributer of the news and Paddy was overwhelmed with calls on his mobile and with people 'by chance' popping by the gardens and congratulating him. They'd all known there was something in the wind but they had never imagined it would come to anything. Out of his hearing, more than a few said what a strange marriage it would be, they weren't a bit suited, but neither Paddy nor Tamsin heard these remarks and remained blissfully unaware.

They were far too busy anyway, organising the wedding, and far too happy at the reception their news got from Peter and Caroline when they went to arrange a date.

'I am so delighted! What lovely news! Let me go and tell Caroline, she'll be thrilled.'

Paddy and Tamsin waited in the study, hoping Caroline would come to see them. They weren't disappointed. She arrived with a great rush and kissed and hugged them both. 'I am so delighted. I'd no idea.'

Tamsin disengaged herself from Caroline's hug. 'You must be the only one who hadn't realised then!'

'I honestly didn't know. So when's the date? Have you decided on it yet?'

'Not yet, but as soon as possible.'

'Oh! Wonderful! I love summer weddings. I wonder, would you ... I don't want to interfere, or make you feel you're being organised when you're both perfectly able to organise yourselves, but would you let me, well, Peter and I, pay for your wedding cake? As our present to you both? Please?'

Tamsin hesitated and Caroline encouraged her compliance by adding, 'Of course Jimbo and Harriet would make it to your design, not ours. Mmm?'

Paddy said, 'We didn't expect … We thought …' He glanced at Tamsin. 'It is most kind of you both, we didn't expect people would be so pleased for us.'

'Of course we are! All of us will be. You belong, didn't you know that? You try and stop us being interested.'

Tamsin's eyes brimmed with tears. 'Thank you so much. We both of us sincerely appreciate …' Then she cried and Paddy hugged her, then Caroline hugged her. Finally, she stopped crying and they fixed the date and time and Peter took down the details for reading the banns. Then the pair of them fled, hand in hand, back to Tamsin's house and revived themselves with a gin and tonic, and then another, before Paddy left for home, only to find that Vince and Greta had been making plans too.

Vince sat Paddy down in the sitting room and said a little nervously, 'Now, Paddy. Tamsin has no one to give her a hand getting things sorted, having no mother and father, so we wondered if Greta could help in some way. Not to tell her what to do, but to give her a hand with making lists of things to do and that. Especially with the reception after.'

'Reception? I never gave it a thought. Should we have one?'

Greta stepped in almost before the words were out of his mouth. 'Have one? Of course you must have one! We all want to enjoy you getting married.'

'But Tamsin and me want a country wedding, nothing fancy, just happy and jolly and everyone enjoying themselves. Not big and posh.'

'Of course not, you're not those kind of people, are you?' Vince embarrassed himself with this remark. 'I didn't mean you weren't good enough for a big posh wedding. Of course you are! I meant ...'

'I know you didn't, Vince. Tamsin wants it lovely and comfortable and surrounded by friends.'

'You know, Paddy, I wish you'd been able to say friends and *family*. I know you've not seen your family for years, but you should ask your mother, if no one else. You only get married once and she's still your mother, whatever it was she allowed to happen between you and your Dad. Remember, Tamsin unfortunately can't ask hers, but you *can*.'

Paddy looked embarrassed. 'Tamsin wants me to.'

'In that case, write and ask her,' said Vince, full of enthusiasm for the idea. 'Send a photo of yourself and Tamsin and say you want her to come. Tamsin's such a beauty your mother will be delighted for you. We could put her up, couldn't we? No problem there. Put your address on the back of the envelope in case she's moved. Then, if it comes back, you'll know you've done your best.' It wasn't often Vince smiled out of kindness, at a bawdy joke maybe, not kindness, but now he did and it convinced Paddy he should write.

'All right then, I will.'

'Good lad. Greta's got some nice writing paper so you could do it tonight and post it on your way to the garden tomorrow morning. It would be best to give her plenty of time to arrange things.'

So Paddy wrote that very night. It took him a long time, longer than it should have done because of the memories that flooded his mind and made his pen falter, but finally it was in the envelope and the stamp stuck on it. Now all he had to do was post it. Paddy lay in bed for a long time before he got to sleep, mulling over old memories, wondering about the rightness of marrying Tamsin and thinking about whether his mother would come and what he'd say to her. Perhaps he shouldn't post it. Or maybe he should make one last attempt to heal the breach. After all, it was his father to blame for making his young life hell, not his mother; all she'd ever done was attempt, admittedly unsuccessfully, to mitigate the horrors their father heaped on them.

So finally he fell asleep with a lovely picture of Tamsin in his head. She was standing by his favourite vine, touching a bunch of grapes with her long sensitive fingers and smiling at him because she loved him. That memory was Tamsin, the *real* Tamsin, without a doubt. What a lucky man he was.

Chapter 18

Jimbo had learned from Tom that the procedure for banking the money had been changed while he was away sunning himself. At the time, it hadn't registered because there was so much to do on his return and it had been such a shock when he found the takings were down so much. So there was a lot to catch up on, but one day when he was adding up the takings, an idea crept quietly into his mind and wouldn't go away. What was it Tom had said about being incredibly busy? That was it! He'd said that Harry had to go to the store each morning, remove the takings from the safe, count up the money, the cheques and the credit card slips in Jimbo's little office, then enter it on the banking slips and take it to the bank simply because Tom had no time to spare.

He couldn't blame Tom. Realistically, he'd left him with far too much to do. The store was open for six days a week and there was no one to let him take a day off. There were the rounds to do, collecting the produce for the mail order business and for the store, keeping the shelves well stocked, ordering the stock and, on top of all that, being responsible for the post office too. Tom, being Tom, had not complained and had found the only possible way to lighten his load.

But it had meant that the one person Jimbo didn't really know, the one person for whom he had no references and the one person who wasn't supposed to actually handle the cash had been left to do it. Harry Dickinson! As soon as he said his name out loud Jimbo felt ashamed of himself. He was an OK chap.

Nothing wrong with him. Look how he'd been accepted so easily by everyone in the village. A good drinking companion, a good friend, a nice chap. Look how he'd taken on old Sykes, and Sykes definitely liked him.

Jimbo pulled himself up with a jerk. Had he lost his marbles? Fancy Jimbo, that long-time hot-shot in the City thinking that if a dog took to you you were a good bloke. He needed his brains examining. That was it. That blasted Harry Dickinson had stolen his money. The owner away, Tom under pressure and Harry seized his opportunity. But staying on after he'd done it? That took some style!

Jimbo leaped up, got out the till rolls for every day he and Harriet had been away, took out the appropriate bank statements from their file and sat down to a long session of comparing till rolls to money paid into the bank, matching cheques, though there weren't many of those nowadays, and checking the credit card payments, and there were lots of those. This was what he hadn't done in the rush of catching up on his return. So he painstakingly did it now.

Two hours later, he had found several discrepancies. Jimbo realised that Harry had removed the till rolls, presumably hoping that Jimbo wouldn't find time to match them up to the daily cash payments into the bank.

He'd kill him! Stealing from Jimbo Charter-Plackett! It was bare-faced robbery! Jimbo rang Harriet at the Old Barn and told her what he'd discovered.

'I don't believe it! Harry? That can't be right!'

'Come to the store and see for yourself. Right away. I'm absolutely incensed!'

'I don't believe it! You must have got it wrong.'

'See for yourself. Don't say a word to anyone though, I don't want him doing a runner.'

'I'm coming.'

But when she saw the evidence with her own eyes, Harriet knew Jimbo was right.

They looked at one another in horror.

'How do we tackle it?'

Harriet suggested speaking to Harry in front of witnesses.

'Call in the Fraud Squad?' said Jimbo.

'If it was millions, yes, but not two thousand eight hundred and one pounds and forty-five pence.'

'Get Sergeant Mac?'

'That would be a start.' Harriet ran her fingers through her hair, a sure sign she was upset. 'But it'll be round the village in an instant if Mac's seen coming here. Harry'll get the wind up and do a bunk.'

'Get Mac to meet me at the Old Barn office. The two of us could then confront him?'

'Wait till morning, it'll give us time to think about what we should do without him getting an inkling. We'd look ridiculous if we're wrong.'

'Harriet! How can we be wrong? It's there for all to see.'

'Could Tom have done it?'

'Tom? He wouldn't. Believe me, he's completely honest.'

'You're right. He's an ex-policeman and he just wouldn't, would he?'

'No. We'll keep it to ourselves and sleep on it. We'll decide what to do tomorrow. If he doesn't know we're on to him, he won't just disappear, will he? He's got no reason to.'

'I've got to get back to the kitchens. I won't be late.' Harriet hesitated at the door. 'I'm so disappointed, he seems like such a nice man.'

'It just goes to show.'

Harriet didn't know what it showed but, when she got back to the Old Barn, she took it upon herself to go and see Harry.

He was busy as usual, typing in the data from the previous

day's business. He looked up and smiled when she walked in. The lovely, welcoming smile they'd all come to like.

'Hello, Harriet, how nice to see you.'

'Nice to see you, too. I've been so busy since we got back that I thought I'd pop in and see how you were.'

'That's nice of you. Enjoyed your holiday?'

'It seems light years ago since we got back. But yes, we did. It's been a long time since we had a holiday together. I've been wondering, is Venetia back yet?'

'No, not yet.'

'She's gone to see her mother, I understand.'

'Yes.'

'Is she ill?'

'Her mother? Yes, she is.'

'Is she getting better?'

'Yes. Venetia says she is.'

'Oh, good, you've heard from her then?'

'She's not much good at letter writing but yes I have. Another week, she says.'

'Oh, good, Jeremy will be glad.'

'He said that the other day. Nice chap.'

'Indeed he is. Must press on. Bye!'

Totally confused now, Harriet retired to think about what Harry had said. Everyone who was anyone in the village knew for a fact that Harry had not heard from her, but now he was saying he had. But letter-writing in this day and age? Using her mobile, emails or texting were much more Venetia's scene. And calling Jeremy a 'nice chap' when he, Harry Dickinson, was having it off with his wife? It didn't add up. A deep, bottomless pit of distrust seemed to open up inside her. The man was a twister. He wouldn't know the truth if he met it in the street. Jimbo was right, she was sure of it.

So where the blazes was Venetia? Had their passionate love affair ended in a flash? He hadn't done away with her, had he?

Now she was being totally idiotic. But they all knew Venetia was a million miles away from being loyal. Had she told him it was all over and he'd finished her off? On the other hand, surely to goodness Jeremy would be panicking by now if he hadn't heard from her? He'd be ringing the hospitals and reporting her disappearance to the police. Wouldn't he? Had she gone to her mother's as Jeremy said she had?

Sykes came trotting past, heading for Harry's office, and it did occur to Harriet to wonder what secrets old Sykes had in his head. Did he have the answer? Because she certainly didn't. Harriet tried to remember the sequence of events and what had happened first. Venetia had disappeared, Harry had gone away to that funeral, well, he said a funeral but was it really? She now didn't believe a word he said, and she hated it when people she knew couldn't be trusted to speak the truth. Well, she and Jimbo would talk it over tonight when they'd had a chance to absorb the horror of it all, and tomorrow they would act.

Fran had no homework to do that night so she had decided to take a night off. She was sitting on the floor, her back resting against the sofa Harriet was sitting on and Jimbo was in his favourite leather chair watching TV with them.

Fran reminded the world at large that she was watching *Crimewatch* at nine and not to let her forget.

'I think you're going to be a policewoman, you always want to watch police programmes.'

'Mum! I find them so intriguing, you know the way they go about investigating and things, the ghastly things they see. They must have very suspicious minds, never wholly accepting anyone at face value but wondering all the time what's going on behind their pleasant exterior.'

To Harriet her comment seemed remarkably apt for today's revelations. 'Mmm. Right, we'll watch it then.'

So they did.

Harriet had made a drink for the three of them before *Crimewatch* began and she also provided some delicious biscuits she'd made during the day in the Old Barn kitchens, having brought home the misshapen ones she had no use for.

'These are lovely, Mum, all coconutty and tasty. I'll have another one, please.'

So the three of them sat companionably together, sharing out the biscuits and enjoying their drinks. Jimbo was more occupied with the criminal he employed though rather than those of the nation at large.

There'd been a bank robbery and the perpetrators had been caught on CCTV. For one appalling moment Harriet thought one of them was ... but it couldn't be. She was becoming completely obssessed, she really was. It was that tall, upright army-type stance she thought she recognised. They showed the robbers' faces again, all four of them, and there he was, half profile, half full face. Harriet shrieked, 'It is him, isn't it?' Jimbo leaped out of his chair, stunned into silence.

Fran demanded, 'What are you talking about?'

'It can't be possible. We must be wrong. It can't be him.'

'It is! It's him! There, look! Look again!'

'My God, it is!'

'Is it though? I mean ... It can't be ... but I'm sure it is.'

'Get the number!'

Fran interrupted. 'What is the matter with you two? Is it someone you know?'

Harriet frantically searched for paper and pen, Jimbo leaped about the room as though he was walking on hot coals, and Fran adopted the pose of a scathing teenager bored with her middle-aged parents apparently taking leave of their senses yet again.

'Who is it? I demand an answer!'

'Harry Dickinson! It must have been when he went to that funeral. But he didn't go to one, he was doing a robbery. A *bank* robbery. Oh my God!' Fran feigned a faint on the carpet.

Rather dramatically, Jimbo shouted, 'We've been harbouring a viper in our midst! To think that I gave him a job, and asked Mother to rent him her cottage.'

'Dad! What now?'

Both Jimbo and Harriet were lost for words. What did you do when you recognised someone on *Crimewatch*?

'Ring the number!' shouted Fran, thrilled by the position they found themselves in. Fame at last. This would put Turnham Malpas on the map and not half! 'Go on, ring the number!'

'Harriet!' Jimbo pointed dramatically in the direction of the front door. 'Pop into the Royal Oak for a word with Georgie or something and see if Harry's in there. Then come back and tell me and I'll ring Sergeant MacArthur.'

'What shall I say?'

'Anything you bloody well like, but *do* it.'

'I'll go as well!'

'No you won't, Fran. You never go in there so it would alert him that something is up.'

'Please!'

Jimbo shook his head.

'I'm going and you can't stop me.'

'You're not going if I have to tie you to a chair. You are *not* going, do you hear? Harriet! What's the delay?'

'I'm thinking.'

'There's no time for thinking, get gone woman!'

So she did.

The bar at the Royal Oak was busy, with scarcely a chair, nor a stool, to spare. Harriet walked as steadily as she could to the counter and fixed her eyes on Georgie. She still hadn't come up with a reason for being there.

'I just wondered ...'

'Yes?'

'I just wondered whether Craddock Fitch was in tonight?'

A rather surprised Georgie answered, 'Well, no. He hardly ever is.'

'Oh! Right. Orange juice please.' Then it hit her straight between the eyes that she'd no money on her. 'Cancel that. Sorry.' She ran her fingers through her hair, then casually turned to check the bar. There was Harry, sitting comfortably for all the world to see, innocently enjoying a pint of home-brew and talking to Zack, Vince, Sylvia, Maggie and Dottie. She twinkled her fingers at them as they waved to her, then said to Georgie, 'Sorry, got to go' and left, walking as slowly as her racing heart would allow.

Once outside she dashed for home. The door was ajar and waiting behind it were Fran and Jimbo.

'He's safely ensconced with a pint, only a quarter drunk.'

'Right. Sergeant MacArthur it is.'

They were still all sitting in the Royal Oak enjoying their drinks and having a good laugh about anything and everything at ten o'clock. They'd thoroughly discussed the outcome of the cricket match on Saturday, gone over yet again Peter's idea about selling the silver and all but one had agreed he shouldn't, Harry having said he'd no preference seeing as he hadn't lived in the village long enough to have an opinion. The imminent annual village show had been discussed and more than one had said it wasn't like it used to be, it had gone all modern and didn't feel the same, not like it did when they were young and ...

At that very moment, three men walked in, followed by Sergeant MacArthur.

You could have cut the atmosphere with a knife because, in an instant, panic was written on every face. Mac coming in? He never did that unless there was trouble, and those three men with him looked suspiciously like plain-clothes detectives. The strangers' eyes were searching every single face in the bar.

Dicky bravely stepped forward. 'Good evening, gentlemen, how may I help?'

But Sergeant Mac walked straight across to Harry and asked him to accompany him to the police station in Culworth to help with police enquiries. Everyone in the bar heard what he said. Every single one of them. There was still a mouthful of home-brew left in his glass, and Harry calmly finished it, winked at Dottie, got up and went out, hemmed in by the three detectives. Sergeant Mac left last and, just before he closed the door behind him, he gave a triumphant thumbs up to Dicky.

There had been many exciting events in the Royal Oak bar over the years, but this one, well, it took some beating.

'He winked at me!' said Dottie. 'It can't be very serious if he winked at me?'

'It took four of 'em to arrest him though.'

'He wasn't arrested, they said helping them with their enquiries.'

'Same thing, different words.'

'But Harry won't have done anything serious, now will he? He's such a nice man.'

Through the door burst Zack and Marie, obviously very upset.

Marie was breathless and trembling from head to foot and Zack helped her to the chair Harry had just vacated. Zack was too worked up to care that he'd sat down in Jimmy's chair. When he'd caught his breath he said, 'We're looking for Harry, he's not at home. Has he been in here tonight?'

They all solemnly nodded.

'Where is he then?'

They all knew how attached to Harry Zack and Marie were, and so people hardly dared to tell them what had happened. But someone earwigging from another table, it would have to be that vulgar man from Penny Fawcett that no one liked, said, 'You've just missed him. He's been taken to the police station.

He's helping them with their enquiries, that's what they said.'

Marie broke down in tears and Sylvia passed her a tissue and asked Zack what he knew about it. Zack cleared his throat and attempted to tell them about *Crimewatch* and seeing Harry in a hoody raiding a bank.

Willie protested. 'Raiding a bank? Never. You must have got the wrong m—'

'But he didn't, did he, Willie? Get the wrong man. They've just been for 'im.' This came from Dottie who was still puzzling about the wink Harry gave her.

'So who rang the police, then?' asked Zack in an accusatory tone.

'You're not going to say they shouldn't have, when they'd recognised him? Just like you did?' asked Sylvia. 'He must have done it when he went to that funeral.'

Dottie backed her up. 'Some funeral. I remember reading about that bank raid in the paper. In Essex it was. If it's the same one, one of the bank staff got shot. I hope it wasn't Harry who fired the gun, else he'll be in for it.'

Marie suddenly came to life. 'Are you suggesting that Harry had a gun? I hope not. I'm certain they've got the wrong man.'

'But, Marie, you watched *Crimewatch*, and the way you're crying, you do believe it was him don't you?' Sylvia said this in such a kindly manner that Marie burst into tears all over again, whispering between sobs, 'I won't believe it. I won't.' Zack put an arm round her shoulders and squeezed her, while privately wondering how they could have been so taken in by Harry. But they weren't the only ones; everyone who met him liked him. Every single one. They'd all been taken in by him, even Jimbo had trusted him. It was no good denying it, the despair he felt inside himself told him it was true; Harry had been involved.

Dottie argued, 'When you think about it, he never did tell you anything about himself, did he? He could talk about anything, but never about his family or what he'd done in his lifetime like we do. You know, funny incidents about when we were young, school and friends and that. Did he have any family? Did he have a past?' Dottie looked at them each in turn and none of them denied what she said. 'He must have been a con man and none of us realised it. Not even Jimbo, and he's very astute.'

Maggie, getting into the spirit of the thing, said grimly, 'I wonder if he'd just got out of prison, what with him never talking about his past. He was very pale at first.'

Marie gasped in horror.

Sylvia said, 'Maybe he's really an undercover policeman and the detectives came to rescue him, to whisk him away to safety. Arresting him was all a sham. That's why he hadn't a past, he was undercover.'

Marie responded to Dottie's remark by looking more cheerful. 'Oh, yes! Of course, that'll be it.'

Vince dismissed this idea abruptly. 'Now we are getting daft. Why should he be undercover in Turnham Malpas? There're no robbers here.'

Eyebrows were raised by the ones who had dismissed the undercover idea right from the start.

They were still at it at closing time. Dicky had kept very quiet while all this was going on and, in fact, at one point had put a finger to his lips to warn Georgie to keep silent.

After everyone had left to spread the news of yet another dramatic night in the Royal Oak, Dicky and Georgie sat upstairs in their sitting room to question whether they should tell what they knew about Harry. They still hadn't resolved the question when they went to bed at one o'clock in the morning.

Chapter 19

Before he'd stocked up ready for opening at eleven o'clock Dicky had been round to the little police station attached to the police house where Sergeant Mac and Mrs Mac lived. He dinged the bell on the counter and out from the house part of the police station came Mac, dressed in mufti.

'Morning, Dicky. What can I do for you?'

'The arrest you made last night—'

'It wasn't an arrest, he's helping the police with their enquiries.' Mac rested his forearms on the counter to lower himself to Dicky's short stature.

'Well ...'

'Yes?'

'I feel uncomfortable coming here because this is only a suspicion but, in the circumstances, Georgie and me, well, we think we need to tell you something.'

'Yes, what's it about?'

'Harry Dickinson. On two separate occasions we were convinced that it was Harry who paid us with counterfeit twenty-pound notes. We didn't mention it to him because we weren't one hundred per cent certain it was him who gave them to us, only pretty sure it was.'

'Right. Still got 'em?'

Dicky dug in his back pocket and brought them out. 'Here we are.'

'I shall take these to Culworth this morning. They have him there. Anything else of value you would care to impart?'

'Well, again, this is only a suspicion, but we did notice that while Jimbo was away and Harry was in charge of going to the bank with the takings like we do, he seemed to be very flush with money. Right from when he first came, he always appeared very eager to pay his round but in fact when he opened his wallet, there was very little in it. Enough, but not more than enough. But then Georgie spotted a real load of notes in his wallet on two occasions while Jimbo was away, and Harry tried to get his money out while he shielded his wallet from view. Now, it may have been coincidence, but on the other hand it did seem odd. Georgie's sharp. Having been in the trade for years, she knows what she's talking about when it comes to money, believe me. Maybe we're being too over ... whatever ... But there you are.'

'Has Jimbo said anything about any theft to you, as one businessman to another?'

'No.'

Mac found a brand new plastic bag and placed the two twenty-pound notes in it. 'Thank you for this information, it'll all add to the case.'

'He's guilty then? It was him on *Crimewatch*?'

Mac tapped the side of his nose, 'Police business, can't talk about it,' but he gave Dicky a wink and a thumbs up.

'OK.'

'I need to report this,' said Mac and drew out a report sheet.

Later that morning, Jimbo, who was working at home for the day, went to answer the very demanding hammering on his front door.

There stood Mac, with his serious police face on.

'Mr Jimbo Charter-Plackett?'

Jimbo was rather puzzled by this question as he knew Mac knew him and that Mac knew Jimbo knew him, but Jimbo nodded his head.

'Can I have a word please regarding your 999 call last night?'

'Were we wrong then?'

'Well, no, our enquiries indicate that you were not wrong, so far.'

'So it was him? On the TV?'

'May I come in?'

In a long, roundabout way Mac asked Jimbo if he had thought over the last few weeks that he had had money stolen from the business.

'Well. You see, between you and me ...' Jimbo explained what had happened to him while Mac took notes. It all appeared very confusing as Mac didn't want to give out too much information but, on the other hand, he knew Jimbo like a friend and dancing between the two situations in which he found himself, both policeman on duty and friend, got confusing at times, so Jimbo gave him a strong coffee from the machine in the hope that it might clear the air a little.

It was only after Mac had gone with a sheaf of notes in his file that Jimbo remembered the money that disappeared from the Organ Recital Fund tin. He could bet his last dollar that Harry had come in for something or other, spotted the tin, and taken the chance to pinch the money while Bel or Tom had left the till unattended. An opportunistic theft maybe, but stealing just the same. The two of them hadn't counted Harry as a customer. After all, he was staff, wasn't he? Too late now to expect either Tom or Bel to recollect if he came in that day. How could they all have been such idiots not to sense what he really was?

Mac's next call was at the rectory. Peter was on his way out, visiting the sick, but he gladly delayed his departure to accommodate Mac.

'Reverend, I thought you might know.'

'Come in the study, Mac, and sit yourself down. Might know what?'

'Well, you will have heard about Harry Dickinson being featured on *Crimewatch* last night? In that bank robbery?'

'Harry Dickinson? No! I know nothing about it.'

Mac told the whole story in lurid detail and concluded by asking Peter if he had had any suspicious exchanges with Harry that might have led him to suspect anything.

'No. He didn't come to church except the one time when I met him in there looking for Sykes, but that was the only time. Once or twice, he assisted Zack with mowing the churchyard, but that was all.'

'Right. So, basically, you have nothing to report.'

'Nothing to report about Harry, but there is something else.' Peter hesitated.

'Yes?'

'I am concerned about the disappearance of Venetia Mayer. Harry disappearing off for a few days and Venetia going, we are told, to stay with her mother all happened at the same time. I've spoken to Jeremy about Venetia, because she's the church youth club leader now Liz has left, but he appeared confident that she would be back from her mother's any time now. But she isn't. Now, as you know, she was having a rather steamy and very public affair with Harry ...'

'I heard about that!'

'Yes, well, it was me who came across them in Home Park. I stalked past, ignoring them, but I went to see Harry the next day. Harry was very sharp and to the point, but at the same time it was obvious to me that he was very much in love with her. However, it's not like Venetia not to communicate. If nothing else, Venetia was a great communicator, and it's quite out of character for her not, at the very least, to phone.'

'Are you suggesting he might have ... ?' Mac drew his index finger across his throat and gurgled rather realistically.

Peter studied him for a moment and then answered with, 'In a way, I suppose I am. But not necessarily Harry.'

Mac's eyes widened with surprise. 'Who then?'

'The injured, seriously embarrassed, badly let-down husband.'

'My God! No, not Jeremy. He wouldn't say boo to a goose.' Mac shook his head. 'No, you've got it wrong there, Reverend.'

'Sometimes they are the very ones. It was heartbreaking for him, very shaming, you know, especially when he found out from the gossip that was going around that I'd witnessed them that night in Home Park. However, you're the police officer, I leave it up to you.'

'She certainly had the hots for Harry, didn't she? So why go away?'

'Exactly.'

Mac left the rectory weighed down with evidence, suspicions and amazement that there could be so much going on in three small villages. The *Crimewatch* incident had given him amazing kudos with the force in Culworth. It was all rather surprising to him as he'd always thought he'd been dumped in the police house because they couldn't find anything else for him to do, his police career having been uninspired right from the start. And here he was with two mind-boggling incidents on the same day. He'd go and visit Jeremy straight away. That incident of the petrol being siphoned out of the Culworth market inspector's motorbike could wait till tomorrow.

Jeremy was actually at Home Farm when he finally found him, so it was in a cowshed that he had to tactfully ask Jeremy about the whereabouts of his wife.

'Sorry to be troubling you, Mr Mayer, but I've had two people asking me,' – that was an exaggeration, but it made his enquiry sound more urgent – 'about your dear wife, Venetia. They are very concerned about her disappearance, do you have cause for concern at all?'

Jeremy dropped his pen in the cow muck but ignored it. 'Seeing as I had a letter from her yesterday, no I am not, sergeant.'

'I see. Would it be possible for me to see it?'

'No you may not. I don't allow my p-private correspondence to be bandied about around the p-public at large.'

'It would put my mind at rest.'

'There is no reason to put your mind at rest. She's s-safe and well and if I was concerned about her, I would be asking you for help, wouldn't I? She *is* caring for her mother, who has been very poorly just recently.'

'I see. I didn't mean to give offence, I'm just concerned, you understand.'

'Understandably, officer. Now, may I get on with the b-business that b-brought me here?'

Mac replaced his hat, turned on his heel, then paused and turned back saying, 'Don't forget your pen.' He pointed to the very messy pen still lying at Jeremy's feet, and left the cowshed.

He was covering up, was Mr Jeremy Mayer. The stammer and the beads of sweat on his top lip were all signs of panic. To say nothing of his trembling hands. Amazing control though, to speak so commandingly. Perhaps it was all to do with his upset about Venetia leaving him though? Yes, of course, that would be it. The reverend had got it completely wrong.

But Sergeant MacArthur's day of being at the hub of the best gossip in Turnham Malpas in years was not yet finished. At eight-fifteen that evening he received the message that a yellow-and-black Mini had been found abandoned, minus its registration plates, on a derelict industrial estate in Culworth that had become an illegal graveyard for unwanted cars. It belonged to Venetia.

Chapter 20

Two people who were not the slightest bit interested in the Harry/Venetia/Jeremy drama were Tamsin and Paddy; they were far too busy enjoying their new relationship and organising their wedding. The day the news broke about Venetia's car, Paddy got a reply from his mother. His stomach churned as he opened it.

> *Dear Paddy,*
>
> *Well, I never! My Paddy getting married! Now all the children have left home I am free to come! She looks a lovely girl, you are a very lucky man. I thought I'd come and stay a few days. Could you put me up?*
>
> *I shall hire a car from the airport and drive straight to Turnham Malpas. I will let you know definite times in a few days when I've booked my flight.*
>
> *So looking forward to seeing you! I shall bring photos of everyone, including all your nieces and nephews.*
>
> *Love to Tamsin and to you.*
>
> *Your Ma. X X X X X*

Paddy was reading the letter sitting in his favourite lunchtime position; in his wheelbarrow, leaning his back against the wall of the peach house where, ever since he'd first come to work at the big house, he always ate his lunch, summer and winter, unless it was raining.

The letter fell from his hand onto his sandwich box and

lay there while he sat there stunned. How on earth had that downtrodden, regularly beaten up, useless mother of his become this apparently brisk, modern, up-to-date one with a mind of her own? He checked the handwriting, suspecting that his letter must have got into the wrong hands. How could this be her? He hadn't known she was literate even, because he'd never seen her read a book or newspaper in all the sixteen years he'd lived at home. Hire a car! Drive to Turnham Malpas! His memory of her was of someone eternally pregnant, always struggling to get through the day, burdened with a houseful of children. He'd never expected a reply, still less one that sounded so positive. Somehow, as he sat there eating his slice of ground rice tart that Greta had packed for him, Paddy slowly began to realise that maybe he wouldn't need to feel ashamed of her any longer, as he had done the last twenty-four years.

It felt ridiculous, but suddenly he felt better about himself, felt able to hold his head higher. Apparently he could be proud of her which, in a way, made him feel less of a waste of space. Perhaps he wasn't such a wastrel, after all. Something within him had made him decide to take up Mr Fitch's offer of paying for his course at the Horticultural College, had he got that from his mother?

He drank the last of his coffee, screwed the lid back on the Thermos, then packed it carefully away. He decided to spend the next few minutes talking to Tamsin.

She was utterly delighted that his mother was coming. 'Oh, Paddy, that will make the day so very special for us. I'm so pleased. Aren't you glad you wrote?'

'Yes, thanks to you and Greta. More so to you for persisting. She's changed so much, you've no idea.'

'What's her name?'

'Bridget Clodagh Mary Cleary.'

'She sounds lovely.'

'Wait till we see her. It all sounds too good to be true.'

'Nonsense. You've read me her letter and she sounds great. Be glad, Paddy, your mother is still alive. I would be if she were mine.'

'Yes, of course. Sorry.'

'Got to go, I've a pupil waiting for me. Love and kisses. Only four more weeks to go!'

'Exactly.' Paddy switched off his mobile and carefully put it back in his trouser pocket. Then he leaped out of the wheelbarrow and went back to work with a song in his heart. No mention of his dad, then. That was odd. She didn't say 'we', but 'I', so that must mean he wouldn't be coming. Because he couldn't or wouldn't? Paddy didn't care. If he was dead, so what? If he was alive and wouldn't come, so what? He shuddered to think of Tamsin having to shake hands with the man. He couldn't bear the idea of it, not him with his cruelty, degradation and lies. Not likely. He felt relieved. Tonight he'd ask Greta if his mother could use the small bedroom, or maybe he ought to use the small one and let her have his bigger one. He'd talk to Greta about it.

Then he suffered one of the deeply disturbing moments when he doubted that he should be marrying Tamsin at all. He'd have to cancel the wedding. He would tonight, cancel it, tell her he couldn't go ahead with it. Not Paddy Cleary, he didn't deserve her. She wasn't in his league and that was important in a marriage. He'd let his mother come, Greta wouldn't mind, but not get married. In fact, he'd go right now and wait for Tamsin to come home to tell her outright, no beating about the bush, straight from the shoulder. That's what he'd do. He dropped the drum of plant food he was about to open and left without a word to anyone. If he tried to speak to someone he'd break down. Best if he just left without a word.

Paddy sat on the seat by the village pond, his sweater sleeve pulled back so he could see the time without hindrance. He nodded at a little girl and her mother who had come to feed the geese and he tolerated them honking and squabbling around his feet as they fought for a share. He heard a helicopter trailing steadily through the sky, round and round, lower and lower, and watched it surge away suddenly as though tired of Turnham Malpas, just like he felt. He'd leave and go somewhere else, make a fresh start, and forget her. It was the only way. He'd overpersuaded her and he shouldn't have done.

Then the familiar sound of her VW Beetle invaded his subconscious and Paddy got to his feet to make his way towards her as she searched for her keys. His legs felt like jelly, but he knew that he wasn't the right person for her, she deserved someone so much more handsome, charismatic, someone higher up the social strata than him. His heart bled as he called out to her, 'Tamsin!'

Tamsin heard him and turned to watch him crossing the green, promptly falling in love with him all over again. Since her parents died, there hadn't been anyone who loved her as he did, despite all her faults, and they were many. She wasn't going to turn her back on him now, not when lifelong happiness was within her grasp. But something in his gait alarmed her. She pushed open her door and went inside to wait for him to arrive, anxiously puzzling about what could be wrong.

Paddy came stiffly into the sitting room.

Tamsin watched him from the kitchen doorway.

Paddy felt shrivelled inside.

Tamsin prepared herself for something shocking that she guessed she wouldn't want to hear.

'It's like this, Tamsin.' As he said her name his guts knotted. 'Yes?'

'It's like this. I'm not good enough for you. I can't possibly give you the kind of lifestyle you are accustomed to. We'll have to cancel. I shall love you till ...'

'Yes?'

'... the end of time. But I can't let you tie yourself to me. I'm sorry. I shall drag you down, I know it. I should never have asked you to marry me. Never. I'm not reliable.'

Tamsin knew Paddy was close to collapse. His face was ashen, those blue Irish eyes with their dark lashes were almost black with pain, and he was shaking from head to foot.

'Sit down. I'll get you a brandy.'

Paddy took the glass from her and downed it in one gulp. His mouth seized up, his tongue seemed to have grown too big for it and he couldn't speak. He groaned. It was all he was capable of.

Tamsin stood beside him, not knowing how to respond.

The silence between them filled the house.

'It's no good. I can't marry you, I'm just not good enough for you. I'm really not. I'm so sorry. So sorry.' Paddy shuddered. What the blazes had he done? He'd given up all chance of happiness with the woman he loved, but it was for the best. He'd done the right thing by her. He'd never find another woman like Tamsin. Oh God. He struggled to leave the depths of the sofa but the message from his head didn't reach his legs.

A voice said in commanding tones, 'Stay where you are!' Paddy couldn't think who'd spoken.

'You dare move one inch from that sofa. Just you try. I mean it.'

There it was again. That voice.

'If I have to chain you to it for the next four weeks, I shall. You're not getting out of this, Paddy Cleary. Believe me, I'll die first. We are destined for one another. You may not believe it now, but you will. I have never in all my life met anyone I would want to have sleeping with me for the next forty or more years. Understand? I've haven't reached thirty-five without opportunities, but believe me or believe me not, you are the *only* man I have ever met to whom I would give that opportunity. Right? Waking up and seeing your face on the pillow next to me every day for the rest of my life is all I want, even when we are both really old. Not good enough for me! That's … that's … that's balderdash.'

'Balderdash?'

'Yes. Rubbish, nonsense, silly, foolish, total madness. To me …' Tamsin tapped her chest sharply, 'to me, you are the man I want. Right? And I'm not going to let you go. So. What do you have to say to that?'

Tamsin stood in front of him, arms akimbo, lips pressed tightly into a thin line, waiting. Her mouth began to tremble with laughter but she grimly held her stance. For a moment she thought Paddy was going to begin smiling too, but he didn't, and then he couldn't hold it back and before they knew it, they were both laughing their heads off.

Momentarily, Paddy controlled his laughter and said, 'I meant it. I really did.'

'I know you did. You frightened the life out of me. Don't you dare do that again.'

'I daren't, not after that telling off. Help! What have I done? I'm marrying a harridan.'

'A lovely one though.' Tamsin flung herself down onto the sofa beside him and clutched him to her. 'Oh, Paddy! I love you so much.'

'And I love you, too.'

'Isn't it lovely? The two of us finding each other, don't you think?'

'After the life I've led, it's like reaching paradise, being with you.'

'I'm no angel, you know. I have a temper the like of which …'

'After that exhibition I know you have.'

Tamsin sat upright. 'And I hate shellfish, I never eat 'em.'

'Neither do I, so that's all right.'

'And I've never learned to ride a bike.'

'That's OK. I don't like bikes, far too energetic.'

'And another thing, I can't go on rides like the Big Dipper, they make me terribly sick.'

'We'll avoid those then.'

'And there's something else you ought to know …'

'Yes?'

'I don't like lovemaking first thing in the morning.'

'Better make a note of that.' He took out his diary and wrote in it. 'Doesn't want sex before breakfast. Anything else while I've got my diary out?' He sat there, pen poised, looking at her.

'I shall get my hair cut off in time for the wedding.'

'What?'

'I'm getting my hair cut off, to just about two inches long all over. I've always worn it long so a change would be good. What do you think?'

Paddy protested. 'I love your hair just as it is.'

'Oh! I see, all right then. That doesn't mean to say I shall keep it long for ever. I have an independent spirit and you'd better accept that before we embark on this marriage business.'

'Right.' Paddy made another note in his diary. 'Anything else?'

'I have a very loving heart and I love you and only you. And always will.'

They had a long kiss then, to seal some kind of deeper understanding between them.

'I'd better go.'

'Yes you had, or the promise we made to each other could be broken and I don't want that.'

'Neither do I.'

As he walked down Shepherd's Hill, Paddy's heart felt as if it was going to leap out of his chest with joy. When he got back to Greta's he gave her his mother's letter to read.

She was amazed. 'I thought you said …'

'Yes, I know. It's come as a shock. I never thought she'd find the money, never mind the time, to come. And learning to drive, I can't believe it. She doesn't say what's changed her so much, does she?'

'No. I wonder, would she like to stay with us, do you think?'

'I was going to ask if you would mind.'

'I'd love her to stay. Would she mind?'

'I think she'd be delighted.'

'Good. That's settled then. You know, Paddy, marrying Tamsin is doing you good. You look ten years younger.' She reached towards him and kissed his cheek. 'We're so looking forward to the wedding, but I shall miss you, you know, living with us. It's been great having you here. I miss my boys. Still, there it is.'

'Won't they ever come back?'

Greta shook her head. 'In Canada they are. They daren't come back 'cos of what happened. They were two very naughty boys. Well, Kenny was and our Terry did whatever he was told. Barry's lovely, as you know, but I miss the other two.'

'Have you never thought about going to see them?'

'Never had the money and I don't know if we'd be welcome anyway. But there we are, I've got you instead and that's enough for me. Reception organised?'

'Oh yes. Georgie's being wonderful. We shall have the whole of the Royal Oak for ourselves that day until 6 p.m. It'll be classed as a private function, you see.'

'I don't know if Tamsin's told you, but she's asked Vince to give her away. She said she thought it would please you.'

'Vince? I didn't know that. She's hasn't said.'

'Don't let on. She hasn't got a dad of her own you see, has she? Vince is that proud.'

'Ah! Right. Couldn't have happened to a better man. I'm so pleased. All we have to hope for is wonderful weather.'

'They say the sun shines on the righteous.'

'Best behave myself then.'

'I'll get supper. Enjoy every minute of looking forward to

your wedding, Paddy, and don't let thinking you're not good enough for her put a stop to it. Understood?'

Paddy had to smile, he'd come so close to doing that very thing. He nodded in reply to Greta's advice. Thank God for Tamsin and her down-to-earth approach to life. He could sense that the best part of his life was still to come. And he had to admit that he was looking forward to his mother coming, if only to find out about the change in her fortunes. Perhaps it meant that either his mother had given his dad the elbow, or he was no longer on the scene, namely that he was dead. Hallelujah to that!

Chapter 21

Sykes, bereft of his best friend Harry, had been taken in again by Grandmama Charter-Plackett. She didn't want him, not any more, but what was one to do with him? He was ownerless all over again. He really wasn't having much luck just lately and that kindly corner of her heart she kept for her family and her dearest friends, though there weren't many of those left nowadays, decided that, despite her better judgement, she'd better have him back with her.

Sykes accepted his change of circumstances with a good heart and kept to his routine as closely as she allowed. She didn't really approve of dogs wandering about all on their own, but he knew the village and its environs so well that he wasn't likely to go missing and because he was so well behaved she allowed him to roam within reason. His favourite place was the church, followed by trotting across Home Park round the lake and up the stairs to where Harry used to work. When he found Harry wasn't there any longer, Sykes dropped the office from his route, and instead popped home via Sykes Wood. This was a much longer way round but there were plenty of rabbit warrens to stick his nose down and it made for a much more interesting way home than covering the same ground across Home Park.

Without fail, he always managed to come home just as clean as when he left it, mainly because he hated the rain so tended to stay home on muddy days. Then, two days in succession, Grandmama had to wash him all the way up his short legs and along his chest before she would allow him in the house.

'Digging for rabbits, I expect, you scoundrel. You should bring one home and we could have it for dinner. I'm good at skinning rabbits. I bet you didn't know that, did you? Off you go.'

She laughed at herself for conversing with a dog, but somehow one always had the feeling he knew exactly what one said. Harry had said that very same thing. Pity him turning out to be a first-class thief, though she supposed being charming was part of his stock-in-trade.

When Sykes came home three times up to his elbows in soil, his claws and pads thick with the stuff, she decided to keep him in and take him out herself the next day for a walk on the extending lead she'd bought the first time he'd been hers.

She intended crossing Home Park, a short trip round the lake, and then home but Sykes had other ideas. He insisted on going on into Sykes Wood. 'Oh! Well, all right then. But that's it, definitely it, otherwise I shall be in bed for a week after this and look at the time, it's already ten minutes past ten, and so far I've done nothing this morning. You're spoiled to death, Sykes, you little charmer.'

She climbed with difficulty over the stile and began admiring the beautiful green trees, now in their full summer prime. The lead kept getting twisted round the tree trunks as Sykes dashed about sniffing for rabbits but she tolerated that, after all he'd only come in because she allowed him to, so it was her fault. Suddenly he disappeared the full length of the extending lead and was pulling so strongly on it that she could do nothing but follow where he led.

He rounded a huge beech tree in the very densest part of the wood and began digging. 'So this is where you've been getting so muddy, you've been digging and digging here, haven't you?' She saw he'd dug and dug, first in one place and then another. And here he was, at it again. She became wary, his digging appeared so purposeful, as though he knew something she didn't. There was more to this dog than she'd ever imagined ... 'Oh my God!' Surely it couldn't be …'Come away, Sykes!' She reeled in the extending leash as fast as she could; the trouble was, it brought her closer to what she knew by instinct she wouldn't want to recognise. 'My God. It is!'

A gold, high-heeled shoe she'd last seen being worn by …

'Oh no! Come away, Sykes. Leave!' But the serious state of agitation she found herself in made her relax her hold on the leash and Sykes plunged immediately towards the shoe and picked it up. Right there in front of her, he worried the shoe as though it were a rat, then went back to digging. This time he exposed not a shoe, but the bare foot of its owner. It was only partly revealed, sticking up out of the soil at a peculiar angle.

Grandmama screamed as she had never screamed before. On and on, screaming and screaming, with Sykes free to dig as he wished, except she didn't want him to dig any more. Finally, she pulled herself together, reeled in the leash until he was beside her and began to run. And running was not her forte. She didn't know where she was going. She kept getting hit in the face by branches that stuck out over the path, stumbling on stones, turning her ankles on the roughest bits and, once or twice, narrowly avoided falling over Sykes. Eventually, she had to pull up to get her breath. Was that a chink of light there through the trees? Had she reached the stile in Shepherd's Hill? Please God! That's it, it is. She was right. She breathed long and deep, then headed for the stile, struggled over it, threaded Sykes through and went straight away to Laburnum Cottage.

She fell on the knocker and banged it continuously until Marie and Zack came running to answer it. The sight of Grandmama, dishevelled, perspiring, her immaculate hairstyle blown to pieces, clothes in disarray, and gasping for breath came as something of a shock to them both.

'Why Mrs Charter-Plackett, whatever's the matter?'

The relief of reaching civilisation brought the realisation

to Grandmama of just what a horrific thing had happened to her. 'S-S-Sykes has found a body in the w-wood. It's terrible.'

'A body?' Zack didn't believe her. People were always talking about Sykes Wood, saying it was haunted and such but no one had ever said they'd found a body before.

'Now, come now. You've frightened yourself. Who'd put a body in the wood? It doesn't make sense.'

'Get the p-police. It's ... Venetia, I-I'm sure.' Whereupon Grandmama fell in a dead faint on their doorstep.

Sergeant MacArthur appeared first on the scene, before the detectives came from Culworth in response to the 999 call. He rang for an ambulance for Grandmama, and called the police in Culworth again while Marie tried to bring Grandmama round. Zack held on to poor Sykes who couldn't be let in the house until Zack had washed him down. Then they thought better of it, in case the soil on his legs held clues.

Marie rang Jimbo and explained as gently as she could about Grandmama and the body.

'A body in Sykes Wood? Whose body?'

'She said she thought ... Well ... She's sure it's Venetia, you see.'

'Venetia? Dead? In the wood? But she's gone to her mother's.'

'Your mother says she's buried in the wood. Sykes dug up first her shoe, those gold strappy things only Venetia could wear, and then, well believe it or not, her foot. She's seen her shoe and then her foot. Your mother's going to hospital because she fainted on our doorstep. Do you want to go with her in the ambulance? If so, come right now.'

'She fainted on your doorstep? And she's going to hospital, you say? Right. Thank you. I can't believe it. Be there in less than five minutes.'

Shepherd's Hill had seen nothing like it. There were two police vans, three police cars, people putting on all-over white suits and white boots with masks hanging round their necks, and men with spades. Carrying their equipment, they all, in turn, climbed over the stile and disappeared into Sykes Wood.

One officer, rather more astute than the others, suggested taking Sykes with them so he might pinpoint exactly where the body was, otherwise they might never find it in such a dense wood. He took Sykes's leash from Zack, intending to go immediately into the wood with him, but Sykes had very different ideas about that.

Sykes, being a rather private kind of dog, was reluctant to assist the police in their enquiries, and fancied staying at Laburnum Cottage instead. But the police would have none of it and marched him off as though he too might soon be under arrest.

Greta, who'd been in Shepherd's Hill visiting a neighbour with a message from the WI, had been passing Marie's and had overheard what Grandmama had said just before she collapsed on the doorstep. She sped home on winged feet to tell Vince and he got the car out, drove into the village, parked in the Royal Oak car park, and went in to spread the news. This was the answer then. Venetia wasn't at her mother's, after all. She was dead.

Georgie blanched when he told her. 'Never! You must have got it wrong. She's gone to her mother's, everyone knows that.'

'Well, she hasn't. She's been murdered. *Murdered!*'

'Who found her?'

'Mrs Charter-Plackett.'

'Oh no! Not Harriet?'

'No, the old lady.'

'Of all things! And at her age. In Sykes Wood, you say? How did she come to find the body?'

'Don't know. She had Sykes with her on a lead, Greta says, and he was covered in mud. The police have taken Sykes into the wood with them to help find the body. I expect she was walking him in the wood, seeing as she's taken him back from Harry.'

213

At the mention of Harry's name, he immediately became Georgie's prime suspect. She would hardly dare say it, but when she looked at Vince she could see, from the look in his eyes, he thought the same. 'He couldn't have done it, could he? I mean, he was dotty about her. He wouldn't. Would he?'

'Well, we could speculate till the cows come home, couldn't we?'

'Yes, yes, we could. And they say living in the country we don't see life. They haven't tried Turnham Malpas if they think that. Have a brandy, Vince, you must be shocked.'

'I don't mind if I do.'

Out of politeness, he patted his pockets as though searching for his money, but Georgie said, 'Don't worry about paying right now.'

She handed him the brandy for which he was most grateful and then added, 'I'll put it on the slate.'

'Oh! Right. Thanks.'

That was the thanks you got for bringing such astounding news.

It being too soon for the early lunchtime punters, only he and Georgie were in the bar so Vince decided that the next person who should know was the rector.

He rattled on the knocker and waited for someone to come to the door. It was Dottie, so she asked him to step inside as the rector wasn't in and did he want to leave a message? Vince knew from past experience that Dottie would be more than mildly interested in his news and so he told her the whole story.

'Dead? Oh my word! I've never approved of her goings-on, but then who am I to talk, with my record? But I wouldn't wish this on anyone. Buried, you say? In Sykes Wood. How dreadful. Poor Grandmama, finding her. What a shock for her. How did she know it was her? No, don't answer that.' She backed away from Vince.

'Sykes dug up her shoe and then scraped away, and Grandmama saw her foot.'

'Oh my God!'

'Sykes is helping with the search. I reckon he knows more than he's letting on.'

'Well, he did live with Harry, didn't he?'

'I never said it was him that did her in!'

'No. But you're thinking it, the same as everyone else will. I'll tell the rector when he comes back. He will be upset. He's gone to see the bishop again about selling the silver.'

'Oh has he? He's not let the matter drop then, even though we don't want it sold.'

'Well, Vince. All I can say is that you should find the money for the repairs if you don't want it sold. He's only doing his best for us all.'

'That's a matter of opinion. Don't forget to give him my message.'

Peter wasn't back in Turnham Malpas until half past seven that evening. On being given Vince's message by Caroline, who'd been told by Dottie, he went immediately up to the big house to see Jeremy, having first confirmed with Sergeant Mac that he had been taken to identify Venetia, and had agreed that it was she.

He found Jeremy at home, a mere shattered remnant of the man he'd known almost since his first year in the village. 'Jeremy. I've just heard about Venetia. I'm so sorry. May I come in?'

Jeremy nodded. He moved like a man twice his age. He slumped down in the first chair he came to and sat still. Peter stood in front of him and it was left to him to speak first. 'It must have come as a dreadful shock. Is there someone I could phone for you? A brother or a sister or a friend? Perhaps they could come to stay, keep you company, you know.'

Jeremy shook his head.

'Are you sure? I think you do need someone.'

Jeremy didn't even shake his head this time.

'Have you had something to eat today?'

No response.

'In that case, neither have I. I'll make some scrambled eggs on toast for the two of us.'

Peter walked into the kitchen and cobbled together the eggs, found the toaster, made a pot of tea, and carried it all into the sitting room.

Jeremy was still sitting like a block of stone in the chair, so Peter pulled up a side table and served the food on there. Jeremy made no effort to begin eating and gentle persuasion on Peter's part had no effect, so he poured the tea and placed the cup and saucer carefully into Jeremy's hands. Suddenly, after two sips of tea, Jeremy spoke. 'I loved her, did you know that?'

Peter nodded.

'I loved her so much. I have done since the day I first met her. She just had that something special, you know?'

Diplomatically, Peter agreed. 'She must have been an exciting person to live with.'

A gentle smile flitted across Jeremy's face. 'She was! In her own way, she loved me too. She stuck with me like glue when I had the heart attack. I owed my life to her persistence with my diet and such.' He drained the cup right to the bottom and handed it back to Peter, indicating he needed a top-up.

'She was a beautiful woman, you know.'

Peter nodded.

'I don't know how I shall live without her.'

'Have the police told you anything?'

Jeremy looked up at him and raised his eyebrows.

'About ... how it happened.'

'Oh! She was smoth ... smothered, they think. They haven't done the post-mortem yet though.'

'Now, I've finished my scrambled egg, how about you eating yours? You have to keep your strength up, you know.'

In five giant mouthfuls the egg and toast were finished.

'Can I get someone to come to stay with you, just for tonight? Is there anyone?'

'There's no one in this damned place would willingly come to stay with me. No one at all. None of them like me. I haven't a single friend in this place and not likely to have, not now. I'm a figure of fun, perhaps you haven't recognised that. But I am. I've always known it. After her funeral I shall move away. It's the only thing I can do after what's happened. I'll have to leave my job. It's the only one I've enjoyed though. Mr Fitch and I get on really well now, you know. We didn't used to, but we do now.' Jeremy's mind went somewhere else and then he came back saying, 'The humiliation of it all. Time after time. But this time was once too often. I'm told it was you who saw them in Home Park. I'm sorry you saw what you saw. She'd have come back to me, you know, now that devil's been recognised for what he is.'

Suddenly the old Jeremy was back. He looked Peter straight in the eye as though seeing the rector for the first time since he'd arrived. 'You'd better go before I say too much. Thank you for coming.'

'You have only to ask and I shall come. Whenever. OK?'

'Thank you for that.' Then a scornful sneer crossed Jeremy's face as he added, 'Ever the good Christian is our Peter, such a good chap. Goodnight.'

Peter had never seen such a look on Jeremy's face before and he found it deeply disturbing. If Caroline had just been found dead in a wood he knew he wouldn't look normal either, but there was something very nasty about Jeremy's expression and it did alarm him. He began to wonder if what he'd said to Sergeant Mac the other day about Jeremy being the wronged husband might have been nearer the truth than he'd first imagined.

Peter put his key in the rectory door with thankfulness. 'Caroline?'

She emerged from the kitchen, a gentle, considerate smile lighting her face. 'Darling! At last. How is he?'

'Very low, my darling. Hardly knows what he's saying.'

'It is Venetia then, they've found?'

'It is, he's identified her.'

'How ghastly for him. Do they know how?'

'Too early. The post-mortem is tomorrow. Jeremy says she was smothered.'

'Do you realise what you've just said?'

'What?'

'You said Jeremy said she'd been smothered, so how does he know that? It's rather odd of him really. '

'He did say "they think".'

'However, you've had a long day and you must be exhausted. Have you eaten?'

'Scrambled egg with Jeremy to encourage him to eat. I don't really fancy anything, to be honest.'

'How about a large slice of your favourite carrot cake to round it off, you poor darling? You must have had a hell of a day.'

'Yes, indeed. I'll come in the kitchen. Children OK?'

'Both upstairs getting ready for bed. Coffee or tea?'

'Coffee with rum in it. I could do with a boost.'

Caroline put her arms round him and hugged him tightly. Neither of them said anything for a few moments and then Peter said, 'How do we come to have a murder in the village? Tell me that.'

'Why not? Passions can run high wherever you live.'

'But we've no drug problems, no drink problems, no abuse, no neglected children. Nothing to cause it as far as we know.'

'Except a sex-mad woman and, let's face it, that's what she was. It was only your clerical collar that put you off limits.'

'For heaven's sake, Caro, you always imagine every woman in the district is after me.'

'They are. So would I be, except that I got you first.'

'Thank God for that. Where's that carrot cake you promised me?' Peter smiled down at her, and she grinned back.

'I do wonder if it is Jeremy. Why should Harry murder her, when he loved her so much?'

'You forget, Jeremy loved her too. He said so tonight. Poor chap, he said he'd loved her since the first day he met her. She was a beautiful woman, he said.'

'Ah! He said that, did he? So it could be either of them who killed her? And all because they loved her too much. How dreadfully sad.'

Chapter 22

The entire village heaved with the gossip about Harry and Jeremy. The night following the revelation of exactly who it was Grandmama had found in Sykes Wood, the Royal Oak bar as well as the dining room, was filled to bursting with people coming in to find out the latest developments. From Penny Fawcett and Little Derehams they crammed in, and Dicky, Georgie and Alan the barman kept the till pinging regularly. Mentally, Dicky rubbed his hands with glee. They could do with a few more murders if this was what it did to the takings. No, he didn't really mean that, of course not, he thought as he rang up eight pounds twenty-nine and paused to wonder if he needed to bring in another barrel of his renowned home-brew.

Even old Jimmy's chair was occupied, so packed was the bar. In it sat Willie Biggs who'd arrived later than he'd intended because of a leaking tap that Sylvia said she would tolerate no longer.

'Sorted that tap, have you?' she asked as he sank gratefully into Jimmy's chair.

'Of course. Well?' Willie looked round the group seated at their usual table. 'Anything else happened? Like Jeremy's been arrested?'

Vince enquired why Willie thought it should be Jeremy.

'Ah! Well, why was he saying that he'd had letters from her when he knew for a fact that he couldn't have received letters from her because she was already dead?'

'To save face?' suggested Dottie sympathetically.

Sylvia nodded in agreement. 'He had to say something, didn't he? If he thought she'd run off with Harry? Though now we know she didn't, but he would, wouldn't he? To save face.'

'It would be terrible for him when it was Peter who saw them ... You know ... at it in Home Park. So embarrassing.' Vince commented.

'I wonder if the two of them felt embarrassed or only angry when he caught them? I mean, the rector himself!' They had no answer to Greta's question, and they couldn't ask either of them, seeing as one was in prison and the other dead.

'Of course it could be Harry.'

'Harry! It was him raiding that bank. Surely to goodness he didn't murder one day and then rob a bank the next? I mean, honestly.' Sylvia shook her head in disbelief. 'No. No, he wouldn't. He was so nice, wasn't he, Marie?'

Marie, who'd had her faith in human nature sorely tried by what had happened with Harry, replied, 'Given what's happened this last two or three weeks, I could believe anything. You know, do you, that Harry robbed Jimbo while he was on his holidays?'

A chorus of astounded 'No!' went round the table.

'And I wouldn't mind, but he paid his rent to me with it,' said Marie, both embarrassed and indignant at the very thought.

'You don't know that. Maybe he paid you with his salary from Jimbo.'

'Out of the same pocket, though. Mmm? I've never been so let down by anyone before.'

Zack, still burning with resentment at the way he'd been taken in by Harry, said indignantly, 'A very practised thief he was. Raiding a bank, armed, how much more professional can you get, I ask you? He's such a low-life he'd steal from his own grandmother, he would.'

'Mentioning grandmothers, how's Mrs Charter-Plackett?'

'She's had a mild heart attack apparently, brought on by the shock,' said Maggie Dobbs. 'She's home, under strict instructions to rest, and she has another appointment at the hospital for tests at the end of the week. But she was out shaking her doormat this morning, first thing, so it doesn't look as though she's resting. I told her, "I'm doing your shopping and there's no need for vacuuming and cleaning because I shall do it."

'She said to me, "The day I need someone to clean for me is the day I die. Thank you all the same." Anyway, I told Jimbo when I went in the store for my groceries and he said he was going to make her stay with them for a few days and then he could keep an eye on her.'

There was a burst of laughter at this and Zack said, 'I doubt Jimbo could persuade her to do anything unless she *wants* to. I bet she's descended from Boudica or someone, tough she is. In 1938 they should have sent her to sort out Hitler, not that fool, Chamberlain. Hitler would have gone back to his bunker and not come out again and the war would never even have started.'

This brought on another burst of laughter.

Zack said, 'It was an amateur who did it.'

'Did what?'

'Murdered her and then dumped her car on that old industrial estate where them cars are all piled up that nobody wants.'

'What makes you say that?' asked Vince.

'Because, OK, whoever it was did it, took the registration plates off. But they forgot about the chassis number. The DVLA has them on the paperwork and her car was brand new. It would have been a matter of minutes to look it up.'

'Well, what little we know about Harry tells me he'd be wise enough to know that. A man who can raid a bank with a gun would be clever about that.'

'Exactly, Vince, and who does that point to? Jeremy. No doubt about it.'

Entirely convinced they'd definitely found the murderer, conversation turned to more fun subjects, but they never quite forgot the dreadful incident which had brought everyone in the village up short with its drama and its ghastliness. Seeing her shoe and then *her bare foot*! It was too ghoulish for words, it was.

Grandmama Charter-Plackett, in a moment of weakness, had agreed to stay at Jimbo and Harriet's until she'd been to the hospital for an ECG and got her results. She was enjoying the attention she received and the company of Fran as she was on holiday from school. Now Sykes was no longer helping the police, he was living a life of luxury, petted and spoiled like never before. Fran took him out every morning before doing her holiday stint of inputting data into the computer now that Harry was no longer employed. Harriet, despite her mother-in-law's loud protests, got quickly into the habit of feeding Sykes snacks when she was cooking and Jimbo, much to his own surprise, found himself taking him out each evening before bed for a walk. Though why, he couldn't say, when the little blighter took himself out whenever he could escape through the door to disappear for hours.

In fact, everyone in the village took note of where Sykes was going as they'd all realised there was more to Sykes than they had ever imagined.

Grandmama was determined that she wasn't taking Sykes back home with her. He was good company seeing as she lived alone, but the responsibility for him, especially given the way in which he wandered about on his own, was really too much for her. Truth be told, though she would never let on to anyone, finding Venetia had been altogether too much of a shock. It had brought on a rush of old age she'd never anticipated she would reach. To find a new home for Sykes obsessed her, and it was only when Peter happened to call to see Jimbo about bell-ringing that she realised she might well have solved her problem.

Sykes, accustomed to seeing Peter in church, was delighted to see him, wagging his tail in greeting with lavish enthusiasm.

And, as luck would have it, Peter spoke about the matter first. 'Poor old Sykes, he doesn't have much luck with owners, does he? He seemed so happy to be with Harry in the office and living in Jimmy's cottage, it's such a pity he lost out there.'

'That Harry was not a suitable companion for Sykes. That poor dog had more than enough to upset him with Venetia and Harry's relationship. He found her and dug her up because he knew her very well indeed. Besides which, Sykes is honest and Harry most certainly was not. Have you been to see him?'

'Not yet.'

'You should. That young man needs your kind of help. I don't approve of what he did, but he does need help. Could you go?'

'He told me he had no time for the church, nor me for that matter.'

'In that case, you should definitely go.' She offered to make him a cup of tea but he refused.

'Peter, now Caroline's cats have all gone to pussy heaven, is there a chance you would have room for another?'

'Another cat, you mean?'

'Well, not exactly.' She glanced significantly at Sykes, now curled up on Peter's feet.

'Ah! Mmm.'

'It would be very appropriate. After all, he does visit the church a lot.'

'I would have to consult the others. In particular, Caroline.' He bent down to pat Sykes's head, who promptly snuggled down and closed his eyes.

'There you are. You see, he does take to you very nicely indeed.'

The front door banged shut.

'That sounds like Jimbo back, I'll go and find him.'

'Will you do what I said about Harry?'

Peter smiled at her. 'Very likely I will. Thanks for prompting me.'

Sykes got up and followed him out and Grandmama smiled to herself, closed her eyes, and took a power nap, well satisfied with the idea she'd planted in Peter's mind.

Peter took the opportunity the following day to visit Harry and, to be frank, he wasn't looking forward to it. The man needed a visit, especially now that Venetia had been found, and he decided to concentrate on that aspect rather than the armed robbery.

His telephone call to the remand centre to ask if it would be possible to visit him in his capacity as rector of the village where Harry had lived, was met with enthusiasm.

The prison chaplain had been to see Harry, but he'd told him not to come again. Maybe someone he knew might have a better chance.

Harry was seated at a table, waiting for him. The lean man he had known was now more akin to a skeleton.

Peter offered his hand to shake and, somewhat reluctantly, Harry eventually shook it. 'I decided I'd better come to see you, Harry, with news of the village. Sykes is living at Jimbo Charter-Plackett's at the moment, along with Grandmama, as she's not well. I've been thinking of taking him on. What do you think?'

Harry summoned a slight smile to his lips at the thought of Sykes. 'I'm glad. I know he's only a dog, but he's very perceptive. He seems to know what you're about.'

'True. I've spoken to Caroline about the idea and she's very willing, so if you approve, I think we'll take him in. Grandmama seems set against the idea of keeping him herself.'

'Grandmama! Ah, yes. I'm almost glad it was her who found Venetia. Better her than some hooligans, at least she'd have respect.' Harry's eyes dropped so he was no longer looking at

Peter. 'I knew her for what she was, but I loved her just the same. I couldn't help myself. The difference with me was that I didn't use her like all the others did. I loved her, and she knew it. It wasn't me that did it, you know. I just thought, though I couldn't understand why, that she'd gone to her mother's like Jeremy said.'

'She was rich, she had *two* men who loved her to distraction.'

'She despised *him*.'

'She stuck by him when he had his heart attack and I admired her for that, Harry. That was before you knew her.'

'She told me. And about all the others. There was no shame there, in her mind. All that time I was pining for her, wondering why she hadn't contacted me, and she was buried. She was dark and cold, filthy and neglected in that blasted wood, with no one to care. She was always amazingly fresh and smelled like a tropical flower, as though she bathed three times a day.' A sob rose up in Harry's chest like a scream, and the tears poured down his cheeks. He hid his face in his hands, his shoulders heaving.

Peter was shocked by the intensity of the sound Harry made. He might be a thief of the first order, but right now he needed someone. He left Harry to weep for a short while, then rang for a glass of water for him.

He took the warder aside and spoke quietly to him. 'Could he have a glass of water? I'm rather afraid for him. Has he been like this before?'

'No, padre, he hasn't. He hasn't really spoken, not until you came. Do him good, I expect. I'll get the water, I won't be a moment.'

The warder returned with the water, shook Harry's shoulder, and got him to take it from him. Harry took a few gulps, then wiped his eyes. He sat staring at his hands and then looked up at Peter. 'Have they arrested the murderer?'

'Who?'

'Jeremy Mayer!'

'Who says he killed her?'

'I do, and I'm right. There was no other man than me, and I didn't do it, so it must have been him. Believe me, I'm right.' He blew his nose, then sat back waiting a reply.

'He's been interviewed, obviously, but not arrested.'

Harry banged his fist on the table. 'Tell them they must do.'

'Very well, I will.'

'You see, she told me he was beside himself when he found out it was you who saw us in Home Park that night. He blethered on at her about the shame of it, and I must admit she was upset. She seemed to hold you in high esteem, you see. Anyone but you, she said.'

'Right. I see. Now, Harry, is there anything I can do for you?'

No reply.

'Like contacting someone who should know, bringing in anything at all for you while you're in here?'

Harry, his equilibrium restored to some extent, looked him full in the face. 'I don't want anything. I have books. I read crime, you see.' He laughed. 'To pick up tips. You haven't mentioned why I'm in here. No sermons on honesty and truthfulness, when I've lied since the very first moment I came to Turnham Malpas. Not to Venetia though, not to her. Not your scene, then, sermonising self-righteously?'

'It can be when appropriate. I think you are soon going to be full of regret for what has happened, full of remorse. When that time comes, I may be able to help. But you're not ready yet. I can still feel your belligerence towards me. I'd be of no use to you right now.' Peter stood up, getting ready to go. 'I'll come next week.'

He held out his hand and Harry took it with both of his. 'Thank you for coming. Thank you for not sermonising, because that's what I fully expected.'

'See you next week then. If you want me to visit, any time,

you only have to send a message and I'll be here absolutely as soon as I can.'

'Thank you for that.'

Peter sat in his car for a full ten minutes before he drove away. Thinking. He was wondering how on earth Harry had come to such a pass. Armed robbery, loving a woman who desperately searched for love from anyone who would offer it and then, when she found the real thing with Harry, lost it in terrible circumstances. How much fear had she felt while dying? Or had she laughed right to the end, never suspecting the depth of Jeremy's feelings? Was it Jeremy? Or was it in fact Harry who'd murdered her? On his own admittance, lies and deceit were the norm for him.

He'd have to pull himself together and change his mood, scrape together the remnants of his peace of mind, because he had Tamsin and Paddy coming to see him for the final talk before their wedding. He glanced at his watch. Only an hour and they'd be at the rectory. He must put his time with Harry to one side. Two people shining with love didn't want a rector in the depths of despair. It would show. He drove home and showered and changed, feeling that might help him shake off his maudlin mood. The magic worked and, when they rang the doorbell, he greeted them smiling and was rewarded by their beaming response.

'We've news!'

'You have, Paddy? What?'

'My mother's come already for the wedding. She thought she'd spend some time with us to get to know Tamsin. Well, get to know me again too.'

'That's wonderful news. I'll see her I expect, out and about. Where is she staying?'

'At Greta's. In the spare room.'

'It must be strange seeing her after all these years.'

'It is. She approves of Tamsin. I'm glad about that, though I'd have married her even if Ma didn't approve.' Paddy laughed. He was almost unrecognisable, full of self-confidence and intensely happy.

Tamsin looked at him with such loving approval that Peter wondered why on earth he'd suggested another meeting before the wedding, they were so obviously made for each other. He had no doubts about that.

They left him half an hour later, full to the brim with joy. Tamsin was to fit in some much-needed practice for an organ recital before the wedding and Paddy was going to spend the rest of the evening with his mother.

He'd had such a surprise when he'd met her that lunchtime for the first time since he was sixteen. Gone was the crushed, hopeless mother of his childhood. Instead, there stood before him a confident, energetic, jolly woman who was well dressed, good-looking, and full of charm. How had this incredible transformation come about?

They were sitting together in Greta's front room, having been left tactfully alone by Vince and Greta. He poured her a whisky which she declared she preferred and sitting opposite her, he raised his glass to her. Then he asked, 'How did it come about that you have changed so much?'

Bridget downed her whisky in one go, put the glass on the little table Paddy had pulled out for her, and said, 'In one word ... money.'

'But where from?'

'It must have been about five years after you left that your Dad became impotent, so that put a stop to a child every other year. Thank God! He could still hit me though. If anything, it got worse. But his health went rapidly downhill. He developed every ailment under the sun and then suddenly, without warning, he was dead. I think he died because he felt he was no longer a man. He just withered away really, what with the drink and that, so he did. A week after he died, I got a job. I was housekeeper to a lovely man. It was a big house, well furnished and he was kind as kind. The older children had all left home by that point. They were disgusted with your dad and his pathetic self-pitying carry-on, so there was only me and the three younger boys to look after. It sounds daft, Paddy, but I loved cleaning that man's house. He paid generously and treated me like a lady. He gave me a car of my own and taught me how to drive it so that I could collect the shopping or whatever and take him to the doctor's. I cared for him like he was the most precious person, because he was. He showed me such kindness.'

'What was he called?'

'Joseph Byrne. When he died and the will was read out, it emerged that he was the black sheep of a titled family. He left some of his money to charity and the the rest to me. His family had wanted nothing to do with him. I think probably because they didn't realise just how well off he was, so there were no disputes, just a quiet handing over of all the money. The house was sold and the money from that was mine too. So there I was, to be sure, with more money than I'd ever dreamed possible, and that ratbag of a father of yours dead and buried so he couldn't spend a penny of it. I've laughed many a time about that. If he'd been alive he'd have spent it and left nothing for me in my old age. It's like a fairy tale.'

For the first time in twenty-four years Paddy reached out to take hold of his mother's hand. 'You deserve every penny of that money, Ma. Every single penny and you hang on to it. Don't let anyone take a penny off you. He wanted *you* to have it or he wouldn't have left it to you. Enjoy.'

She rooted in her bag and pulled out a well-fingered photograph. 'That's him. It was taken about ten years ago, I suppose.'

Not wishing to give offence, Paddy studied the photo very thoroughly and saw a man he could well have liked. He was a tall, smiling man. He seemed relaxed and happy, with thick white hair brushed back and deep-set bright eyes that looked out in a kindly fashion. To Paddy, he looked a generous man and he was glad. 'Good-looking man, Ma. I can see he'd be kind.'

She took the photo back and gazed quietly at it. 'The best. The very best. Pity I didn't meet him twenty-five years previously, but then I wouldn't have had you, would I?'

'No, but then I haven't been much help.'

'Thanks, Paddy, for liking him. He wanted us to get married, you know, but I wouldn't.'

'Why not?'

'I'd had enough of that side of life and I just didn't want it again. Not likely. Everything else but not that.'

'Where do you live now? I'm so glad you got my letter. I did wonder if you'd still be there.'

'I live in one of those houses alongside the river that I used to envy so much back in the bad old days. You know, the ones with the balcony and the wrought ironwork over the front door. I've done up our old house and I rent it out and, since then, I've bought two more in the same row and I rent those out too. So I'm well set up, I am. Like I've never been in all my life. Isn't it grand?'

'I've always regretted leaving you with him. I should have stayed and protected you, but when he knocked me down after the school sent me to have my broken arm set, that was the final straw.'

'I was glad you had the courage to leave. He didn't deserve to be a father to you children, and see, you've turned out so good. I'm so proud, and marrying that girl! Well, I can't believe it.'

'She is lovely, isn't she? I shan't treat her like Dad treated you. He should have been horsewhipped for it.'

'All water under the bridge, Paddy, and I'm not going to let it hurt me any more. There's too much life to be lived, you know. And don't let it hurt you any more, either. You did the right thing and now you and I have a chance to live our lives like we should. You seeing your Ma as and when, and me getting to know you again. Aren't we going to have a good time, you and me? I almost wish I lived here in one of those nice little cottages on the green. I saw a poster nailed to a tree saying about the embroidery group. I could join, couldn't I? Fancy me embroidering! All ladylike! Paddy, I'm tired and I'm going to bed now, if that's OK with you. It's been a long day. Goodnight. What time do you leave in the morning?'

'Ten to eight.'

'I shall be up and have breakfast with you before you go. Won't that be nice?'

She opened the door and then turned back to say rather shyly, 'Greta tells me the reception is at the Royal Oak. Well, I have the money to do better than that for you and Tamsin and I shall set about it in the morning. No. No protests. It'll still be a country wedding, but I've plans to, shall we say, upgrade it. I know about the cake that's already been planned, but I've visions of a carriage and such to bring the bride to church and—'

'Ma! She lives too close by for that.'

'Well, there's got to be something. I know! You could have it to leave the church and go ...'

'Go, where?'

'The Old Barn! Greta told me about. How beautiful it is. I really fancy the idea of that. I'll talk to Tamsin first thing.'

'But we have it all planned.'

'I know you have, but we can invite the whole village if we do it my way.'

'We wanted a quiet wedding.'

'A quiet wedding for my eldest son! Not likely. Come on, let me have my way.'

'Only if you can persuade Tamsin and she's not upset.'

'Right! You're on. Night, Paddy. Sleep tight. Leave her to me.'

The bubbly Irish woman who was Paddy's mother swept Tamsin along on a tide of such enthusiasm that Tamsin could not resist her. 'But …'

'No buts. I want to make it the loveliest of weddings. Not formal, but jolly and really happy, because that's what you are and so you should be. So that's what the wedding will be like. I'll square it with the pub.' She rubbed her fingers together as though fingering fifty-pound notes and winked. 'Sure, money goes a long way in circumstances like these and I shall sort it, believe me.'

Bridget hugged Tamsin till she was breathless. 'You're the best daughter-in-law-to-be any woman could hope to have. So beautiful and talented … Just gorgeous. You and I will be real friends.' She smiled at Tamsin and then said so softly it was barely audible, 'You see, I've a lot to make up to Paddy for failing him all those years. Now it's my chance to put things right. Will you let me?'

'Mrs Cleary—'

Bridget wagged her finger. 'No. What did I tell you? I'm Bridget.'

Tamsin laughed. 'Bridget then. Of course I will. I love him more than life itself and I would be delighted to be able to ask all the village. It was only the cost that was holding us back. You see, I don't have parents to help.'

'Then if you will, you can have me for a substitute mother. Well, perhaps a second mother, not a substitute. If that's all right?'

'I think maybe that could be lovely.'

'Good! Then we'll get cracking. You and I together. We'll make it fabulous for Paddy.'

Chapter 23

It was the following Sunday when Peter announced at the ten o'clock service that he was intending to leave the parish. The shockwaves that went round the congregation were almost palpable. 'I can no longer be your guide and mentor when we are at such odds with our objectives. This church and its survival as a vibrant anchor for everyone in the parish is at risk and I honestly feel, despite praying long and hard about it, that I can no longer hold my place as rector of this parish. Everywhere I go, in spite of all the very dramatic happenings that have taken place here recently, I am met with such opposition to my suggestion that we solve our financial problems by asking permission to sell the church silver that I feel I can no longer justifiably continue here as rector.

'Caroline and I have spoken endlessly about this question and we both feel the opposition is too strong. Therefore I shall be leaving the parish as soon as it is possible. We have had all these wonderfully happy years here, we've seen Beth and Alex born and grow up here, but as this year they will hopefully be leaving for university, it feels the best moment to leave. You will be for ever in our hearts and I hope and pray that my time here has been beneficial to every single one of you in some way. I have been serving this parish for almost twenty years now, maybe I should make room for another.' He paused to regain control of his voice and then continued, 'Our final hymn this morning is that well-loved hymn of Charles Wesley, "Love Divine, all Loves Excelling".' Tamsin Goodenough began to play, but the heart of the congregation was not in the singing of it.

Peter was so deeply affected by what he'd announcd that he couldn't have spoken another word at that moment. Despite all his persuasive powers, he had totally failed to change anyone's mind, so he felt his decision to leave was inevitable.

He knew all about the upset he would cause, but there came a time in everyone's ministry when difficult decisions had to be made for the good of everyone, and this was one of them. He had to let the congregation sing the hymn because he had no voice with which to sing himself. He looked up to catch Caroline's eye, but her head was down and she obviously wasn't singing either, so he could get no reassurance there.

For the first time ever in his ministry in Turnham Malpas, Peter's heart was so heavy that he didn't stand at the door to shake hands with everyone, but disappeared into the vestry and began disrobing.

Zack knocked on the door. 'It's Zack Hooper, sir. Can I come in?' He carefully closed the door behind him. Then he said, 'I'd no idea it would come to this. No idea at all. After all you've done for us. It's a truly sad day. I can see what you mean. But this ... How can we ever replace you?'

'I don't know, Zack, but someone will fill my shoes, believe me.'

'We don't want someone, we want *you*.'

Peter straightened his leather belt and secured his cross in it. Then he said, 'Nothing and no one will change my mind, so don't even try.'

'As you wish, but ...'

'I'll go out by the vestry door and go straight home. Good morning, Zack. See you at evensong.'

'Yes, sir. Right.'

Peter went straight to his study when he got in, closed the door firmly behind him, and sat at his desk. He knew his decision was the right one. If the congregation wasn't behind him, there was nothing more he could do here. It was almost twenty years since he'd taken his first service and now it was at an end. He knew deep inside himself that it was time he moved on, but at the same time …

'Dad!' It was Alex. Peter couldn't help noticing how closely his son resembled him. He was tall with thick, red-blond hair, bright blue eyes and a serious expression. It was himself to a T.

'Yes?'

'Sorry it's come to this, Dad. It must be rotten.'

'It is. But what can I do? There's just too much opposition. I can see what they mean, their arguments are very sound, but they're not really founded in reality. More on sentimentality.'

'But they love you so. Wherever I go, everyone loves you. I've never heard a wrong word about you all my life until now. They are saying such cruel things. I simply can't believe they could turn like this. It isn't fair, not after everything you've seen them through.' Alex slumped down on the sofa and stared at the carpet.

Beth came in and slid her arms round his neck. She kissed the back of his head. Coming round to face him she said softly, 'Love you, Dad.' Putting her arms around his neck again she laid her cheek against his. 'Love you, Dad, so much. I'm so very, very, very sorry it's come to this. They must all have taken leave of their senses to be saying the things they are. I overheard someone talking in the store when they didn't know I was in there and it took all my self-control not to leap out from behind the soups and give them a piece of my mind.'

'You never said.'

'I know. I didn't because I was too scared. I saw what was coming. But if it's how you feel, that you must leave, then so be it. But we love you, don't we, Alex, even if they don't.'

Alex didn't look up, but he did nod his head.

Caroline kicked the door open and walked into the study

carrying a tray of four mugs of coffee. 'Here we are.' She handed them round and then sat herself beside Alex.

'If that doorbell goes,' she said, 'or someone knocks, we'll ignore it.' So they sat in silence, sipping coffee and trying to come to terms with Peter's announcement. They'd known it was coming that morning, but hearing it actually said had come as a shock. All three had been convinced Peter would change his mind. But he hadn't so there they were lamenting their predicament.

'Of course,' said Alex, 'they haven't had a chance to change their minds yet, have they? They might when they understand what they've brought about.'

'It's too late for that.' Peter put his coffee mug down on the tray. 'Now that I've said I can't stay. Maybe, in the end, it will be a good thing. Perhaps I'm needed elsewhere.'

'But,' wailed Beth, 'I love it here.'

'I know, I know. It is very comfortable living here. Too comfortable, perhaps. Perhaps I need a new challenge.'

'Perhaps,' said Alex, 'we all need a new challenge.'

Beth burst out with, 'Our results next week might provide us with that very thing. A new challenge and perhaps not going on to university like we'd hoped for.'

Alex rubbed his face to refresh himself. 'Maybe I'm not destined to be a doctor then.'

'Nor me an archeologist. But I wouldn't know what else to do. I've always wanted to be one. Well, nearly always. What on earth would I do if I don't get in? Thursday's coming all too quickly. Hell's bells.' Beth laid her head on Peter's shoulder. 'Dad, what shall I do?'

'Darling child, at this moment I have absolutely no idea about anything. Sorry.'

'I propose we leave the house by the back door and let everyone stew whilst we recover ourselves. Come on. Strip off your cassock, Peter, and let's just *go*.' Caroline leaped to her feet in an effort to inject some energy into them all and they fled out to the garage, got the car out, and just went. Anywhere but Turnham Malpas.

Chapter 24

'My God! Did I hear you right? Why hasn't the man consulted me? I would have dealt with it immediately.'

'What would you have done?'

Craddock Fitch poured his coffee out into his porcelain cup and sipped it, black, hot and sugarless. His secretary watched warily. It was his tone of voice she was unsure about and she really wished she'd never told him.

'I'd have given him the bloody money, wouldn't I? I won't have him resigning, it's ridiculous. How will we manage without him?'

'Perfectly well, I imagine.'

'What's got into you this morning?'

'Nothing. But he is a bit on the holy side, isn't he?'

'What else can you expect, woman? You are being plain daft. The man is our conscience, our collective conscience, didn't you realise that?'

'Not especially, no. It's the command he has over people round here, the "only if the rector agrees" type of authority. Well, now he's got his comeuppance. They won't agree, so that's that, he's off.'

'Much more of that attitude and *you'll* be off for good! Maybe it's time *you* went too. You're an idiot, woman. He's what holds us all together. He's the glue.'

'That's not what you said when it was you wanting to sell the church silver all those years ago.'

This remark brought about a pause in Craddock Fitch's

onslaught. The fool was quite right. He pushed that acknowledgement aside and remarked instead, 'Your trouble is that you're not religious.'

'And you are?' His secretary raised a sceptical eyebrow.

Mr Fitch was so angry he could have struck her down. In fact, he wished for a biblical plague that really would strike her down. She'd worked for him for far too long, that was obvious. She'd become insolent.

'One more sarcastic remark like that and it'll be you leaving. Right?'

'Are you sacking me?'

He hesitated briefly and then said, 'If you fancy it, yes, I am. You can go out that door right now. I've had enough of your kind of insolence.'

'Right! OK then. As of this minute, I am no longer in your employ. I'll let Human Resources know what you owe me.'

'I never said I was paying you *money* to leave.'

She paused at the door, her hand on the knob in case a quick exit was needed. 'You will though. It's the law. I shall need to be paid off.'

'You'll be laid out if you're not careful. Right!'

'That's threatening, that is. I could sue.'

'Sue away, I shall be glad to see the back of you.'

So, to his surprise, she left. They'd had rows before, but she'd always turned up the next morning as though their upset had never happened. It appeared to him that this time was very different. All this because he was so upset about Peter. How could this have all taken place without him knowing? Kate was his eyes and ears, but this had landed on him without warning.

Peter! What he'd said about him being his conscience was absolutely true. He mightn't attend church regularly but he did rely on the man for keeping him straight on moral questions. One look deep into his eyes and he, Craddock Fitch, was putty in his hands and all the best in him came to the fore. He stormed up and down his office thinking up schemes to keep Peter right where he belonged.

Then he remembered what Kate had said to him once in the first year of their marriage: Don't brandish money about in broad daylight, but let people benefit from it by stealth. Of course, that was it. He'd donate the money the church needed anonymously. How? He tapped the side of his nose with his index finger. And then he realised that he knew exactly who would help him keep it secret. The person in question followed in the same footsteps as his father, able to keep secrets better than anyone he knew. A chip off the old block, but much nicer.

Then the church could keep the silver and he could keep Peter in the church. Of course. Immediately, as of now, he'd do that very thing. The repairs could be done and no one would be making a single wasteful, unnecessary sacrifice. He rang for his secretary and was surprised to find he got no reply. He marched into her office to find her collecting her bits and pieces together.

'Now, now. Our little tiffs don't really mean anything, do they? Come now ...'

He struggled to remember her name and couldn't. Was it Penny? Paula? Pat?

Damn it. 'I need my car. I'm going out.'

'You know where it is, go and get it. Remember I'm no longer in your employ.'

'I didn't know you meant it.'

'I certainly did and so did you. I can find far more pleasant work than being a secretary to a mean-minded, arrogant man like you. Good morning.'

So Mr Fitch set out on his mission of mercy sitting in the back of his Rolls muttering about women this, and women that, and then he remembered he was married to one and smiled. He patted his pocket to ensure he had his cheque book with him and marched into Neal and Neal Chartered Accountants. He saw Hugh Neal and made all the arrangements. He choked slightly when he made out the cheque, but it salved his conscience and made sure, he hoped, of a place in heaven for him when the time came. Then he remembered Kate and hoped heaven wouldn't be round the next corner for a long while yet. He followed this up with a visit to the rectory and, to his delight, found Peter in his study.

Dottie had answered the door and, while she was dying to put her ear to the study door to find out what he'd come about, she didn't. Instead she polished every surface in the sitting room to within an inch of its life, as always.

Mr Fitch had come up with a clever plan. He was going to try to persuade Peter not to leave as a way of putting him off the scent of tracking the donation to its source. Peter would assume, from their conversation, that it couldn't possibly be Craddock Fitch who made the donation since he'd tried to get him to stay with no mention of a massive contribution to the church funds to help persuade him.

Craddock Fitch went home rejoicing at his tactics and the first person he met was Jeremy Mayer. He was outside, smoking a cigar on the terrace, and Craddock was forcibly struck by how dreadful he looked. My God! The man was dying on his feet. Surely he wasn't pining for the slut who'd been his wife. He was well shot of her, as Craddock knew from personal experience.

'Jeremy! You OK? You don't look too good.'

Jeremy nodded his head.

'I didn't know you smoked.'

He got another nod.

'Not heard any more about, you know …?'

Jeremy looked at him, straight in the face, and Craddock saw the pain in his eyes. Suddenly he felt ashamed of what had happened in the past.

Jeremy shook his head.

'I'll join you with one of those. It's years since I smoked one. After the morning I've had, I could do with one.'

Jeremy offered him his cigar case and Craddock helped himself. Then Jeremy lit it for him and the two of them stood smoking on the terrace, their backs to the big house, staring out across Home Park towards the Old Barn.

'I always knew.'

'What?' asked Craddock Fitch.

'About you and Venetia.'

Mr Fitch coughed a cloud of smoke from his throat and lied, 'I guessed you'd think that. You're quite wrong on that score, I'd nothing to do with her.'

'Beggar you for it. She was mine.'

'Let's be honest here, Jeremy—'

'No, it's for me to be honest, not you. I'm the honest one. I didn't stray with someone else's wife.' He remained staring into the distance. 'I loved her. People might think she wasn't worth it, but I loved her. I put up with that actor fellow Hugo, this man, that man, even her passion for the rector, though that never came to anything of course.'

'I should think not. You shouldn't even think along those lines. The rector, indeed. I'm shocked.' And he was too. Not just shocked, but *appalled*. What was the matter with the man? How had he landed himself with Jeremy letting his hair down like this? In an intuitive flash he saw the truth; this was guilt talking. It was Jeremy who'd killed her.

No, he must be wrong. Not old Jeremy. He'd bullied him for years until he'd grown bored of it and Kate had persuaded him to treat Jeremy like a human being. They'd got on much better after that.

'Is there something you're trying to tell me? If so, spit it out.'

Jeremy turned to face him instead of staring across at the Old Barn. He slowly brought his arm back and Craddock Fitch, totally unaware of the man's intention, watched as Jeremy's fist shot out and landed fair and square on his nose. In spite of his very evident exhaustion, Jeremy's punch was powerful and the blood flowed.

'That's from Venetia, for using her as a prostitute.' Then Jeremy walked back into the house, leaving Craddock Fitch mopping up blood with his immaculate handkerchief. It didn't seem to want to stop, so he went inside to find his secretary. Then he remembered, too late, that she'd sacked herself that morning. And all because of him. Damn everything this morning. Everything and everybody. What was the point of giving all that money to the church and then having a morning like this one? But somewhere deep down, Craddock Fitch knew he'd got the punch because it was well deserved and nothing to do with God, nor the donation.

The church treasurer, Hugh Neal, rang Peter early on the Wednesday morning to tell him about the massive anonymous donation the church had received.

'*How much*? Have I heard you right? We're talking six figures here?'

'Yes, we are. Fantastic, isn't it?'

'Who from?'

'It's anonymous, Peter. I can't say, can I? I paid it into the bank before they changed their minds.'

'Who on earth can it be, Hugh?'

'Not the faintest. If I were you, I'd get using it for the repairs in case they ask for it back! Only joking, but it is a godsend. Literally. Be glad.' Hugh refrained from saying, 'So you won't need to resign now.' But he did say, 'Is someone on high telling you something here, Peter? Be seeing you.'

'I can't believe it. What a huge surprise! I'm completely overwhelmed. Are you sure you've got it right? I mean, it is such a colossal sum.'

'Of course it's right, I counted the noughts! Several times! Be thankful. Rejoice!'

'I will. Thank you, Hugh.'

Peter sat staring into space thinking about this enormous windfall. Was it money from Ralph's estate, perhaps? It would be the kind of gesture he would make. Maybe there wasn't anyone to inherit the money so he'd left it to the church instead. No, of course not, he was quite wrong. Craddock Fitch? No, he'd been that morning to beg him not to leave and he hadn't mentioned a bribe, so it wasn't him. He rang Caroline at the practice and told her the good news.

'Oh, darling! Talk about pennies from heaven. My word. That's marvellous.' It was on the tip of her tongue to add that now he needn't leave Turnham Malpas, but she left it unsaid because it might well be that he needed to go just the same, in spite of the money. But who on earth would give that enormous amount to the church? As far as she was concerned, it must be Craddock Fitch, though he'd never given money on this scale before.

The news broke in the bar that night. It was Zack who told everyone about the phenomenal good fortune. 'True as I'm sitting here. It was someone who wishes to remain anonymous. Not even the rector has been told, so it's no good quizzing him. It's a vast sum of money. The rector told me this afternoon in my shed over a cup of tea. He's absolutely gobsmacked and he's got no idea who's given it.'

Dottie said, 'Mr Fitch came to see him this morning. Is it 'im?'

'Apparently not. No.'

'Never mind who's given it, how *much* did they give? Do we know that?'

Zack knew they'd be amazed, so he delayed his reply for as long as he possibly could till eventually Sylvia said, 'For heaven's sake, put us out of our misery.'

'Guess how much you think it'll be.'

Someone suggested twenty-five thousand pounds, but then they said that that would be ridiculous.

Zack shook his head.

'More?'

Zack nodded. So the estimates went up and up and when they'd reached one hundred thousand, they couldn't believe it when Zack nodded his head again.

Dottie declared that they couldn't go on guessing. 'For heaven's sake tell us, Zack,' she said.

So he did. 'One hundred and fifty thousand pounds.'

Every single person drinking in the bar stopped what they were doing, overcome with disbelief. Georgie, coming back in after a quiet ten-minute break to recoup her energy, couldn't understand the silence. 'What's the matter? Has someone died?' Then she remembered Jimmy and wished she hadn't said that.

'My God!' said Willie. 'My God!'

'Bloody hell!' said someone else.

'Blimey!' said the Londoner called Royston, the one with the weekend cottage.

'Cripes!' muttered Sylvia and took a great gulp of her gin and tonic. She didn't swallow it properly and choked. Willie had to bang her on her back to bring her round. She wiped the tears from her cheeks and said croakily, 'Whoever in all this world could give all that to the church?'

But there was no answer to that. It was some time before anyone thought of the consequences of this vast sum, and it was Zack who said the most important consequence out loud. 'We shan't have to sell the church silver now.'

'More importantly, the rector, bless him, won't feel he has to leave now.' This was said by Dottie, who had felt ill ever since the big announcement on Sunday in church. She didn't think she could bear the idea of the rector leaving because she so loved her housekeeping at the rectory. She knew full well that, with her past, they shouldn't have allowed her over the doorstep, but they did and for that she would be eternally grateful.

'You'll be pleased, Dottie, that they won't be going?' said Vera.

'Oh yes. It's a privilege to work there, all their lovely furniture and that, and such nice people. I love Beth as though she was my own. I love Alex too, so like his dad.'

'Like me, you never had no children, did you, Dottie?'

'No, I didn't, Sylvia. I never really wanted any till it was all too late. When you're young there's all the time in the world, then suddenly there's none.' She stood up and raising her voice said, 'I propose a toast, everyone, to whoever it is who's given that money. God bless 'em, I say.' And they all clinked glasses and were grateful for the anonymous donor who'd stepped in and saved the day.

The anonymous donor, at this moment, was entertaining a police superintendent in his sitting room. 'The man is dying on his feet, superintendent, believe me.'

'We have no evidence. Not a scrap.'

'I'm sure I'm correct. In his right mind, he would never have punched me, ever. He's just not that kind of man. He's an educated man. He may have been married to a tart but he always treats everyone as a gentleman should. '

'Grief can do funny things to people.'

'Well, I find it hard to believe he's grieving. You see, she wasn't worth that kind of loving. Honestly, believe me. Did you know her?'

'Never met her actually.'

'Tart through and through. She was free with her favours and it didn't matter who it was. Dustman or duke. And, what is significant is that the rector caught them at it in Home Park one evening. Jeremy must have been absolutely mortified, enough for his temper to get up and to do her in. How did he do her in?'

'Strictly speaking, Mr Fitch, I am not permitted to reveal that. The post-mortem isn't complete anyway and, even if it was, I still wouldn't.'

'Of course, of course. Quite right. I know I've no evidence as such, but he is talking like a guilty man. He is. But I can't convince you, can I?'

'We can leave no stone unturned and, other than Harry Dickinson, we have absolutely no clues as to a possible murderer. Therefore I will question Mr Mayer again and see if I can—'

'Good man. Good man.' Mr Fitch got to his feet and held out his hand. 'Thank you, I'm sure I'm right. He's got guilt written all over him. Thank you. If it is him, I shall be very upset. The poor chap's had a rotten time with that wife of his playing away. Go carefully with him, won't you?'

'I will. I'll interview him again tomorrow. I'm sure it's Harry Dickinson though. He lies better than anyone I have ever known. One lie after another, and we can't catch him out.'

'He certainly fooled everyone in the village.'

'Must go. Thanks for the whisky.'

'A pleasure, believe me. What seems so surprising to me is that they both loved Venetia to bits. Both of them. Amazing, isn't it? A woman like her?'

'Nothing so queer as folk, Mr Fitch.' He examined Mr Fitch's swollen face. 'Hope the face improves. Goodnight!'

Peter and Caroline were both late to bed that night. Peter because he was reading and didn't stop until he found his eyes closing and the book falling out of his hand, and Caroline because she'd not been keeping up with new medical research and was working hard to catch up.

Peter turned on the alarm, Caroline switched off the light and the doorbell rang with an urgent clamouring which couldn't be ignored. Beth appeared on the landing and Alex shouted down from the attic, 'There's someone at the door. Shall I go?'

'Stay where you are, it's most likely for me.' Peter snatched his dressing gown from the back of the bedroom door and fled downstairs. Whoever it was had now begun hammering with their fists on the door. Peter undid the bolts and the person begging to be allowed in fell on his knees on the hall floor as Peter undid the lock. 'I need to talk. Sorry it's so late. Just need to t-talk.'

'Come in. Let's go in my study.'

It was clear that Jeremy had a terrible weight on his mind. One didn't have to be exceptionally perceptive to see that was his problem: the deep grooves down either side of his mouth, the ashen, almost grey-green colour of his skin, his bowed posture and, most of all, his tortured eyes, told a story.

'I always keep a bottle of brandy hidden in my study for cases such as this. OK?'

Peter didn't even get an acknowledgement, but he poured out a measure in the small glass he kept for the purpose and put it into Jeremy's hand. 'Drink it steadily and that's an order.'

Minutes passed and, so far, Jeremy had said nothing so Peter decided to speak up. 'Now, Jeremy. Do you need to unburden yourself? Perhaps you want to tell me something you can't keep to yourself any longer? I'm more than willing to listen, if it will help.' Peter took the empty glass from him and waited.

'I had to come. I had to tell someone. I just can't hide it any longer.'

'You'll feel better when you've told me. I make a good listener.'

'It's Venetia. You know I loved her.'

'You did, you told me so.'

Jeremy nodded. 'All along I knew she wasn't, shall we say, top drawer. No education that counted, not like you or me. I got a first at Cambridge, when I was young and full of life. You wouldn't think so to look at me now.' He half laughed at himself. 'Heading for great things, me, they all said. But I'd no interest in succeeding. Anything for a quiet life. With a name like Sidney Milton Mogg, how could I possibly succeed at anything?' Jeremy paused and gazed into space, a sob occasionally breaking the silence. Suddenly he hauled himself out of the sofa and blindly headed for the door to escape. Peter protested, 'Don't go. Don't go. Stay and talk to me.'

Very softly, Peter said again, 'Don't go, Jeremy, stay and talk. Please. I know it's late, but I don't mind if you have things you need to speak of for your own good.' He laid a restraining hand on Jeremy's arm. 'Please, just sit down and let me hear you out.'

Jeremy stood looking at him, his eyes full of pain. 'You'll listen, won't you? You won't be judgemental? You won't laugh at my foolishness?'

'I'll listen and I won't be any of those things. You know that.'

Jeremy sank down again, dropping like a stone as though he had no strength left.

'I met her in a massage parlour in the West End. She worked there as the receptionist. We got talking and when she asked me what I did for a living I said "nothing". I hadn't got a job at the time so it was true. She mistook that for thinking I was so well off I didn't need to work and, when I happened to mention that I'd been to Cambridge, that did it. She thought I must definitely be well off.

'To my shame, I didn't enlighten her because she thrilled me and I wanted her so badly. She was so fascinated by me, I can't think why, that before we'd known each other a month she was living with me. She found out soon enough that there wasn't much money about, but for some reason she stuck with me through thick and thin, and I loved her for that. I loved every inch of her, her clothes which were usually outrageous, her overdone make-up, her body because it was good, everyone could see that. I also loved her for her sense of humour. You know what it's like to love someone.' He looked up and half smiled at Peter, as if acknowledging that they were one of a kind. 'At that time I could impress people and get them to lend me money, almost without asking. My CV was impressive, you see. Public school, a first in classics, it all spoke of reliability. How mistaken could they be? Venetia could spend money faster than anyone alive could earn it.

'I've always known you are a man of the world, not some soft in the head, self-righteous cleric, so I can tell you what she did and it won't cause offence. She began making money as a prostitute, with taste, if that's possible. She wasn't standing on street corners, you know. Night after night, I had to make myself scarce so she could have the flat to invite them back to.

'It tortured me. It broke my heart but, when you've no money and no job and you've sunk so low you haven't enough money to buy food, you do whatever you can. Anyway, she met this man with more money than sense and he offered to help us buy Turnham House, which we longed to do as soon as we saw it up for sale. We wanted to set it up as a health club. The money we spent. Oh, God!' Jeremy drew in a great, shuddering breath and started to stutter. 'As you k-know ... it failed, f-failed almost before it got s-started. It was a terrible blow. You see, I thought it was something I could really make a go of. Fortunately, Craddock Fitch saved the day when he bought it from us and we've never looked back since. We did so well out of it there was no need for her to ... There was no more need for her to ...' Jeremy fidgeted with his hands as though that explained what he meant without the need for words.

Peter was tempted to break the silence but he found the words simply wouldn't come. He was horrified by what Jeremy had gone through. Imagine, he thought, loving Venetia like he did and knowing that was happening, night after night.

'Then, as you know, Harry Dickinson appeared these last few weeks. This time I knew for certain it was different. This time it was for real. She didn't know that to start with, but I did. I saw the signs and I could see she would leave me, that was the way it would go. Worse, she was so taken with him that she told me everything they got up to. She taunted me with it.'

By now Jeremy was shaking with distress, yet he appeared to have a strong inner core that made him determined to make a full confession, leaving nothing out. 'She came home the night you saw them in Home Park and told me. She said how shaming it was. Anyone but you, she said. Absolutely anyone, but you. But she loved him so much she could still laugh it off, it was all just another part of the excitement of their affair. I still had some standards left then, and I was destroyed by that. She was dead that night really, but it took me a while to get round to doing it. She'd had too much to drink one night, much too much, and I'd encouraged her so she wouldn't realise what I was going to do. I wanted to make it easy for her. She would be too drunk to know, if you see what I mean. And I did it. I smothered her while she was full of the drink. She lay there on the bed wearing one of her beautiful nightgowns, dead, but still beautiful in my eyes, and I wished to God I hadn't done it. It was the most appalling betrayal. But there she was ... she was gone, and it was all far, far too late.'

Peter knew it was coming, but when it was *said* out loud, he was struck dumb.

Eventually, having sat there for a few moments unable to speak, Peter said, 'In view of what you have told me I think we'd better go and see the police.'

'No, no. You tell them to come and arrest me.'

'I can't. I really can't. You were provoked beyond what any man should have to endure. She tormented you, telling you it was me who saw them and she knew, full well, what it would do to a man like you.'

Jeremy came out in defence of Venetia. 'You can't blame *her*, she couldn't help herself. She loved him like I loved her. It was all my fault for letting it all happen, for allowing her to sell herself, instead of getting stuck in and earning the money myself. She couldn't help herself loving Harry, it was true love for the first time in her life. It was my fault for not loving her enough.' Jeremy groaned out loud in despair.

'I'm going to get the car out of the garage and take you to the police station. You must tell them like you've told me. It's the only way to regain peace for your soul. If we go quietly now, while everyone is asleep, it will be so much more dignified for you. If I call the police they'll be here with all their bells and whistles and everyone will know. If I take you, we can slip away down Pipe and Nook Lane and no one will know. The police will take the circumstances into account, I'm sure. And if you give yourself up it will help your case.'

'They are on to me, I feel it in my bones.'

'Then let's go. Now.' Peter put a hand under Jeremy's elbow and heaved him up.

'May I use your bathroom before we go?'

'Of course. The downstairs lavatory is under the stairs. There, look. I'll just tell Caroline where I'm going and get my clothes on. Right? I won't be a moment.'

Peter shot upstairs and found Caroline still sitting up in bed reading. 'It's Jeremy, isn't it? Is he confessing?'

'Mmm. I'm taking him to the police station. Right? Be as quick as I can.'

'Take care, darling.'

Peter flung his clothes on and raced downstairs. He picked up his car keys from the hall table, unlocked the back door again, and waited for his passenger. He was taking far too long. He put his ear to the door and could hear him sobbing. Women's tears hurt, but men's tears were ten times worse to listen to. Peter knocked on the door. 'OK in there? I'm ready for the off.'

It took a moment for Jeremy to unlock the door and, when he did, he'd wiped away the tears and it was as though, having made a decision, he was more composed. 'I'll go home. I'll go in the morning myself.'

There was such desperation in his voice that Peter guessed exactly what it was Jeremy would do in the night in his house all alone. He'd kill himself. But he couldn't deceive Jeremy by pretending he was driving him home but instead speed away to Culworth and the police station. That simply wouldn't be honourable.

Peter sat Jeremy down on the chair in the hall, stood in front of him, and asked him outright, slowly and firmly, 'I believe you are thinking of killing yourself in the night. Am I right?'

Jeremy shuddered and Peter could scarcely hear his reply, he spoke so softly. 'I should have known you'd see through my subterfuge. I was a fool to think I'd get away with it. I'm in your hands. You decide for me. I can't make any more decisions, I'm lost.'

'My one and only decision is to take you straight away to the police station in Culworth. I can't, in all conscience, take you home knowing what you might do. You'll have to make this a time for being as honourable and truthful as any self-respecting man should be. I'm sorry, but that's how I see it.'

Jeremy looked up at him with dead eyes, got to his feet, and followed him out of the back door.

Chapter 25

Paddy's mother Bridget had got her own way. She'd rearranged the wedding reception, organised a harpist, consulted Jimbo about the menu, the flower arrangements, the gifts for each guest, the place name cards, and the dancing with a smart band from London. Finally, with everything in place for a wonderful wedding for her eldest son, she visited Grandmama with a fresh idea she had in mind.

Grandmama, now at last back in her own cottage having recovered from her ghastly experience in Sykes Wood, was beginning to enjoy life again. Especially as she didn't have Sykes to walk each day. Caroline and Peter, with eager support from Beth and Alex, had decided to give Sykes a home.

So when she opened her door and found Bridget Cleary standing there, she was absolutely ready for any proposal.

'Bridget Cleary, Paddy's mother.'

'Yes, I've seen you around. Nice to meet you, do come in.'

Bridget appreciated the delights of the cottage and said so in no uncertain terms. 'My, this cottage is beautiful, sure it is. So unusual and much bigger than you'd expect from the outside. Such character and very much enhanced by your interior design skills. I love the curtains, may I see the kitchen?' She stepped straight into it without waiting. 'Small, but everything you need is there. And a larder, wonderful! I love larders, they're so easy to keep clean. Did you plan it? You must have, it's wonderful. Up to the minute but so ... so appropriately country style. I love it.'

'Thank you. Yes, I did plan it. I love it too.'

'It's so light, that's what's lovely about it. Some of the cottages round the green are really quite dark, aren't they? Small windows, you know. But this ... I've come with a proposition. Shall we sit down?'

Grandmama found Bridget rather overwhelming, yet so nice with it. She thought to herself that she could do with someone like her for a friend.

Bridget plumped herself down on the sofa saying, 'Now, this proposition. Tamsin is a dear, beautiful girl and my Paddy is so lucky to have her. She's a delight and so talented. She played some pieces on her piano for me last night and it was out of this world. What a talent. What a talent! Now, this proposition. I would like to rent the cottage that belonged to Jimmy. Paddy tells me you've redesigned it, refurbished it, and it's vacant at the moment. Is that right?'

'Yes, but ...'

'Yes? Can I have it?'

'The thing is, I want it to be a long-term let, not a week here and a week there, you understand. Not like a holiday cottage.'

'Oh, that's what I want. A home I can come to as and when I have the time. I'd like to stay for a few weeks, go home and come back. I'd pay the rent three months in advance, no messing, every three months on the dot. How about it? I'd move in after the wedding. What do you say?'

'You mean long term?'

Bridget nodded her head vigorously. 'Of course long term. For years, and I shan't expect a discount for long term. I pay my own way and thank God I can. God has been great and glorious to me these last twenty years. Let's hope it stays that way. We could have some rare old times together, you and I. Eh? Don't you think?'

'Well, yes, we could. I'd enjoy the company.'

'First of September for three months in advance. I tell you

what, I'll write the cheque this very mimute, no time like the present.' Bridget whisked her cheque book out, rested it on the little table by the side of the sofa and wrote rapidly. Then she signed it with a flourish and handed it over. 'There we are, all signed and sealed.'

'You've not seen the cottage yet. You'd better see it, surely?'

'Sure I will. Tell you what, I'll go and take a look round while you put the kettle on. How about that?'

'Certainly. Here's the key. It's furnished. I cleared a lot out when Jimmy died, I got rid of his old furniture and put new furniture in. New beds too. The bathroom and kitchen are new too. I decorated everywhere as well.'

'Just what I want, furnished. It'll save me a lot of bother. Key?'

'It's next door but one. It's called Jimmy's Cottage. Jimmy left it to me in his will.'

'Wonderful. Won't be two ticks. Milk, no sugar.' Bridget clutched the key and left in a whirl, leaving her handbag on the sofa as though they'd been friends for years. And that was what Grandmama liked about her; her spontaneity. Wonderful.

The tea tray was ready and the tea brewed when Bridget came back. There was a light in her eyes that was a pleasure to see. 'Like it?' asked Grandmama.

'I most certainly do.'

'You can call me Katherine.'

'You call me Bridget then.'

'I'll pour the tea, shall I?'

Bridget nodded. 'Isn't this nice? It's lovely at Vince and Greta's but not like it is here. This is great. Thanks, yes, I'll have a biscuit. A great one for biscuits, I am. I could live on 'em, though I don't. I'm a great believer in good food well prepared, plus plenty of exercise.'

'I like the idea of good food, but not plenty of exercise. My exercise days are over.'

They sipped their tea and ate their biscuits in complete harmony, chatting in general about absolutely anything. Then Bridget looked at the clock. 'Heavens above, I promised I'd go and visit the rector about the service. Got to go.' And she did, piling their things on the tray and carrying it into the kitchen and leaving in a flurry.

What a thoroughly pleasant person, thought Grandmama. She'll be a friend for me when she's here, a friend of the kind I haven't got in this village. They're kindly and friendly in the village, but they don't like me much. But Bridget Cleary has become my friend in an instant, and I like her very much. She carefully put the cheque away in her handbag, ready for the bank the next time she went into Culworth. She wasn't without money, but that cheque four times a year would be very useful. Strange how things work out. Harry goes, Bridget comes. She dwelt on Harry for a while and wondered how he was getting on and what his sentence would be when he finally came up in court.

Bridget arrived breathless at the rectory five minutes late. 'Oh, my word. You must be the rector's daughter. I've heard all about you. I've an appointment to see your dad?'

Beth invited Bridget in saying, 'Good afternoon, Mrs Cleary.'

'Name's Bridget to everyone, whatever their age. Nice to meet you. Beth, isn't it? What a lovely girl you are. Finished school, I guess?' She cocked her head to one side while waiting for Beth's reply.

'Yes, I've just finished. Results on Thursday.'

'Then where?'

'If I've got what I need, I shall be doing archaeology at Cambridge. If I do get the right results, that is.'

'I'm not going to be such a fool as to say, Don't worry, of course you will. One just never knows with these things. What I will say, is good luck. Your dad?'

Peter appeared as if by magic from the kitchen. 'Here I am, Mrs Cleary.'

'Bridget to you, Father.'

'Bridget then. Do come in. It's about the wedding, I understand.'

As he shut the study door, Bridget said, 'Well, it is and it isn't.'

'Please sit down.'

She dropped on to the sofa saying, 'I've been Catholic all my life but then, for various reasons, I stopped.'

'I see.'

'Will it be all right for me to come to your church to a service? You knowing I'm a lapsed Catholic. Would you mind? I don't want to cause offence, Father.'

'Peter's the name. So far as I am concerned, the church is there for everyone.'

'Right. That's it, is it?'

'Yes. There's nothing more to say.'

'If I felt able to change to C of E, would you have me?'

'Of course.'

'As easy as that?'

'Yes, if that is what you genuinely want. We, you and I, would need to talk about things. Not lessons so much as a discussion, so that you know where the Church of England is coming from.'

'Or going to!'

'Yes. Quite right.'

'I could try it and see.'

'Of course.'

'Oh! You see, I thought you'd be difficult and ask me all sorts of questions and want to know this and that. My pedigree, almost.'

'Why should I?'

'I don't know.' Then Bridget looked into his face trying to understand the simplicity of it all, and she saw the compassion and understanding in his eyes. She knew then that he meant what he said.

'Thank you. That daughter of yours is beautiful.'

'Thank you.'

'Well, I'll go then. You're clearly a man of few words.'

'But I mean every one of them. I'm glad you're coming to the wedding. Paddy is delighted and so is Tamsin. It's made all the difference to Paddy. I suppose some people would say they're an odd match, but in fact they're very well suited, I feel.'

'I think so too. Different as chalk and cheese, but right for each other. And if our Paddy steps out of line when I go back to Ireland, you've my permission to put him straight.'

She grinned at Peter and he laughed. 'OK then. I shall say it was you who told me to.'

'Exactly. Just because he's forty, it doesn't mean to say he can misbehave. Where's the rest of your family?'

'My wife Caroline should be home any minute and our son Alex is upstairs, lying on his bed, worrying about his exam results.'

'I'd love to meet him. Would he mind?'

'I'll give him a shout.'

Bridget watched Alex as he walked down the stairs to greet her. She shook him by the hand and wished him every success with his exam results. 'My word, you are so like your dad it's unbelievable. Almost, but not quite as tall yet, and identical in looks. Are you following in his footsteps?'

Alex smiled. 'No. I'm hoping to qualify as a doctor like my mother.'

'Wonderful. Now, I must go. I'm just getting things sorted with your dad. I'm Bridget, by the way, Paddy's mother. We'll see you at the wedding? Come and enjoy yourself. It'll be a real Irish wedding party. Love to your mother. Say I'm sorry she wasn't in.' And with that, Bridget swept down the hall and out of the house waving both hands above her head and shouting, 'Bye!'

Before going back to Vince and Greta's, Bridget decided to call in at the pub and have a quick drink, and see if there was anyone in there she'd already met.

Alan the barman served her drink and helpfully, for him, carried it across to the settle, which he remembered she liked the best. There were three other customers in, but she knew none of them.

'Where's Georgie? Day off?'

'No, she's just having a bite to eat before the rush begins. She won't be long.'

And she wasn't. Georgie burst into the bar, excitement in every inch of her. 'He's out! He's out!'

Alan broke out of his somnambulist attitude to life and said, 'Who's out? What d'yer mean?'

'Harry! He's escaped. It's on the radio. Just now.'

Georgie sat down on a bar stool and fanned herself. 'I can't believe it. He was taken to hospital for an appointment and, while he was there, he walked out, bold as brass.'

'No! Honestly?'

'I haven't made it up, Alan, it's on the news. Apparently the warder left for just the briefest of moments. Harry got dressed and hopped it, the warder came back and assumed he'd gone in to see the consultant, but Harry was away on his toes before anyone knew.'

'D'yer think he'll turn up at Zack's?'

'Alan! For God's sake, he isn't daft! It's the first place the police would look for him.'

'Would it be though? Maybe it would be the last place they'd look, them thinking he wasn't daft.'

Trust Alan to have a skewed viewpoint on absolutely everything, thought Georgie. 'Well, you may have a point.'

Bridget asked, 'I take it this Harry is a rogue?'

The three customers, Georgie and Alan couldn't wait to tell her the whole story.

★

Bridget laughed herself helpless when they'd finished. 'He's the kind of bloke I would love to meet. What a guy.'

The other people in the village were not as amused as Bridget by the situation, remembering how he'd duped them so cleverly. They were scandalised, but they didn't find it funny. Would he come back to borrow money perhaps, or take someone's car or ... Finally they all decided that he wouldn't dare, not after what he'd done. But they did remember to lock their windows, just in case, despite the hot weather.

Harry did arrive in the middle of the night at Zack and Marie's house, tapping gently but persistently at the back door and eventually waking Zack.

He put his finger to Zack's mouth the moment he stuck his head round the door. 'Let me in.'

Zack, still half asleep and not thinking properly, opened the door wider and allowed him in. He whispered, 'What the blazes are you doing, coming here? Marie's frightened to death, all that knocking.'

'I left some money here and I need to get it.'

'Like hell you did.'

'I did, Zack. In my bedroom. There's not someone in it at the moment, is there?'

'As luck would have it, there isn't. We have got guests in, but not in your room. Luck of Old Nick you have.'

The kitchen door opened and there was Marie in her dressing gown. 'Oh!'

'It's all right, Marie, I've not come to murder you. I've come to collect my money.'

'What money? We don't owe you money.'

'The money I hid.'

'Where?' Marie demanded. She was so wild with him for

deceiving them that she honestly wondered whether it would be right to let him have it, wherever it was.

'Under the floorboards.' Harry was exhausted. He'd walked all the way from Culworth without any food since his breakfast.

'In your bedroom, you mean?'

'Yes. Is there a chance I could have a sandwich?'

Zack would have protested but Marie got in first and said, 'Yes, you can.'

She rinsed her hands under the tap and began to prepare a sandwich for him, and she made a pot of tea too. The three of them sat round the kitchen table and drank tea and she and Zack watched him eat his sandwich. It was filled with fresh home-grown salad and a thick slice of Jimbo's ham with mustard.

Marie told him where the ham had come from. 'You shouldn't have pinched from him, you know. He offered you a lifeline and you abused it. You should be ashamed.'

Zack shook his head at her to stop her belligerence because he didn't want Harry turning nasty. He might even have got himself a gun, but Marie ignored him.

'You really disappointed me, you did. I gave you a nice home, kept everything lovely for you and that's what you did. What have you got to say for yourself then?'

Harry cleared his mouth of sandwich and said, 'I can do nothing but apologise, Marie. I must have been mad.'

'You did all right out of it though, didn't you? Friendship, a job, the money that you stole, a roof over your head, a woman.'

'Venetia, you mean. I love her and always will. She wasn't my sort, but I couldn't help myself.'

Marie put her oar in again. 'She was someone else's wife and now he's paying for it, or he will do. That's something else you should be ashamed of. Poor Jeremy.'

Harry put down the sandwich he was so desperate for and said, 'To be honest …'

Marie spluttered her disgust. 'You, honest! Huh!'

'I am being honest. Right now. Under the floorboards I've got three thousand pounds to pay Jimbo back and the rest is yours. I'm giving myself up. OK?'

'Well, now,' said Zack. 'That's good to hear. But I don't know that I want tainted money.'

'The rest isn't tainted, it's what I saved from my salary. Honest.'

Again he used the word that so angered Marie, but this time she sympathised. 'I do believe you mean it.'

'I do. I've been an idiot. I'm thinking of turning Queen's evidence, you see. I've had enough of being a liar. You and the people in Turnham Malpas have taught me that.'

'Do you mean it, Harry?' asked Marie.

Harry reached across the table to squeeze her hand. 'Yes, I do mean it.'

Zack was understandably cautious. 'I'm not too sure about giving us money we've done nothing to deserve. We might keep it for you, but I ... that is, we ... don't want it. Thanks all the same.'

'I'll get it out, and give you the money for Jimbo. The rest you can hide for me, then you can ring the police and tell them you've found me.'

'Oh no. You ring the police. It's the first honest thing you've done in years. You do it.'

'Me?'

'Yes, you.' Zack was emphatic about it.

'It's not quite the first honest thing I've done. I did truly love Venetia and I can't bear her death.'

Harry leaped to his feet and set off for the stairs. 'I'll get it for you.'

He came back with it wrapped in a Turnham Malpas stores green carrier bag.

Zack found it rather ironic. 'OK then. You've finished your sandwich and your tea, you've given me the money for Jimbo, now go to the phone and give yourself up.'

'Is my car here still?'

'No, they took it for forensic investigation so you can't buzz off into the great blue yonder. Mine's in Culworth in the garage having a service and MOT so there's no easy escape for you. If you don't ring the police quickly, I shall. Now, go and do it.'

They listened to his telephone call. Zack locked the back door again and put the key in his pocket because he still couldn't believe that Harry would stay around long enough for the police to pick him up.

Marie whispered, 'That's not right,' but the key stayed in Zack's pocket.

They sat still and quiet, each of them mulling over the situation they found themselves in. Zack was furious, Marie distressed and Harry was wondering if he really wanted to be honest. But before he'd come to a decision, the police were at the door. He jumped up, his eyes darting around as though looking to make a run for it, but Marie looked him straight in the eye and shook her head. 'Not this time, Harry, this is for real.' She kissed his cheek and Zack went to open the front door. They put Harry in handcuffs and marched him out to the waiting police car. He took one look round at the houses as though sad to be seeing the last of them for some time, ducked his head, and sat in the car.

Marie waved to him and turned back to the house. 'Zack, that poor boy.'

'I don't know how much sympathy he needs, or if he needs any at all. He's no fool, he knew exactly what he was doing.'

'I'm off to look for the money he's left for us.'

She eventually found it underneath the floorboards in the wardrobe. Two hundred and seventy pounds.

'Well I never.'

Zack said, 'We don't want none of it you know, Marie. It could bring us bad luck.'

'I know. We don't actually need it anyway. Well, we could

find a use for it, but best not.' She carefully wrapped it up, carried it into their own bedroom and hid it under the clutter in Zack's half of the wardrobe. As she closed the door she whispered, 'But I can't help but feel sorry for him. Losing Venetia in such a nasty way. I do believe he meant it about loving her.'

As she was climbing back into bed, Marie said, 'Would you mind if I see Harry when he's in prison?'

'I'll tell you what we won't do, and that is tell anyone about him being here tonight. Not Vera, nor Sylvia, nor anyone. Right? OK?'

'I hear what you say, but Jimbo will have to know.'

'We'll tell him Harry smuggled a letter out and we found the money according to his instructions. But I tell you what, Marie, if a man on his own comes asking for accommodation again we'll have to be a bit extra careful about 'em. We've got off lucky this time, things could have turned out a lot worse.'

'So what do I do? Ask for references? That would be the end of the B&B as we know it. Might I remind you that it was you who recommended that he come and ask for a room, not me. You never suspected anything.'

'No, you have a point.' Zack rolled over and put his arm round Marie's waist. 'Just remember, though. If there's a man on his own, watch out!'

Chapter 26

The following morning, on his way to begin his stint as verger at the church, Zack called in at the village store to find Jimbo already there with everything in full swing.

'I thought perhaps you wouldn't be here as early as this.'

'It's Tom's day off. How can I help?'

'I have this carrier bag for you.' Mentally Zack crossed his fingers because of the lie he was about to tell. 'You see, we had a letter from Harry that he smuggled out, and he told us where he'd hidden this. He asked us to let you have it. He says he owes you it. I have to say, I know what it is. Don't open it in here in case someone comes in.' Zack winked at Jimbo and left him to it.

Of course Jimbo couldn't resist looking in immediately. To his amazement, it was filled with notes. He raced off into his own office and laid the money out in piles. He counted it twice and then collapsed onto his chair. My God! Just over three thousand pounds.

There came the sound of someone shouting from the front of the store, so Jimbo clapped his boater back on and raced to the counter. It was Willie Biggs paying for his paper.

'I could set my watch by you, Willie. How do you do it?'

Willie laughed. 'You look on top of the world this morning.'

'Do I? I don't know why.'

'It's as if you've had some good news.'

'Me? No, not me. I never get good news.'

'Right, I'll be off for my breakfast. Croissants this morning. I love 'em.'

'They taste best eaten in a cafe on the Champs-Elysées with a pot of coffee.'

'Ah! Well, they're not that bad in my kitchen prepared by Sylvia, along with a cup of tea from our shiny brown teapot. Bye!'

Jimbo watched Willie crossing the green and thought about Harry. So he'd turned up trumps at last. Whatever he'd done in the interim, he'd liked him right from the first. He was a bit surprised to find he was a full-scale robber, but there you are. There must be something good in him to give him back the money he owed him. Poor Harry. He really did seem to have loved Venetia. Poor Venetia. All the drama she had created while she was alive and she was still making waves, even from the grave. Well, not the grave because she hadn't been buried yet. If the funeral was here in Turnham Malpas he for one would go, if only to say thank you for all the fun she'd caused. And the gossip, come to that.

The door opened and in came a young man whom Jimbo thought he recognised.

'Good morning, we're just opening up. What can I do for you?'

'Good morning to you. You are ...?'

'Jimbo. Owner of this store. I don't know you, do I?' Over his customer's shoulder he spotted a very expensive car parked outside. 'Should I?'

'No.' The stranger held out his hand. 'I'm Jonathan Templeton. Always known as Johnny, the late Sir Ralph Templeton's great nephew. I'm his heir. I've come to see my house now that it's almost restored.'

'Well, my word, we've been waiting for the day. Wonderful man your uncle, greatly loved. What a surprise! I can't believe it! You've got the Templeton nose, that's why I thought I knew you but couldn't ...'

'That's me.'

Jimbo paused for a moment and saw the likeness, the same sort of kindliness shining from the same blue eyes. 'I'm so pleased to meet you. It's been so long that we thought they'd not found anyone to inherit.'

'Well, they have, and it's me. I've got jet lag and I'm badly in need of a breakfast and bed. Is there anywhere in the village that does B&B?'

'Oh yes. Laburnum Cottage down Shepherd's Hill, just down here to the right, first turn. Your car's pointing in the right direction, it's about halfway down on the left. Nice place, lovely people. Can't miss it. Tell them Jimbo sent you.'

'Thanks. When I've recovered from my jet lag we'll talk some more. I'm barely coherent at the moment.' He reached out to shake hands again, got into his car and zoomed away. A much better proposition as a paying guest than the last one they had, thought Jimbo. At least Jonathan Templeton wouldn't be facing a jail sentence!

Jimbo turned from watching Jonathan leave and started up the day in the store. Two days to go and it would be the wedding of Tamsin and Paddy. Thank God he had Harriet to organise all the food. He'd sneaked a peep at the cake she'd decorated and it was magnificent. She was so talented. The customers could talk of nothing else but the wedding, it was obviously going to be *the* wedding of the year, all thanks to Bridget's money, from which his business would certainly benefit. He thought about life before Turnham Malpas, of the rush and bustle and the competitive world in which he had lived and worked and he knew for sure that coming here had been the very best move he had ever made. Would ever make.

The door burst open again and in came Beth, accompanied by Sykes. 'Sorry! Out, Sykes and wait. *Stay*! Jimbo, I've come for a bottle of champagne, we're having a champagne breakfast!'

'Champagne breakfast? It's not your ... is it? It is!'

'Yes, our results.'

'Go on then ... tell me.'

'We've both got three As and Alex has a B too. We're so excited.'

Jimbo put his arms round her, hugged her and kissed her on both cheeks.

'Wonderful! Fran's got her GCSE results next week, just the three she's taken early. Her nerves are in shreds at the moment. She'll be so pleased for you and so will Harriet. Wonderful! Look, I'm going to give you your favourite gateau. Chocolate! A present from me. Take it home, it's frozen, but it won't take long to defrost. With my compliments.'

'Oh! Thank you! I wasn't expecting ...'

'Of course, I know you weren't. Remember when you were ill and you struggled round to the store to get some slices of gateau for Dottie and everyone? I was so proud of you that day. What a brave girl you were. Here you are, carry it carefully.'

Beth said, 'I was so sad when you closed the store and so thrilled when you reopened. I don't know what we would do without being able to come in here and talk. And cheer ourselves up.' Her eyes filled with tears and she couldn't say any more. So Jimbo patted her arm, opened the door for her and, when she heard the doorbell jingle, she smiled at the sound of it and left.

'See you at the wedding, Beth!' Jimbo called out to her.

When Saturday morning broke, the sun was shining as they had all hoped it would. The bridegroom was experiencing a bad case of panic. His mother had brought him his breakfast in bed and told him to have another hour before he began to get ready.

Another hour in bed? It was time to think about what he was doing. Time to contemplate being married to Tamsin. Time to worry about his speech. Time to be glad his mother had come. Time to ... Paddy hid under the duvet to pretend he didn't exist. Here he was, with all the luck in the world in the palm of his hand, and he was petrified. Mainly because he'd had a letter from Michelle telling him there was a job for him at Kew if he wanted it. He hadn't opened the letter till late yesterday and when he did, he'd rapidly returned it to the envelope and pretended it hadn't arrived. If he couldn't see it, then it hadn't arrived, had it? But common sense told him he was being pathetic. He was forty, not four, and he had to pull himself together. Now that he was soon to be married, he'd have to learn to share everything, not just the bed. He came out from under the duvet, ate a hearty meal, leaped out of bed and headed for the bathroom. Today was the day he'd dreamed of and he was going to make it the best day ever.

The bride, on the other hand, was weeping. No mother, no father, no sisters at her wedding. Just two old aunties, one of whom was in a wheelchair, so there was no flurry of women helping her to dress and her friends, well, either they lived thousands of miles away, had very young families, or were about to give birth. Tamsin just wished there was someone, for it seemed to her to be a day for family, not just for friends. Then she thought about Paddy and wondered how he was feeling. So she dug out her mobile and in defiance of all the rules, dialled his number. As the phone began to ring the front door opened and a voice called out, 'Tamsin! It's me!'

'Oh! I'm upstairs, come up.'

She cancelled the call and listened to the footsteps coming up the stairs. She didn't know why, but she was puzzled by them.

And there, standing in the bedroom doorway, was her sister Penny. They hadn't met for years and seeing her now, it was just as if she'd never left. The same disordered hair, the same disregard for fashion, the same beaming smile and welcoming arms held wide to embrace her.

'Oh, Penny. I'd no idea. I'm so glad you've come. So glad.'

Then they both burst into tears. Which turned to laughter, which turned to tears again, and then laughter. 'Couldn't miss the wedding, could I? For heaven's sake. The sun is shining and it's going to be a good day.'

'I don't care if it's thundering and lightning, it'll still be a good day.'

'It is still on then? The thought occurred to me that it might be cancelled and then I'd look a fool!'

'No, not cancelled, I love him too much. You'll like him. He's not what you'd expect him to be though, but he loves me and I love him.'

'He's not full of music then?'

'He's trying. He's started on the flute and I must say, considering he's had no training whatsoever, he's doing quite well. This is him, look.' Tamsin showed her a photograph of herself and Paddy. 'He's a qualified gardener and works at the big house in the glasshouses, with the peaches and the grapes and such. He's well respected.'

Penny sat on the bed and said, 'There's a but, isn't there?'

Tamsin nodded. 'You know too well, just as you used to do.'

'I'm still your sister. What is it?'

'The trouble is ... well ... I've got the offer of a job at Dame Celia Collingswood Girls' School in London. The post is Director of Music, with time for playing at concerts and such, as part of the bargain. It's a fantastic job, it's just right for me, but now I've got Paddy to consider. I didn't even apply, they just contacted me and said the job will be vacant in January next year when their present director retires. I'm in one heck of a mess.'

'How did they know about you?'

'The head of the school heard me play at a recital in Smith Square and made enquiries. We've spoken on the phone and they've more or less offered me the job subject to an interview. Apparently that's just a formality.'

'Look! I need a shower, you need to get ready. We'll talk, afterwards, shall we? There's nothing set in stone, you can say no, and Paddy could say yes. Maybe he needs a move too. You never know. Stunning job, though. And just right for you. Definitely not for me!' Penny scooped Tamsin up in a great big hug, just like she used to do when they were young and suddenly life didn't seem quite as complicated as Tamsin had thought.

'Oh, Penny, I'm so glad you've come. Are you staying in England?'

'For a while, yes, then I'm going back. I love it out there. I'll see you back from your honeymoon and then we'll see.'

Tamsin's wedding dress was a romantic, dreamy affair, floaty and gently sparkling with crystal butterflies embroidered all over it. It so suited her personality that Penny gasped when she saw her in it. 'Why, it suits you beautifully. It's absolutely you.'

Her bouquet of flowers was neat and strikingly suited to Tamsin, being sweet and countrified, not designed with high fashion in mind. 'Well, sister dear, there couldn't be a lovelier bride. You look wonderful.'

'So do you. Look, I haven't got a bridesmaid. Would you be my bridesmaid?'

'Me? A bridesmaid! Well, if you think my outfit is suitable. I didn't intend it to be a bridesmaid's dress.'

'I know you didn't, but it could be. We'll get a rose out of my garden and you could carry that, how about it? Your dress is coppery coloured and I have a rose in the garden that's kind of apricot and coppery coloured round the edges, it would look just right.'

'OK then. We will. Don't you come out in that dress, I'll go and get it.'

Penny chose the loveliest rose on the bush with a long stem and just perfectly opened, not too much, not too little, and she snipped off the thorns so she could hold it easily.

The two of them stood in the hall and smiled in triumph at each other. 'What an auspicious day. I always thought it would be me who'd marry and not you, but here you are, looking fabulous!'

'Thank you. You'll love Paddy's mother, she's called Bridget and she's wonderfully kind and full of laughter. Is that the car?'

'Tamsin, you've got your slippers on!'

'Oh, good grief. I brought my shoes down and forgot to put them on. Could you open the door and tell the driver I won't be a minute?'

The groom, meanwhile, had been ready for the last half an hour, sitting in Greta's lounge, almost trembling with trepidation. His mother was insisting he had something to eat before he left, so he had one of Greta's aprons draped over his suit and he was eating, very reluctantly, a toasted teacake. 'That's what you want, comfort food. Your mother knows best, and I know nothing better than a toasted teacake for giving comfort. Now, give me the plate, and you have a drink of tea.'

'You haven't put whisky in, have you? I don't want to smell of drink.'

'Shut up, Paddy, and drink it else you're going to be late.'

Bridget looked down at him and remembered the love she had for him when he was born. She was so proud of him, prouder still of his future wife. What a pair they made. She leaned over and kissed his cheek. 'Love you, Paddy. You've got a great future ahead of you.'

Paddy thought to himself, a future I'm going to have to turn down, but there you are. It's one of the sacrifices I shall make in the cause of happiness. Kew comes second to Tamsin. 'Time we left.'

Paddy turned to watch his bride come down the aisle. She glided towards him, smiling as though he was the only other person in the whole wide world, just as she was for him. As for Vince, he looked ready to faint due to the enormity of giving away the

276

bride, but he held on and solemnly placed her hand in Paddy's when they reached the altar.

Peter smiled at them both, waited while the music ended and began, 'Dearly beloved, we are gathered here …'.